MORE AND HARDER

Skinhead sex is cock, boots, piss and spunk, and helping your mate come. Skins are into being skins together, sucking each other's shaved cocks, running hands through cropped hair, rubbing oil over smooth bodies and pissing over each other's jeans and boots, licking each other's boots clean, feeling boots on hard cock, kicking up the arse, grinding balls with boot-sole, running the laced-up boot between your mate's legs and wanking your mate real hard so he comes heavy and strong, knowing he's a skin with a skin mate.

MORE AND HARDER

Morgan

idol

This book is a work of fiction.
In real life, make sure you practise safe sex.

This edition published in 2002 by
Idol
Thames Wharf Studios
Rainville Road
London W6 9HA

First published in 1999 by Idol

Copyright © Morgan 1999, 2002

The right of Morgan to be identified as the Author of
this Work has been asserted in accordance with the Copyright,
Designs and Patents Act 1988.

www.idol-books.co.uk

Typeset by SetSystems Ltd, Saffron Walden, Essex
Printed and bound by Clays Ltd, St Ives plc

ISBN 0 352 33697 8

*All characters in this publication are fictitious and any resemblance
to real persons, living or dead, is purely coincidental.*

This book is sold subject to the condition that it shall not, by way
of trade or otherwise, be lent, resold, hired out or otherwise
circulated without the publisher's prior written consent in any form
of binding or cover other than that in which it is published and
wthout a similar condition including this condition being imposed
on the subsequent purchaser.

CONTENTS

INTRODUCTION _____ 1
ROUGH BIKERS IN BERKSHIRE _____ 3
CPBB AND THE METROPOLITAN BIKERS _____ 8
SUBURBIA _____ 12
REPLIES TO YOUR QUESTIONS, SIR _____ 16
THE WIRRAL _____ 17
BIKER BONDAGE IN THE WOODS _____ 19
BIKER IN THE CELLAR _____ 21
NEW CROSS AND DEN HAAG _____ 23
BALL-WEIGHT STUCK ON _____ 25
NEW YEAR IN HOLLAND _____ 27
HOLLAND AGAIN _____ 29
JERSEY, CHANNEL ISLANDS _____ 30
LOCKABLE BALL-WEIGHT _____ 32
UNSUSTAINABLE SKINHEAD LIFESTYLE _____ 34
REDHILL SLAVE TRAINING _____ 36
AMSTERDAM NEW YEAR 1985 _____ 39
MASTER JIM, FROSTERLEY, COUNTY DURHAM _____ 41
SKINHEAD VIDEO _____ 44
BLIND DATE AT LAX _____ 45
THE BLACK PARTY _____ 49
SKINHEAD SHAVING _____ 51
PRINCE ALBERT _____ 55
QUESTIONS FROM A RESPECTFUL SLAVE TO HIS NEW
    MASTER _____ 57
BUTTPLUGS AND BOXING _____ 59
FANTASY TRAINING SESSION _____ 61

CONTENTS

CP SKINHEAD RICK	68
JOSEPH: LA COP	70
'THE GREEN SHORTS' AND DARTMOOR	72
GREASE, BELT AND BOOT SLAVE	75
SKINHEAD PARTY	78
GREASING AND BLACKBALLING	81
SKINHEAD NEW YEAR PARTY	84
THAILAND	86
WEST BERLIN	88
THE EARLS COURT LEATHER BAR	89
DEVIL'S PUNCH BOWL	92
WIMBLEDON COMMON	96
PETER W: RIP	100
MARK GOES TO JAIL, PART I	106
TA BFT	121
START OF A NEW DECADE: NEW YEAR 1990	124
CHRISTENING MY NEW BOOTS	127
MARK GOES TO JAIL, PART II	129
CP FANTASY: THE TAWSE	135
DARTMOOR HIKING	137
MARK GOES TO JAIL, PART III	138
NIGHT-RUN TRAINING	143
MARK'S TWO-MONTH US HOLIDAY	146
'The Stockade'	146
South Holland, Ill. – City of Churches	153
Charleston, South Carolina	157
Merced, Yosemite and San Francisco	159
Tucson, Arizona	160
Casper, Wyoming	162
Sunny Downtown Burbank, California	165
Toronto	168
New York Wrestling	168
CORPORAL PUNISHMENT IN WALES AND LONDON	169

CONTENTS

CAMERONE '92 – LÉGION ÉTRANGÈRE	171
BIRTHDAY IN SWITZERLAND	175
DENVER, COLORADO	176
THE BEAST OF CROYDON	178
BRABANT SOLDIERS CAMP '92	181
RUNNING STEVE TO SOUTHFIELDS	186
LAKE DISTRICT IN THE SNOW	188
POTENTIAL BRIG-RAT	191
CANAL-TOWPATH RUNNING	195
HARD-STEEL GIFT FROM OTTO	196
MILITARY TRAINING	198
OBEDIENCE TRAINING AND A LIVING SCULPTURE	204
BERLIN, MAY 1993	207
GAY-SOLDATEN KÖLN UNIFORM-WOCHENEDE	214
BERLIN MILITARY TRAINING	219
RECRUIT TRAINING AT THE BUNKER	225
COTSWOLDS ADVENTURE TRAINING	229
RECRUIT TRAINING	233
TRAINING AT THE BUNKER	236
CP FRAME	239
LÉGIONNAIRE ENCOUNTER	242
THE MASOCHISM OF URBAN RUNNING	244
GAY-SOLDATEN KÖLN: EIFEL	247
ADVENTURE TRAINING – DARTMOOR	252
GAY-SOLDATEN KÖLN – 'FÄLSCHER HASE' (FUNNY BUNNIES)	254
WEEKEND AT THE BUNKER	260
SEVERE PAIN ON THE NATIONAL HEALTH SERVICE	262
SQUADDIE TRAIN TRIP	263
PONY DAY OUT – SHROPSHIRE	267
'PLAYPEN' SLAVE NIGHT	270
MORE AND HARDER	274
AUTHOR'S END NOTE	277

The following items have previously been published:

'Skinhead Shaving' and 'Training Session' published in *Toy*;

'Peter W' published in the *Body Positive Newsletter* (London);

'Mark Goes to Jail' published in *Dungeonmaster* and reprinted in Leyland Books' *Sir, More Sir*;

'Military Training' published in *Itch*;

'Recruit Training', 'The Masochism of Urban Running', a part of 'South Holland, City of Churches', 'Hard Steel', 'Pony Day Out' and '"Playpen" Slave Night' published by *Checkmate*, PO Box 354, Wyoming, Pa 18644–0354, USA.

Introduction

This is an erotic autobiography of Mark, a submissive English sadomasochist: an 'SM sub' or 'slave'.

The story begins in late 1970s England, which was an era of 'Suck it and See' experimentation rather than SM manuals or groups. Friends encouraged and warned him. Mark's instincts for safety and fun developed and allowed him to enjoy for real some serious sadomasochistic fantasies beyond the scope of the gay-bar scene.

Morgan
London, 1999

Rough Bikers in Berkshire

October 1977

When I was young, sweet and innocent, and fresh out of university, I came to London for my first career job and ended up living 25 miles out, in Slough.

Although I had an open mind, I knew nothing practical about sex apart from the biological basics and had not yet had a sexually aware relationship. My expectations of a career probably included a wife and the average 2.4 kids; although, had anyone actually asked me about it, my public-school-rebel attitude probably wouldn't have been particularly keen on the prospect.

To travel to work from Slough by rail was unattractive for shift hours and I bought a motorbike and started learning to ride it. I knew nothing more about engines than I had learnt from the family lawn mower. The bike shop delivered the bike (a Kawasaki KH250 two-stroke triple) in a pick-up as I didn't have a driving licence. I rode the bike up and down a service road near our rented house until the engine coughed and stopped. I gave up for the night. Things got better next evening when I found the petrol supply on/off tap!

Next problem was I couldn't get it to start – the bike shop asked had I 'juiced it up', which turned out to mean 'flooded'. I was totally naïve on sexual talk.

I cautiously rode the bike to work in London and it fulfilled its primary economic objective but I instinctively hankered after social contact with 'real' bikers and, on enquiring locally, was directed to a pub outside Slough.

The rough bikers there – a few were Angels – soon informed me that I'd bought a 'Jap-crap' bike and I was consequently the lowest of the low. To ride with them I'd have to pass a few tests and prove myself. My hair wasn't exactly short at this time but theirs was longer and that was the first issue. My 'sponsor' in the group was Peter – one of several significant guys named Peter in my life.

Part of being acceptable to these guys was riding and part was drinking – at university drinking lots of ale without falling over had not been a strong point of mine and Southern beer turned out to have much the same effect.

I rode pillion with Peter on the Sunday runs but as a probationer wasn't allowed to wear leather except work boots: these were a brand I hadn't encountered previously, known as Doctor Martens. No leather jacket, no leather jeans or gloves, so I was a bit cold in zip-fly Levi's blue-denim flare jeans, navy-blue rugger shirt and button-up Levi's denim jacket.

Lots of interesting stunts. If your guy takes care of your wallet for you on the run then you don't need pockets in your jeans. And a rear seam on your jeans isn't really necessary; it turns out they suspected me of being gay anyhow. Easier to put grease, fingers, ball bearings or Mars bars in there for fun. And on a run, miles from home, no other transport or money, you take it or else get left stranded . . . And, having tried it, I found I enjoyed it.

This clothing was always the same and was worn from new and wasn't washed; my clean upbringing was soon challenged by bike oil and grease as well as pub-spilt beer. Things got even more challenging when it was demanded that I wear a chain padlocked through the belt loops and Peter kept the key. As a refinement, the zip-fly traveller was also padlocked to the chain and kind 'friends' ripped out the pockets.

I also learnt another bikers' trick: how to waterproof jeans. They were removed and returned to me coated on the inside with black engine grease. This certainly stopped any stains from pissing inside – as was necessary with locked-on jeans – and also repelled water from the outside. When I finally had a bath a lot of black grease came off around the bath rim, so as well as cleaning up myself I did a full bathroom clean.

These practices were a far cry from parental toilet training or normal hygiene. Most pubs in the area would not serve anyone in a leather jacket: bikers were almost inherently outlaws and it seemed that you had to conform to strange norms to try to be accepted by them. Perhaps the Angels were taking advantage of my gullibility and innocence, but at the time I thought not. My desire to be accepted as a 'real' biker and to conform to what the group required was stronger than my inhibitions and received ideas. Anyhow, having achieved economic freedom (by working rather than being a student), I was going through a 'rebel' stage and my education had prepared me to accept on their merits new and different ideas: 'Don't knock it if you haven't tried it' and 'Try it – you may like it'.

It wasn't all dirty jeans and drinking – there was the serious business of motorcycle maintenance that justified all the oil and grease. I did have my doubts about the supposed supremacy of British-built motorcycles. The things kept breaking down. My KH250 was temperamental as well but it was usually to do with the battery or the spark plugs and getting it to go faster. The breakdowns with the Triumphs, Nortons, Tritons and 'Beesas' (BSA) seemed much more involved and usually caused total immobility, so we all stopped and stood around watching and offering advice while the bike was stripped down at the roadside.

Their bikes all had names like 'Trigger' or 'Thunder' or 'Tiger'; they also all had oil leaks and it was said that your bike wasn't a 'proper' bike unless it had at least an oil drip. Some even sprayed oil on your jeans as you rode along, from leaks around the upper-cylinder area. Therefore no point in wearing clean jeans.

I wore the approved kit for a memorable, cold bike run to a farm near Barnstaple in October or early November: not the kindest weather for biking. As a probationer ('a moll') I was still not allowed to ride my own KH250 on runs, so I was pillion-clinging behind Peter on his noisy Norton with no grab rails. We didn't go that fast so the coffee that he poured into me soon wanted to be pissed away, but there was no stopping so the grease inside the jeans guided the liquid down to the boots without showing discoloration. Shortly afterwards we stopped – for more coffee!

Getting laid out drunk had become a ritual back in

Berkshire but out here around a campfire and with hurricane lamps inside old Scout tents things were wilder. The curry had dope in it and joints were being passed round more than usual. I collapsed early and awoke a little later finding myself tied on the damp ground with my arms and feet pulled outward and attached by ropes and tent pegs. Despite my protestations to Peter about the cold, he allowed the others to tip beer over me and to piss on my boots and legs. I was untied only when he wanted to crash out in his tent and even then I wasn't allowed out of my usual probationer's locked-on jeans and jacket.

As I was working for a television company and working with the stars, I was 'allowed' to put a big five-pointed star of studs on the back of my Levi's jacket. They said I looked smart from behind, especially when I was riding pillion on Peter's bike. That jacket eventually had the sleeves cut off and I now wear it over a leather jacket as 'colours', although I was never allowed to do that by the Angels. It has never ever been washed.

Sex had never been mentioned by any of these guys until we were all drunk together either at the pub or out on a run. However, they sussed me as a 'queer' (they always said 'queer', not 'gay' or 'poof'). There had been suspicions early on, probably from following my eye; at school and university I remember lusting after other guys' bums in tight jeans: that was the time of flared jeans which had very tight bums and crotch.

One of the first things that happened when I was starting to get accepted (as I thought it) was that the back seam on my jeans and the front pocket linings were ripped out from my zip-fly jeans. It wasn't only me who was treated like this – there was another guy whose zip didn't work and they wouldn't let him change jeans or get it fixed. You didn't wear anything under jeans and I got a big thrill (but was disgusted) when someone first put a finger up my arse and got *into* my bum – the others had just poked around a bit in the crack.

Coming back after spending the New Year with my parents in Bristol, I found I wasn't so well in with them. The next time we met up Peter said that he and the others thought

I was 'queer' and that I should go off and ride with the queer boys' bike club. He gave me a phone number in London of a guy called Jack T.

My 'coming out' story is actually a bit more confusing than that because the first guy I literally went to bed with was Mike; we'd met at university and he was back home for the weekend. It was a rather lovey-dovey affair. We met up for a day quite ordinarily. I got over to his parents' place on my bike – they were away – and we spent an afternoon out hiking, walking and talking in the pine forests near Bracknell. He cooked dinner for us both; we got pissed and ended up in his parents' bed. He was the first guy to stick his cock up my bum. When I asked him to use some olive oil as a lubricant he accused me of being kinky.

There wasn't any animosity from the Angels about my being queer – I was almost one of them but I wasn't the same as them. The interesting thing, in hindsight, is how tolerant (or exploitative) they were of me being gay. It was one of those things. But if you went to the Angels saying you were queer I guess there'd have been a quite different reaction.

About eighteen months later some of them in that Chapter got done for knifing offences at a party that went wrong, when someone from Hampshire picked a fight. Angels will be Angels . . .

CPBB and the Metropolitan Bikers

Jack T turned out to like Black Prince rubberised waterproof riding gear and had a whole walk-in wardrobe of the stuff in the basement of his flat in Ladbroke Grove. He dressed me in that stuff and took me on the back of his BMW bike down to his mate who was a farrier living in a caravan in Aldershot. No gloves again, so I had to wander my hands inside his elasticated Black Prince trousers and hold on to Jack's belt buckle or touch him up as we were riding. At least the Black Prince clothing was much warmer than denims.

One Saturday night he took me to a leather bikers' pub in Earl's Court. It was huge and most of the men were wearing black leather jackets and jeans – but they weren't bikers! I was touched up all the time, which was novel, and I was pissed enough not to be annoyed. The tiny toilet was jammed full and I had to go the whole way round the bar to the other toilet. With all those eyes on me it seemed an enormous pub.

We met some friends of Jack's – I always called him 'Jack' but he was referred to as 'Johnny' in conversation as there were a lot of Johns around. That's a joke from that time – a 'John' was a queer and in straight company 'queer' was a bad thing to be, an insult that would start a fight. There was a shop that was pointed out to me a couple of doors down from the leather bikers' pub where I subsequently furtively bought my first gay wank-book, an early American copy of *The Leatherman's Handbook* by Larry Townsend. I liked the pun in the title, wasn't shocked at all and was highly turned on by several of the stories.

Another Saturday Jack T asked me if I wanted to go to the queer bikers' party. This turned out to be very late at night and we parked in Northumberland Avenue. After that I was to become quite an expert at parking in that area, but this was another first time. We walked into some back streets behind the station and there was a hatch in the ground which you could barely squeeze through, and then you took a bit of a leap to an arched area underneath the brick piers supporting the railways.

Not very big but smoky and sleazy. It seemed oppressive because you knew how much brick was above. We stood around drinking and talking until it was necessary to piss. After I'd done the deed I was appalled when I was shown that the urinals weren't plumbed into anywhere: behind the board on which they were mounted was a flat area with men rolling in the liquid. Although I'd been told by the Angels that you wouldn't catch anything from piss, this sight still appalled me; perhaps it was that those involved actually appeared to be turned on by the degradation. Wet jeans with the Angels had been a 'grin and bear it' situation.

That cellar was run by a group called the Metropolitan Bikers; it was later the subject of an exposé by a Sunday tabloid newspaper and was shut down. When Celestine disco opened a few years later they opened a Cavern Bar, the entrance to which was at the opposite side of the street to what had been the Metropolitan Bikers' cellar.

Some of the non-London bikers had a group going called CPBB. The club badge could be explained to inquisitive bikers as 'Centre Point Bike Boys' but, to any gay man knowing the euphemistic and heavily legally scrutinised language of gay personal ads, CP could only indicate corporal punishment, and BB meant 'bare buttocks' or 'beating and bondage', so the intention of the club was quite obvious really.

I was still just 21 years old and, although no longer technically 'chicken' (which meant younger than 21), I did seem to be popular with the members of the club.

The President of CPBB, Martin, lived in the Rutland area and held parties at his house. Sometimes these were preceded by events that were supposed to bolster the reputation of the club as a real bike club. There were Treasure Hunts and Economy Runs – the latter pandering to the noticeably slower speeds that the queer bikers rode at compared to my real rough biker friends.

CPBB had ten written rules of the usual kind concerning the running of the club and a notorious unwritten Rule Eleven which stated that at club events lights would go out at

10 p.m. and all members must remove their trousers. The sadomasochism interests were well explored before everyone bundled up together to sleep a bit.

One particularly notorious piece of equipment was 'The Board'. This was a large piece of wood which was supported at the ends and on top of which you lay naked and face down. Hands and feet secured and head maybe blindfolded. But the surprises were the holes in the board which gave access to the tits and cock and balls. You got teased and tickled, then tit-clipped and maybe caned, finally thoroughly fucked.

Those days before AIDS you got Vaseline and grease (cooking or metalwork) used on you and you sucked cock till you choked and then some more. It wasn't long before I found myself going to the clap clinic in Windsor; not the local one in Slough in case I was recognised: being gay was definitely a stigma.

I was diagnosed with NSU (urethritis) and given a load of tablets and it went away. Next dose was warts up the bum; they painted on some foul-looking brown liquid that got painful fast and stayed painful for a couple of days even after washing it off.

Another CPBB weekend was in a farmhouse near Shipston on Stour. The farmer was gay and liked bikers. With our bikes all parked up in the yard outside, we had a meal in a big long refectory-type room. Afterwards we went up an open staircase to a loft above. It had no light except cracks coming through from the room downstairs. The farmer went misty-eyed seeing all these men there, saying it reminded him of the time during World War II when he had accommodated some Germans on the farm as prisoners of war.

On that run I made it for sex with a council parks gardener from Taunton; he had tight jeans, brown DM boots and cropped hair – a skinhead. I had long hair then, down to my shoulders, and we grappled and wrestled a bit as part of our sex play: Angel versus skinhead, the old rivalry.

The Royal Wedding in the summer of 1981 marked a watershed; for that occasion and for the month-long InterRail holiday that I took immediately afterwards, I changed to a crew cut. I told people at work it was for practical reasons for the holiday but it was also a deliberate style change. The crew cut was done with scissors by a Cypriot barber near Centre Point. I've been cropped or skinhead ever since.

Suburbia

July 1981

Dear Doug,

I thought I'd write about a guy who also answered that same wank-mag advertisement you replied to – he's a biker, about 5'11", broad frame, broad shoulders, etc. Goes around as an Angel, either as a slave or a Master, depending. Got a pair of nice leather jeans, unlined throughout but flared, with a button and a thong to gather up the flare when riding the bike. Triumph Bonny or Harley Low Rider.

He came back here and we had a few drinks and smokes. It was fairly hot – I'd fixed the heating and he was in his leather jeans and dark-blue T-shirt, biceps just about squeezing through the T-shirt arms – he weight-lifts as well.

So he gets the conversation on to sex, the size of cockrings, dildos and so on, wants to look at a four-in-one belt I won at a disco competition on New Year's Day 1980: it makes into a belt or (usefully) breaks down into four restraints.

Then, while he's looking in my bottom drawer, he notices the handcuffs; he pushes me backward from sitting on the bed and holds me down – remember he's about four times the size of me. Gets the cuffs on – and the game's up. He takes my jeans off and just about gets a 'Four-Gates of Hell' strap on me: you know, both balls through one ring, another in the usual place and two on the prick pulling it down to the balls.

Buttplug in and shorts over. He likes the hook on the dildo showing through the shorts. With my legs over my head and tied to the bed-head, he tore the white shorts off and then he gets the small dildo out and gently eases in a larger one, then screws it about a bit and tries a few of my toys on himself, comes back to me and puts some oil from the kitchen on my hairy navel and starts massaging me about – pecs, shoulders, etc.

He takes out the buttplug and comes himself – I'm bursting inside the Gates of Hell rings but he won't let me come until he's come hard against me. Then he tells me he'll untie my hands. I can take off the rings and wank, while he massages my arse with Deep Heat. Wow, what a lubricant. I was on fire and came enthusiastically.

We met on another Saturday night to go to the East London leather pub – the Princess of Russia, home of a leather club, some of whose members seem more into needlepoint than riding bikes. The club had a party in an old warehouse in Spitalfields which has a fantastic spacious cellar, a roaring fire providing almost the only illumination from a huge open fireplace. We brought booze from the pub and fucked around in the firelight shadows on the broken stone floor. Tough on the knees. No toilets – or they were busy – so he pissed on my colours. Rode home happy with a sore and greasy arse again.

I also had a good night last Saturday, was down in Slaveway in Leicester Square again, and a friend of mine, Walid, won their 'Mr Slaveway' competition – he's the guy who got me into weight-training. They'd got one of the back rooms all lit brightly advertising things, and the other one was very, very crowded, so I left 2.30ish and went cruising up to Hampstead and the Heath. Got fucked gently and came home. Slept till three in the afternoon!

So this Master answered an ad I'd put in a gay muscle magazine: 'slave requires further training . . . etc'. I'd replied to his letter, telling him what I'd done so far, what sort of limits I'd go to and so on. He wanted every sentence, even in a letter, to end with 'Sir' and for me to always use lower-case letters such as 'i' not 'I' when referring to myself. He threatened to punish me when we met if I failed to comply. The next letter was a list of questions asking in detail what I was after: 'Do you want to be shaved? All over? How about nettles wiped over you (the effect dies away after about ¾ hour). Will you be clean when you arrive at the house? How large a dildo can you take? Have you ever had Deep Heat on your arse?' and so on. He said that while I was in training as his slave there would be no normal conversations and if asked to speak I would only be permitted the following words: 'Yes,' 'Sir,' 'More,' 'and Harder,' 'please, Sir.' The omission of any form of 'No' or a 'Stop' word turned me on particularly . . .

I replied and was sent another letter – by now they were addressed to me by name on the envelope and inside I was either called 'slave Nº 26' or just 'slave' – and this letter gave detailed instructions on where to meet this Master, what to wear, etc.

I was to arrive at the door of the house, in suburbia, wearing only my shoes or boots, no socks, leather shorts, buttplug and 2½-inch cock-ring in place, and a chain round my neck. I was not allowed to bring a bag; this was in January. If I was late for any reason I'd be sent to run round the block, timed and punished if too slow, the number of strokes equal to the number of minutes I was late.

So I turned up as instructed. First thing the guy did was to handcuff me on the porch, hands in front of me. Next he put a leather hood which smelt of grease and piss over my head. It had zips for the mouth and slits for the nose and eyes and a blindfold over that so I could not hear or see properly. Then he pulled my balls out through the leg of my shorts, attached a ball-stretcher and weight and left my prick inside the shorts. My legs were held apart by restraints and a pole and he started playing with my prick.

Then he pulled off the shorts and bent me double over a carpenter's saw-bench, feet attached to one side and arms the other. He played with the dildo for a while, took it out and added it to the weight on my balls and started to fuck me. I never saw his prick, but it felt about fourteen inches long and six inches wide and hard as a broom handle – perhaps it was. Then he made me come and then he came inside me, rocking me backward and forward as he did.

There was another guy who invited/instructed me to come round to his place at 2020 hours sharp. He'd told another slave to arrive at 2000 and I was to go into the room on my left, strip and blindfold myself, stand with my hands on my head and wait. He'd already restrained the other slave and left him in another room. Then he came in and handcuffed me, put bicep restraints on, rubbed oil over my body, around my prick and arse, to lubricate me. He put a ball-stretcher and collar on me and made me kneel.

Then he brought in the other slave, also blindfolded, and made him kneel behind me, back to back. He tied the collars together and restrained our arms so that our hands were over each other's prick. (We'd never seen each other and could only feel the warmth of our backs in contact – magic!) He got us wanking together but stopped us before it went too far.

Then he got one of us to lie down on a bare bed – just the springs – tied the slave up to it and told the other to fuck the tied-up slave and to do it nicely as he'd change the slaves round so that next the one being fucked did the fucking. That was nice. Then he put buttplugs up each of us, tied us up standing together – collars and ball-stretchers tied – and told us to wank off, still blindfolded and in hoods. Then he separated us and sent us home. I believe it is called 'lack of closure' by the shrinks – doing something intense with an unknown person.

Replies to Your Questions, Sir

1. I'm clean-shaven and I don't want to be shaved anywhere.
2. Yes, I've got a small buttplug – could arrive wearing it.
3. Got denim, leather, sports shorts. Prefer to arrive in leather jacket, nothing under; jeans (shorts under if required) and DMs or over-trousers, which will come off over DMs.
4. Yes, oil, grease, mud, etc, jeans and anywhere except face.
5. Bike boots and leathers, one-piece leather suit (not to get too dirty), leather shirt, singlet.
6. Short hair, nearly skinhead every two months or so.
7. Clean-shaven.
8. Can't wear dirty clothes to work.
9. Could get dirty Friday (Heath, etc.), go home and do shopping, etc, and come back on Saturday. I work indoors so can't wear leathers all day.
10. Dirty runs fine.
11. No to rings in tits or cock or anywhere.
12. Ditto tattoos or brands.
13. Work in an electronics workshop. Yamaha XJ750 bike from Maidenhead to work in Wembley.
14. Single – live alone.

May I bring a camera along again, please, Sir?
Not too heavy first time. I don't like being cold, Sir.

The Wirral

September 1981

Dear Dave, Sir,

Your letter arrived about twenty minutes ago. I've just washed and must get to work soon on my bike; I work in Levi's, T-shirt and training shoes, and put leather jeans – big, baggy, roomy leather jeans – over my denims to go to work and a scarf *tight* around my face under my crash hat to keep the wind out. I have a feeling that today I'll put my tight leather shorts on under my jeans and be turned on further all day.

I went for a weekend with a guy who has a cottage rented in the country. I took an army tank-suit and was either naked or in that – it's roomy and will go over restraints or ropes and it's warm.

He collected me from the station, put a dog chain round my neck and tied me up in the back of his van and drove me to his cottage. After he unloaded I was put in the woodshed, hands in manacles, and attached to one of the beams. A ball-stretcher parachute was put on my balls. They're relatively big, though my prick's about five and a half or six inches and it's often fun watching/feeling Masters struggling to contain them in T-straps which they can't fit!

No need for a hood (dark). He took me inside, laid me face down on the floor and made me put my Doc Martens on, blindfolded me, gently teasing me with a cat when I got it wrong. Then he put me face down, attached straps and ropes to my legs and a pole to keep them apart, and then he pulled the pole up with a couple of hoists, made it off and gave me a buttplug and then his cock in my mouth.

That session started Thursday evening and I went home Sunday evening. He tied me up at night – ropes all over me and then tied me to the bed.

He supervised morning push-ups and chinning, ordered

me to cook the breakfast (English bacon + eggs + sausage) and during the day we worked on the cottage, him in overalls and me with a cockstrap, a collar, boots and torn denim jeans. We did some gardening but it was mainly inside. Once I didn't work to his satisfaction and he made me get the hoist out and he suspended me from a board with boots screwed into it – leaving my weight on my shoulders. He put an electric vibrator in and got me nearly wanting to come, then threw a bucket of cold water over me!

I've been back to him several times since then – it's fun as it's in the right surroundings and he doesn't overdo the humiliation side – he recognises that it's a game which is being done for both sides' enjoyment in the end.

Biker Bondage in the Woods

December 1981

Dear Doug,

I've met this really nice bondage guy; he used to be an amateur boxer and is now into bikes, racing Yammy 250s. I'm not so much into pain as you seem to be, and he (Geoff) is pretty good at tying one up – chain across the bed, collar then handcuffs attached to it, and legs pulled down hard to the end of the bed – blindfolding and generally turning on. Ball-stretcher then Deep Heat on balls. Buttplug then dildo then vibrator.

He's good-looking as well and has the knack of keeping one turned on for a couple of hours at a stretch – bloody murder but you've got to be cruel to be kind, etc.

Also I've been out with another guy who met me at a motorway junction, padlocked my bike and took me off in his van, changed me into shorts and rugger shirt, had me run from one cottage to another, wanked me and went off with my shorts, throwing me another pair as he went – made of rubber!

Then I had to run to another cottage. He wanked me again, left me another pair of shorts and off I go to another cottage – except that he's put a Ty-wrap on my cock (like a cock-strap but hard nylon and you can make it tighter) and the shorts are flimsy, so the hard-on shows through, if not bounces out. So I'm running along a high street. Then the shorts break under the arse and I'm running with it all hanging out at closing time.

I meet him at this next cottage. He Ty-wraps my hands (like cuffs but removable) and makes me walk in front of him. Passing cars make the broken shorts blow up, hard-on and all.

Into some woods by a stream. He Ty-wrapped me to a tree, with my feet Ty-wrapped apart to a branch. Deep Heat on my balls, shorts in my mouth. He starts stuffing Maltesers up my bum – they make bloody good suppositories. He Sellotapes my legs together, puts shaving foam up the inside of my rugger shirt, axle grease on my cock, then he wanks me a bit more to make the Maltesers hard to keep in. Then he leaves me with my hands free, nearly ready to let my bum go, and with no shorts but a note to tell me where some shorts are.

I just about manage to untape myself and find the shorts buried in some mud, and I follow the directions to run back to my bike: phew!

Biker in the Cellar

October 1983

I recently went out on Saturday to the new leather and denim pub in Shoreditch with rubber trousers on underneath Moto-X boots, leather jeans, rubber shirt, army pullover and bike leather jacket. Plus cock-ring and buttplug. Had a good time talking to friends except that Peter had two skinheads in tow, just coming out of the monogamous love-affair stage. Decided it was impossible to split them so left my phone number with one (who turned up here for a session in my dark, damp cellar last week) and went on to Hampstead Heath – it was a nice night and I needed some 'relief'.

Unusually for me (alcohol?) I got stuck in quickly with the first guy to hand, then a crowd formed around us and this guy in a rubber one-piece suit with a through-zip took me somewhere less public.

He stuffed some rubber in my mouth and put a hood over my head and started pouring oil into my jeans. Rubbed the oil up the front of my shirt and all around; he got me kneeling and sucking him despite the rubber in my mouth. With me thus tied up, both hands to a branch above me with bits of sash-rope, he found I'd got the buttplug in and started playing with it and pulling at my balls and tits through the rubber. Finally ended up fucking me, standing, very thoroughly – big prick, and mine sloshing around inside the rubber.

I gave him my phone number sticker – a week later he turned up here. I have a terraced house and it's easy to bring a visitor into the kitchen, give him a drink of coffee if he's a cold biker, and then go to the cellar downstairs, taking a candle or night-light. The cellar doesn't have many fixtures except an old kitchen unit and two old doors, but in the dark it's great.

He'd arrived wearing bike boots, jeans soaked in chain

lube (bike drive-chain grease, thick and black), T-shirt and leather jacket and colours – also greasy. I slipped a buttplug in me and a candle up him and put gloves on. Although his jeans were greasy he hadn't greased up so he had a lot of cooking fat (cheaper than Crisco) smeared around him. We messed around a bit and went out for a ride on his bike, then stopped near Hounslow and pissed into each other's jeans, the piss running warm inside and down into our boots. He bent me over his bike and fucked me hard and fast, coming all the way out and ramming hard in.

I've been taking more photos for a leather company who design and make high-quality leather chastity belts, shorts and jocks, etc. The photos were fun to do, even if more than 200 pictures of them made my bathroom – shall I say 'untidy'? Some of the photos were taken in an army surplus shop at the Angel, Islington. It got a bit involved as I took a fancy to Jon, who was the model there. It happened that the next Sunday I went to Redhill as a slave, as did Jon, so was able to cuddle him slave-to-slave, tied up and blindfolded, which was quite the best way to meet another slave.

New Cross and Den Haag

November 1983

I became a slave to two Masters who live in southeast London; they replied to an advert of mine in a gay muscle photo magazine and there was one Saturday when I had nothing to do and hadn't wanked in the morning so I ended up phoning mid-afternoon to go and see them.

I was to turn up at 2100 hours on their doorstep, dressed in Doctor Marten boots (14-hole), cammo trousers and leather jacket, and with a buttplug up my bum and a cock-ring on my cock. If I arrived at the correct time then the door would be ajar and I would find a note inside with further instructions. I arrived correctly and the note said to close the door, put on the blindfold provided and then the handcuffs and to kneel, doggy position, and wait.

I hadn't seen a photo of the Master, although he'd asked me if his friend could also do me over. In due course a boot arrived for me to lick and I was then dragged downstairs and chained to a post in a cellar, hands above my head and a chain round my waist securing me to the post. A joint was presented to me. While I was smoking a few drags, the Master's leather-covered hands examined my chest and tits and cock and balls; a chain was put round me to secure the buttplug and a ball-weight was put on my balls.

A ball-weight is made of surgical-grade stainless steel and is a hollow cylinder with a weight of about ten ounces and a hole in the middle just large enough to squeeze the balls through. The effect is fantastic, the more so as I'd never seen anything like it. The Master released one of my hands to allow me to feel the device and asked me if I could get it off; it felt as if my balls had had a permanent shackle put on them.

There were many other things that we did that night. I was given some caning for disobedience and in the middle of it I realised that there was another pair of hands being nice to me, and there were then two Masters.

They threatened me with a complete body-shave, but I resisted, and in the end they only cropped my head hair. I stayed overnight there, tied up on the floor in their bedroom. In the morning I was sent out running in football kit, no jock, still with the ball-weight on, so my balls were well bounced and my hard cock was showing a bit. I was allowed to take the blindfold off when I left the house and had to put it back on when I returned. I was allowed to see the tattoos on their arms and cocks, but not to glimpse their bodies and faces.

I went back for many sessions, one of which culminated in the attachment of a dog chain round my neck and the soldering of the final link so that it wouldn't come off without using tools. Unlike the ball-weight, it stayed on full-time and, as it was winter, it could be worn inconspicuously under clothing.

Ball-weight Stuck On

December 1983

Dear Sirs (Ed and Eddie),
So, I've just finished getting that ball-ring off: I put it on last night when I got back from training at the YMCA (the neck chain got some interested looks) and had a bad (but enjoyable) night's sleep as a result (too much wanking again).

Went out shopping this morning with it on under my jeans making me look as if I've got something like twenty inches there. Returned, wanked again (I'm getting the technique of pushing really hard to overcome the ring, which makes for a great climax) and did some other shopping, by which time I was getting fairly noticeable ball-ache and starting to think about getting the ring off. Fifteen minutes later, no progress, ball-ache worse and me getting a bit worried. I'd delayed putting it on until after training as I'd suspected it would not be too easy to get off, but the possibility of it not coming off hadn't quite sunk in – after all there is the Principle of Reciprocity: what goes up must come down.

So I started trying out different trousers – US fatigues, Brit. Cammo, posh black ones and less tight jeans than normal – just in case it was for ever. Less disastrous to change my trousers for work than some possibilities, like wearing a ring for the rest of my life – or attempts with a hacksaw to get it off and embarrassing visits to Casualty.

This time cold water didn't help; nor did poppers or wandering around the house without any trousers to cool off the blood. Getting desperate – or resigning myself not to cop out of what I'd intended to do (wear it from Thursday night to Monday morning) – I went out walking to the shops – to reproduce the conditions that had enabled me to get it on.

It wasn't so bad anyway, but I was afraid that my balls might swell or something and make it impossible to ever get it off. Got back, despite some interested looks from the checkout boy at the supermarket (I expect I looked almost as guilty as I did when I went there with a buttplug in), and am very relieved to have got it off. Perhaps I should have made myself sign a statement that I won't put it on again as otherwise I wonder how long it'll be before temptation gets the better of me and I'm skating on thin ice again.

There might be something to be said for the lockable ball-shackle – lock it on me on Thursday, and take it off (if I'm good) on Sunday.

New Year in Holland

January 1984

It soon came up to Christmas and I'd organised a trip to a Master (Jan) in Holland. Ed and Eddie were a bit sick about it, but determined not to be shown up.

I returned from a family Christmas and went almost directly to their place, still not having seen either of them. They got me very high, both on grass and on bondage, spread-eagling me against their wall in a kneeling position and making me suck them. They put in their Prince Albert piercing rings and made me suck their cocks, then tied me over a bench and put a dog chain round my neck with a padlock so that it wouldn't come off. They kept me tied up while I sucked one and was fucked by the other.

They cropped all my body hair and my head hair to a Number One, and we generally had a heavy session.

I went home to my place that night and then caught the boat to Holland, and the Dutch guy (Jan) was waiting at the station for me. He was everything I could have wanted at that moment; he is quite different from the London two. I was going to say that he's not physical, but he is and we had really good mind-blowing sex. There was no great equipment involved, but the main thing was that he is the Master and I am his slave.

Second night he made me shave myself totally, which I did without question, unlike in London, and he took me to Amsterdam for the New Year's Eve 'L' party, as his slave. I wore nothing too showy in clothes or gear but I had on a pricker cock strap which slowly made a red feeling around my cock, and there was the newly shaved feeling around my legs and the bruises on my bum.

He chained me to a railing at the 'L' party and left me with instructions to look only at the boots of the men passing and to resist any advances. That was hard, but great, and a great solo ego trip at turning men away.

Back at his place we did some SM gym exercises. I train two or three times a week anyhow so am in quite good shape. He got me doing press-ups and was encouraging me with the cat on each power stroke. We also did bicep curls with tit clamps on, the pain from the tit clamps obscures the pain from the muscles so I really worked hard. We did sit-ups with tit clamps, and if I was flagging he would use the cat across my back.

I came back on the boat really happy.

The two in London and I eventually had to see each other. When I did see them it was amazing: I'd been associating the wrong body with the wrong voice – the heavy voice went with the light body and small cock!

Holland Again

February 1984

I went to Amsterdam with Ed and Eddie in their car but that really marked the end of it sexually: I couldn't take it from them and then the next minute hear them bickering about which postcard to buy.

I stayed with Jan for a week as his slave, staying indoors while he went to work. One day he left me the new edition of *The Leatherman's Handbook* to read but not wank to (that is forbidden while I am his slave) and he asked me questions on it in the evening and punished me for those that I got wrong.

Jan also got me doing press-ups to his boots. Him standing straight up in (army gear, I think) big boots, and using a cat to encourage me on to sets of a hundred (it's all true!) with me doing press-ups, my face to his boots, and being whipped if I didn't keep a straight back or didn't keep going.

Other times we tried bicep curls with tit-clips on (the theory is that you're busy thinking about the pain from the tit-clips so you don't notice the pain on your muscles); also pull-ups to a chinning bar with ball parachute and a weight.

And the old favourite of sit-ups. We've been doing a variation on the end of my weights bench: the guy doing the exercise lies on the floor, legs up on the bench so that his calves and feet are on the seat, thighs vertical. The other guy sits (gently) on his shins; the effect is to come up to suck the guy's cock on every rep, which (I've never done it) could be intensified with tit-clips and chain.

Jersey, Channel Islands

May 1984

Jan, Den Haag, Holland

Dear Sir,
   I've been having a great time. Sitting here with stripes on my bum and thighs, I'm continually reminded of it. Jersey was a long overnight trip on the boat away, although I spent a lot of it talking to a biker in leather and Moto-X boots who turned out to be going to Jersey to work in a theatre over the summer. I saw him again several times as my friends are into the theatre world there.
   Was met by Michael & Michael. The one I'd been writing to is early thirties; his lover's older. He's over six foot and broad, wore cut-off denim shorts, studded belt, boots and short-sleeved denim shirt. You can imagine that the weather was still fine and I was soon in shorts too. Jersey has a lot of disused fortifications, anti-Napoleon and anti-German. He took me to several and belted or kicked me, the other Michael keeping lookout. The more punishment, the more I wanted to suck him and feel his large chest, shoulders and thighs, although he only let me start at his boots. Lookout Michael invariably came back too soon. I'm getting fed up with being a bit on the side.
   Also he took me out to the cruising ground at night, chains in a harness all over me and a buttplug padlocked in, under the cammo trousers, etc, and ended up pissing all over me, belting me and fucking me. He fucks very hard. The morning I left he fucked me in bed, with no bondage but he's stronger than me and was holding me down by my legs, hands on my knees, in a forced doggy position and all sorts of variations. The net result was a well-fucked sore arse – he wouldn't stop even though I was screaming – nothing really,

really wrong – and ended up with me totally submitted, slightly pissing myself and totally relaxed.

Got back Saturday after long, boring day-boat.

Sunday afternoon, phone rang. I was ordered a short way away for an hour later. Was stripped to boots and found there was another slave there: not full-time military but Territorial – his 'Yes, Sir', had the emphasis very much on the 'Sir', unlike mine. I had to hold him down while he was punished, first by the cane and then with an electric machine, then was told to stick needles through his foreskin and scrotum – which I couldn't do, and was duly caned for, being held down by the other slave. Various other things – buttplugs, being fucked, being caned with the two of us both bent over side by side, elbows touching. The feel of the other is great when being punished, and there's a lot of competitive slavery, of not being the one that couldn't take it – it was really great.

Then he had us clean up, me make the food, talk, etc, then more punishment. The other slave had wanted to go home and was punished again with the electric machine. Either I wasn't into it as much, or the Master was getting very heavy with him, which was worrying me. Anyhow, I refused to hold him down after a fairly short while, and walked out (reasonably gracefully in as much as one can: being fifteen minutes away from home one can do that, which is naughty). It worried me as much that the electric pads could do something dangerous as that he might do it to me. As it turned out, when I had a bath this morning, I'm far more marked than the other guy, and I thought he was the one who was getting the heavy treatment, and I enjoyed it. I cut off Ed and Eddie's chain just before Easter; it didn't mean much any more and it wasn't really on in T-shirt weather.

Lockable Ball-weight

September 1984

I reckon I've actually invented a new sex toy: Ed and Eddie had made me wear a metal cylinder about one inch long and two inches in diameter made from surgical stainless steel so it could be worn indefinitely. All the edges rounded and the hole through the centre, just big enough to get the balls through with a bit of pain but too small for the weight to fall off. The 'problem' was that it was a bit of a squeeze to get it on and wearing it made the balls swell so that removing it was not always possible just when you wanted to.

The feeling of wearing it (e.g. for a long weekend) under loose cammo trousers with no jock is fantastic: balls pulled down continually, stairs an interesting adventure! You get to forget about it and then suddenly are reminded of your status as your Master's slave by a surprise tug to your balls when you make a sharp move. In bed at night your balls are pulled down between your legs or you have to sleep face down, screwing the bed. Jacking off wearing a ball-weight is an experience every man should try — there's an ecstatic rhythm you can get up between bouncing your balls and wanking your prick.

Now I've stopped being Ed and Eddie's slave I got a Hell's Angel metalworker friend with a lathe to turn some more ball-weights like theirs and also to make the new one that has the cylinder cut in half so it can be put on and off without trouble. There are holes cut to fasten the halves together using security screws, ones you can't open with ordinary tools. This overcomes most of the problems of the simpler ball-weights and has a much smaller hole in the middle so it won't fall off except when the Master chooses to unlock it.

I collected it on my bike from the metalworker at his home garage. He blindfolded me while I was still in my crash hat and bike leathers. He attached my hands to the chain hoist and positioned me over the engine inspection pit so that I was stretched tight with one boot resting on either side and almost suspended above the six-foot drop. He extracted my bollocks from inside my leathers and my scrotum felt for the first time the surgical steel that it would come to know so intimately.

He was fumbling down there for some while after screwing together the two precisely aligned halves of the ball-weight. He left me for some time. I was swinging slightly, taking my weight on my hands; my prick was showing that it was enjoying the rocking and pull from my bollocks. My 'friend' cheerfully informed me that my new toy had been fitted and that the epoxy glue that he used to cover the security screw-heads was now set. So, although in theory this was a removable ball-weight, it was now up to me to pick out the epoxy glue to free myself.

Unsustainable Skinhead Lifestyle

September 1984

Did I ever tell you why I support West Ham? It mainly revolves around an ex-army skinhead racing biker called Spike.

I'd been going around with him a lot this time last year; he was then working for a motorbike paper and test-riding all sorts of classy bikes. Previously he'd been racing bikes properly, though I think he never really made the big time, i.e. got signed up by one of the big works teams.

My involvement with him came to a sudden end when another friend showed me a small bit in the newspaper saying that he'd been killed in a collision with a big car. We think it was more complicated as he'd been very down at that time; he might well have been drinking too much, but no one will ever know.

Obviously I was very down after that for a while; it wasn't just the fact that he was dead but also that the image that Spike represented was not tenable for very long. He had been one of the few bikers who was able to consistently ride faster than me and appear to get away with it. He carried the skinhead image through all he did as well. He wasn't a no-hoper on the dole: Daddy was rather well off and Spike had several security companies going as well as the journalism.

Anyhow, Spike lived around East Ham and supported West Ham Football Club fanatically; he had the WHFC crest tattooed on his forearm and for a time was sponsored by them, so had a set of leathers on WHFC colours too.

You'll remember that I support the fans; I'm not very interested in the game or the footballers, although some of them are very dishy in nice shorts ... Spike got me along several times to see matches from the terraces and introduced me to some of the characters there – much better than going without a friend as there's quite a bit of rough goes on. So that's West Ham. At least they win matches, too.

I'm back on the Prestel computer network. Maybe Peter showed you his terminal. It's like Teletext except that you receive data over the telephone and you have to pay for it. There are gay personal ads on it which seem to produce replies, although not a lot of them are worth meeting – but it's fun exchanging weight-training schedules with other people. I can leave messages for people to pick up when they next connect up to the computer – they call it 'electronic mailbox'.

Redhill Slave Training

September 1984

I re-established relations with a Master called Sam who has a place south of London and has an attic done out as a playroom with a very large collection of toys and equipment. He has wooden stocks, whipping bench, fistfucking bench, pulleys and suspension gear and (it seems) an infinite supply of toys and ideas about using the place. Also, I believe, a permanent slave; certainly the other slave I've been there with is very into it and seems to know his way around, makes tea, etc.

The conditions of my going there included being clean when I turned up, wearing only cotton clothes (i.e. no belt, etc) and DM boots. When I arrived I had to strip, except for my boots, fold my clothes and then go upstairs into the playroom. I guess the other slave was kept in the cage there – I couldn't see him.

I was immediately made to lick my Master's boots; a hood was put over my head (no eyeholes at all and a strap over the mouth-hole); I was tied very closely to the whipping bench and lightly (heavily enough!) whipped. The other slave was then tied to me and the bench and soundly whipped too.

Being tied to him and each being beaten established a physical bond that grew in intensity throughout. At times when he was being beaten, chained to the bench, and I was licking boot, it was immaterial whether it was actually him or me that was being beaten: it felt the same. When he was near the limit of his endurance I felt so too, and cooling his heated bum (licking his cheeks) reinforced the link.

The night together was fantastic, each restrained by leather chastity belts and secured by iron collar and chain to the cage. No words – all communication was animal – hopelessly turning each other on, our cocks each hurting when hard, unable to come yet increasingly wanting to, made totally helpless by our Master, accepting and revelling in our bondage, tiring each other out, falling asleep in each other's arms only to awake again with a still-hard, still-restrained cock and fellow slave.

The elation I felt driving home, having been released, hearing words spoken on the radio, realising that the night could only have been like that because of the pain and bondage from our Master.

I realise the similarities with other things I get up to – weight-training with a partner, each encouraging the other and getting each other through pain barriers, the military scene, under discipline together. I've had several drawings made depicting the Master–slave relationship and the most recent painting I now see in terms of the slave–slave bond, although that wasn't consciously in my mind when I commissioned the artist to paint it.

To reflect even further, perhaps what it is in SM that has been turning me on is not primarily the Master–slave relationship as I often don't respond as much if I can see my Master or more generally if the Master/slave side gets emphasised. Rather an almost masturbatory image of myself: one part of me being a slave, the other part holding the slave's hand. With his slave that night, I was me, the part of me that thinks, and the other slave was the wank image I have of myself as a total slave, ringed, shaved and beaten.

Another side is being Top. I've got an ad that reads: *Skinhead bootboy for private weight-training and jogging pacing*. It produces all sorts – the easiest to deal with are the corporal punishment (CP) fans: cup of coffee, chat and beat their bum as required.

There are a few who actually want to do some weight-training and then have a quickish massage but even they mostly want to gawp at me doing the training. There is one who does a good hard session, in as much as one can in about 25 minutes, but unfortunately none of them are interesting enough for a heavy SM gym session, which is a shame!

There was one who I went for a jog with, him in skimpy shorts, me in all my army kit and boots. I had a good wank after that one! The others want varying introductions into

SM, which I think I do responsibly; flatteringly they do keep coming back. It's also a way of getting experience of what it is that a Master gets out of SM and so I hope helps me to give you, Sir, a good time.

I feel much more at ease exploring this side of myself while I have a loving relationship with Peter W so that I'm not 'desperate' for human contact as well, i.e. I can explore the animal side without the human side butting in as it's lonely. And as we know, 'a good S is hard to get'. In a way I'm saving myself for Peter, who is not into SM, and the other good S guys I know and I'm having fun getting my experience at playing S. All in all I'm having a good time!

Amsterdam New Year 1985

We went to Amsterdam for the weekend and New Year. We stayed at the Pole Hotel, which was OK, though cheap. There seemed to be some rooms rented by the hour by street boys.

Sunday we got up early and went to a coffee shop downtown for a coffee-and-cookies breakfast at midday! Then to the Stadtsmuseum, which has modern art. Our heads got going and I started seeing all sorts of wonderful things in Klee, Matisse and so on.

I was chucked out at closing time and had a doze at the hotel until Jan arrived in town. We had a meal and then went to the 'A' bar and then the 'E'. 'A' too crowded; 'E' was good. I ended up in the fuck room upstairs with a guy who put some handcuffs on me, restraining me to the vertical scaffolding bars there. I could stand up or kneel but not move away or sideways.

Then he got two pairs of tit-clips and put them on his left tit to my right tit, etc. He started pulling himself away from me and pushing me down on my knees, getting out his cock, which turned out to be covered all over by a rubber sheath and leather strap. I started sucking him right down – no small cock either. He came inside the rubber . . .

Also had a couple of guys down on me, licking my boots and sucking my cock and balls.

Peter met a Frenchman he'd seen at the 'L' party at the beginning of December (the last time we went to Holland) and had a good time with lots of piss and spit. Jan found a cute Berlin biker in a one-piece red, white and black leather suit also staying at the Pole, so we all ended up back in the same hotel.

Monday (New Year's Eve) didn't start until midday, and then we went to Den Haag with Jan, looked around the shops and got very stoned at his place, then to the 'L' party. Peter in full rubber with jacket, shirt, jeans, gloves and 20-hole Doctor Marten boots. Me in rubber shirt, a denim cut-down jacket and tight denim jeans cut short just below the knees to show off my shiny black Commando boots. The two of them ensured I was also carrying in my rectum all four 38mm steel balls, which was heaven: a combination like a buttplug fucking me and my head being in my bum – the momentum sensing had gone from my head to my arse.

Got there and we were then posing around watching the rest of the world arrive. I got Peter hands up against the wall, legs apart, and made as if I was searching him like they do at the airport and got a lot of eyes watching. Lots of action in the backroom and toilet bit but I was having a fantastic body trip on the steel balls and Peter – playing with each other, hands through our newly cropped hair, and generally turning each other on. Got home at about 5 a.m.

The rest of New Year's Day we spent in the day sauna. I cruised two guys in the Jacuzzi, one with cropped hair and built like a brick shit-house (big shoulders and arms) with a peacock on his right shoulder and a couple of other tattoos on his left. His mate was a Leatherman Master. They took me out from the Jacuzzi to the fuck rooms upstairs. I was playing as if I didn't understand the language: it saves everyone opening their mouths and spoiling it! I had the guy with the tattoos underneath me, wanking himself, me doggy position over him being fucked by his mate and giving him a heavy rub down, while we played with each other's skinhead hair. We all had a good time. I also found again a big black guy in the hot room whom I'd seen on our last visit. Peter was equally satisfied.

Master Jim, Frosterley, County Durham

DAILY DISCIPLINES FOR slave mark FROM MASTER J
1. No briefs or pants to be worn at any time – only jocks allowed.
2. Sleep nude every night wearing cock & ball strap.
3. Breakfast to consist of dry Ryvita-type biscuits and black tea/coffee only.
4. Jog 3–5 miles each day wearing jock, tracksuit, socks and trainers only. No shorts or vest allowed.
5. Do twenty press-ups each morning wearing tit-clips & chain.
6. Nightly wank in bed into condom, then eat your spunk – very nutritious.
7. Only allowed to piss freely three times each day – any extra pisses to be made through or into jock, which must remain on your body.

DAY BY DAY DISCIPLINES FOR slave mark FROM MASTER J

MON   Wear tight leather thong bondage on cock and balls under jock all day.

TUES   During evening pack jock with ice and keep in until melted; also push four ice cubes up arse at same time.

WED   Go out in public for two hours at least wearing cock-ring with chain attached, the end of which is hanging visibly over top of jeans on right side.

THUR   Wear buttplug all day, plus spring clothes peg on scrotum behind balls under jock.

FRI   Wear leather belt round waist next to skin all day. Put cock and balls in leather thong bondage so that cock is pulled up tightly through legs over crack and fastened in centre at back. If this is not possible pull it up tightly to belt at front.

SAT Go out shopping or in public wearing tit-clips and chain, also peg on end of cock for at least two hours.

SUN Put five-pound weight (at least) on balls (without jock) and do running on the spot or jumping exercises for five minutes in morning. During afternoon or evening place Deep Heat wadding in jock over cock and balls and keep wadding in for at least twenty minutes.

February 1985

Dear Sir,

Thank you for providing me with the training programme in your last letter. Sir, I fear I have been unsuccessful in following all of your instructions. Daily, I have worn jocks and slept nude (with cock and ball strap in place, though I only wore a buttplug for one night, Sir, had an almighty wank in the middle of the night, Sir, and removed it in the interests of getting some rest). I have been drinking black coffee first thing, and not having breakfast, though a sandwich at 11 a.m. I managed to run for about 35 minutes on Sat, Mon and Tues, though other commitments have prevented me from continuing every day, Sir. I'm afraid that I have been unable to comply with any of your provisions concerning piss, Sir.

Although I have made an attempt to reduce the number of trips to piss, Sir, and tried once to piss in my jock, Sir, by standing in the bath, jeans off, Sir, and letting it flow, then replacing my jeans over my wet legs, Sir. There were some interesting wet marks down the jeans where the piss got absorbed, Sir, and I got quite randy, Sir. I haven't had to piss at night at all this week, Sir.

I've been doing twenty press-ups every day with clothes pegs on my tits, Sir. I haven't eaten my spunk at all, Sir. Would do if I was made to, Sir, but on my own it's more difficult.

I did manage to wear leather thong bondage on Monday, Sir.

Tuesday, Sir, I don't have access to ice cubes here, Sir, so

I put a can of coke in my jock instead of the ice cubes, Sir, and an ordinary buttplug up my arse, Sir.

Wednesday, I did manage to go out to McDonald's wearing a cock-ring and chain, Sir, and then on to an Earl's Court leather bar, Sir. A guy in the bar started pulling on the chain, Sir, and we had a grope, though nothing heavy, Sir. Monday and Tuesday and Thursday I did a lot of weight-training, Sir.

Thursday, wearing a buttplug to work is not possible, Sir, so I did that last Saturday, and kept it in for most of the afternoon, Sir, going out shopping, etc, Sir.

This Sat I'll try wearing clothes pegs on my tits, Sir. Thursday, I did wear a clothes peg on my scrotum, under the jock, Sir, though took it off by 11.30 a.m., Sir.

Today, Sir, my cock and balls are wrapped in a leather thong, again, Sir, though pulling them through the crack of my arse to my back seems impracticable, Sir. I'm also wearing a belt next to my skin, under my jeans, Sir.

Sir, I hope I am not failing too much in your estimation and look forward to a visit to Frosterley. From my point of view it will not be possible until about the 25th March or later, as I have things planned up till then. I look forward to your observations on my training so far, Sir.

Sir, the heat treatment that you mentioned seems like it would be good training and I look forward to it when I visit your place. Sir, would it be possible to include regular enemas in my training schedule. I have a four-pint bag here and would welcome instructions in that direction, Sir.

Skinhead Video

February 1985

Dear Mario and Joachim,

We made a video last weekend – Peter doing over this skinhead he knows. I edited it and put on a little music so that the pauses between them going on about 'fucking skinhead bastard' and 'skinhead wanker' aren't too bad. Peter starts off cropping this skinhead's hair into a Mohican, then shaving off the sides and then getting rid of his eyebrows – again the clippers, then the razor.

Quite a lot of boots and tattoos flying around as they have a bit of a play together on the bed, and a bit of rough, spitting and then pissing – you can't see the rubber sheet, but it was carefully put there beforehand!

Peter comes on screen, but we couldn't get the other one to come at all; perhaps too much poppers – he was certainly very into it all and has a nice cock. Peter's got the edited copy of it at the moment and is happily showing it to all his friends!

Blind Date at LAX

March 1985

Chris H, Australia

Hi, Chris,

My advert was printed in the American leather magazine before Christmas, and it produced a couple of replies. One was from a guy who said he was a doctor with the US military in Los Angeles, and who asked me to visit him. The conditions were that I was to arrive in Los Angeles and he would look after me from then onwards. When I got myself to Los Angeles International Airport and cleared through Immigration and Customs (with my rucksack full of leather and rubber toys that he's specified that I bring), I was to go out of the obvious exit, walk five yards to my left and wait, standing to attention, eyes down, whereupon he would make himself known.

Various friends thought this was the height of folly and advised totally against it, saying that if I didn't get totally stood up and left there waiting for the whole ten days until my return air flight, then I'd be picked up by a mindless psycho and stabbed. So I took out medical insurance so at least the body would get back!

Other people were winding me up, telling me about people they'd heard of who'd done something similar and had ended up being collected, given acid on the way back from the airport, taken into a darkened playroom, totally tied up and restrained, while the acid got going, and then had the heavy scene of their wildest dreams.

In the event the guy did turn up, although I was extremely apprehensive and got more and more worried that he wouldn't. He had a nice car, newly polished and cleaned with shiny red-leather seats. He drove out from the car park and explained the rules: I was his slave for the ten days, I was not to wear any shoes or socks unless explicitly told (I removed them there and then) and at all times in the car I was to have my cock and balls out (I did so).

He drove from the airport to the Hollywood area of Los Angeles and stopped at a motel on Sunset Boulevard, booked us into a room for two nights and got me down on my knees sucking cock. He explained the rules of the hotel room: I was to be completely naked at all times and was to wear a ball-stretcher as well. At night I was to sleep on the floor. He was going to go out to make some arrangements and would return a few hours later; I was to have some food and do some sightseeing. When he returned, he expected me to be naked on the floor wearing a buttplug and ball-stretcher. And he left. I had a shower and recovered a bit from the ten-hour plane journey from London, and dressed and went out shopping.

When I had got only about a hundred yards from the hotel, a car stopped and asked if I wanted a lift. It was pretty obvious that he expected me to be hustling, even though I was wearing nothing more outrageous than a pair of tight jeans, T-shirt and training shoes. Before I managed to get to a supermarket, two other cars and a motorbike (you don't have to wear a crash hat there) had stopped and asked the same. All at about 6 p.m.!

Shopping done, I went for a walk around Sunset Boulevard and Hollywood Boulevard, looking in the shops. Huge place; with the road being twice as wide as at home, the buildings had to be twice as high to match. Even the people looked different: bigger thighs and broader chest and bigger arse; there's a different shape to American boys and men; I can't work out how to describe it and not imply that they are fat.

The man returned and I was waiting as specified. While I was sucking him from the floor he used some of my leather restraints that I'd brought to tie me up. He announced that he liked me and said that the plan was for me to do some more sightseeing the next day in LA and then we would be flying to Lihue. I asked where Lihue is, and was told it's in Hawaii. The same hotel rules would apply and I would travel on the plane in a rope harness and he would obtain a blanket and I was to have my cock out of my jeans for the duration of the flight. The following day he took me to a 24-hour restaurant for breakfast and dropped me at the start point for a day-long tour.

Back at the motel, he had me strip then took me out shopping naked in his car to a sex shop. Also a hardware store to buy lots of rope and a nice pair of handcuffs. That night I slept in the handcuffs, hands behind my back. Once in a while he turned over and played with me a little, just enough to keep me excited and make it hard for me to go to sleep, even allowing for jet lag.

Things came to a head early in the morning: my raging hard-on hadn't abated and he was getting randy too; despite the cuffs I was able to start fondling him and licking his back. He found the buttplug and the new tin of Crisco and quickly put it in me, still doing nothing to stop my stiff prick. I continued making nice to him, and he got some of the rope out, tied my ankles together and to the bed-head, so I was tied there, arse in air, hands now in front of me. Some heavy strokes of the belt later, my bum was much redder, the buttplug still firmly up there and my cock still hard. He took out the buttplug and immediately started fucking my warmed arse. His hair felt great against my newly shaved and tanned bum, his cock getting even larger inside my shit-hole. He fucked fast and deep and screwed me through and through before coming heavily inside me, eventually withdrawing and leaving me still hard, still tanned.

And that was the end of the SM. We did go to the plane at LA Airport with me wearing the rope harness and some BDUs he provided, my first encounter with American Battle Dress Uniform; these were smart and clean in Woodland Green camouflage pattern and I was dressed in the role of his enlisted secretary. I didn't get my cock out on the plane. And I haven't joined the Mile High club of those who've been fucked at altitude. When we got to Kauai, Hawaii, we stayed in a nice hotel and all the SM went out of the window. I had some good runs along deserted beaches, barefoot and wearing only shorts. We saw some wonderful scenic sights there and on another island, Molokai. After we split back at LA Airport he never made further contact. Maybe he was seeking to recruit me as a spy or maybe he just wanted a holiday companion.

The Black Party

June 1985

I went to the 'Black' party on a Sunday night in London's largest disco and it was all-leather that night. My main occupation in the early part of the night was to help look after the leather company stall there. At the party there were six or seven gay business stalls plus Gay Pride march and so on. Peter (my other half) and I were newly cropped skinheads wearing big shiny DM boots and football socks. The idea of the stall was for everyone to wear bits of really effective leather gear to showcase the designs.

For me and the other gay men on the stall it was just for show but, for the four early-twenties staff from the leather business who are straight, it was sheer necessary protection in a potentially predatory environment. Perhaps I should explain that we were all wearing some form of chastity belt, from a simple locking waist-belt to the lockable leather shorts which I was wearing; this had a hard leather insert and locking straps on the waist and thighs.

And we were all sporting a large number of wrist and ankle restraints with various degrees of security, some done up with padlocks, others with secret keys. The stall had a large (two-inch high) metal collar attached to the table in front by a heavy chain, and we locked it on each other in turn and let the guy just cruise or smoke. There were also some smaller one-inch collars which get locked on tight, which were worn without chains. I had one on all evening and got quite fond of it, so I bought it. In time Peter will get it round his neck . . .

We also had fun with the wrist and ankle restraints: I was wearing some on wrist and biceps, and also some marine spring clips, and was set upon, grabbed, and my arms folded behind my back with alternate wrists and biceps attached – 'Parade Rest' position that the Americans use – then led around the place by a dog chain attached to the collar, causing quite a lot of envy!

Peter turned up and we closed the stall. We'd taken some orders for catalogues, etc.; really everyone had seen it and the straights wanted to go home. Kept the gear on! We cruised the disco and the partly refurbished Cavern bar together. The Cavern had a sort of leather grotto: a fountain and a Leatherman statue and its usual dim lighting.

Skinhead Shaving

Skinheads in Great Britain have a subculture of their own whose externals are tattoos, boots and cropped or shaved hair. Football and fascism are, for them, inextricably bound up with their way of life. But a shaved head in our sexual world has an *entirely different* meaning: the man has allowed another to take away his hair, symbol of strength. Who knows how many men we see walking down the street have discovered the secret delights of shaved arse or balls, a constant (yet impermanent) reminder of their sexuality and the scene which led to the shaving.

The two skinheads I'm thinking of, Steve and Peter, keep each other cropped and shaved regularly. The hair clippers used have different combs for the different crops, generally given numbers roughly equivalent to the number of weeks' growth of hair left, thus the shortest is a Number One, i.e. one week's growth, and the longest is a Number Four.

For a kid going to a barber and asking for a Number One for the first time it's really scary: you've been put up to it by your mates, you've had a wank about it at night, and you've probably got a stiff cock while the barber's at you with the clippers. He's done it many times before and knows how you feel. And then he's cut it all off and there's no way to get it back again: everyone knows you're a skinhead.

But if you've been cropped as a slave there's even more explaining to do. A responsible Master will know that most slaves will be able to explain away a Number Four crop without any problem. Although the slave, tied up and blindfolded, may be threatened with becoming a 'real' skinhead, he may even refuse, but once he has heard the hum of the clippers, felt the softness of his own hair falling on his shoulders, the unusual coolness of his head, he will know there is no turning back.

It is up to the slave to explain to the world his new style, but it is up to the Master to choose the right moment to force the slave to take it willingly, perhaps starting by shaving the slave's cock and balls and arse and at a later date progressing to shaving the rest of his body and ordering the slave to maintain it shaved.

On this occasion Steve turned up at Peter's late, as he'd just been buying some new Doctor Martens. Skins always refer to the number of lace holes and these were 20-hole DMs, the biggest yet on sale, with a steel toecap inside. Peter gave him a Mohican cut almost immediately, cropping then shaving the sides of his head. Steve stripped off and started putting on his new boots, showing his tattoos and fancying his Mohican cut in the mirror. Lacing the boots properly was a problem: ideally the knot should be on the outside of the boot and getting it there is an art. Peter got Steve on the bed and got on with cropping and then shaving his cock and balls, the clippers jangling against the cock-ring Steve wears all the time. Shaving followed, to get a really smooth skin. By now they were getting really randy and some oil got splashed around on to their shaved bodies making the skin contact more intimate.

Skinhead sex is cock, boots, piss and spunk, and helping your mate come. Skins are into being skins together, sucking each other's shaved cocks, running hands through cropped hair, rubbing oil over smooth bodies and pissing over each other's jeans and boots, licking each other's boots clean, feeling boots on hard cock, kicking up the arse, grinding balls with boot-sole, running the laced-up boot between your mate's legs and wanking your mate real hard so he comes heavy and strong, knowing he's a skin with a skin mate.

You like the feel of your mate's boots soft yet hard on your body. He won't hurt you as he's your mate. Those same boots have been on the football terraces and kicked bottles on the street, but your mate's being nice to you with them and you'd better be good to him or he'll kick you too, even though you're his mate. Smooth boots, smooth like your skinhead arse, smooth boots on your shaved chest, hands running though your mate's cropped hair, each hair springing up as you brush through it, turning your mate on good. And sucking your mate's skinhead cock, feeling his smooth balls

MORE AND HARDER

outside your mouth, feeling him sucking your skinhead cock too with his skinhead tongue, spitting on your cock then sucking it proper, spitting on your boots and licking it off, spitting in your face and rubbing his skinhead spit into your nose and mouth. Your mate spitting on your hair, rubbing his hands through your cropped skinhead hair, drenching it, changing from rubbing to scratching just to turn you on as you're his mate and he knows what you like 'cos he's a skinhead too and he likes what you like and likes it with you. Then he gets his arm round you, hand on your cock, and rubs it real hard, then spits in your skinhead face. You grab his cock and feel the oil smooth over his shaved skin. You spit at him; he spits at you; you feel his smooth body against yours and you come, your skinhead spunk together all over your skinhead bodies, skinhead mates wanking together.

> *OK, skinhead bootlicker, just get on a real tight cock-ring, your 14-hole boots and short jeans and fuckall else.*
>
> *Lie on the floor with a DM nearby.*
>
> *Screw up your tits hard with one hand and rub your cock hard through your jeans with the other.*
>
> *Feel that cock-head through the denim.*
>
> *Let out a bit of piss for lubricant and rub hard again.*
>
> *Feel that piss cool and the denim shrink.*
>
> *Get that boot doing the rubbing on your cock, then lick it clean – yeah, use the underside to rub yourself with and lick it clean.*
>
> *That's what skinheads' boots taste like after a hard afternoon on the terraces down West Ham: piss and stale lager.*
>
> *Lick it, bootlicker, you need it.*

SLAVE: EVER BEEN MADE TO CRAWL UP TO YOUR SKINHEAD MASTER'S BATHROOM IN YOU DOCS ONLY, COCK AND ARSE FREE TO THE AIR?

MADE TO TAKE A BIG ENEMA TO CLEANSE YOU OUT AND ALLOWED TO DROP IT.

MADE TO TAKE ANOTHER (BIGGER AND TO REMIND YOU YOU'RE A SLAVE) WHILE YOU'RE SITTING ON THE LOO, NO SEAT, YOUR ARSE SPREAD, YOU ORDERED NOT TO LET IT GO.

MORGAN

YOUR MOUTH ROUND YOUR SKINHEAD MASTER'S COCK WHILE HE DROPS YOUR HAIR RIGHT OFF, LETTING THE CUTTINGS FALL ON YOUR SHOULDERS, YOUR HAIRLESS HEAD LETTING NO ONE DOUBT THAT YOU'RE A SEX-SLAVE.

Prince Albert

May 1985

I'm going around with another skinhead, Peter. We each have salaried jobs in electronics. He also does piercings; in fact the reason why I'm writing now is that on Monday (a holiday here) we went out for a ride on my motorbike around Surrey to a big deep valley called Devil's Punchbowl. There's a café at the top where bikers and truck drivers have coffee and a big natural wood with mud at the bottom for fucking about in.

We just messed around there (too many kids and mums) but went on to Box Hill, which is where you pose on your bike. Got even more randy there looking at the bikes and all these supposedly straight bikers and a few army guys all posing at each other.

When we returned to his place he got me smoking a bit and finally got me to allow him to do a Prince Albert on my cock. He's been doing frenum and nipple piercings for a while but this was the first Prince Albert. Thus I can't wank for a while, which is why I'm writing.

I can't say that the procedure was pain-free but it turned me on at the time and wearing the ring now continues to turn me on. I can feel the weight of the metal there in the head of my cock; at the moment it is still healing so I can't really wank, which makes for even more of a turn-on. And I have a ring in my cock: much more relevant than a ring on a finger; it says that I'm kinky to anyone who has got as far as seeing my cock.

It's also a thing between Peter and me – mine was the first frenum piercing he did and this was his first Prince Albert. We've consummated our love sexually of course with fucking and sucking but this is an additional token. It's fun manipulating the ring through a jeans pocket – I can rotate the ball on the ring or I can rotate the ring through the cockhead.

Pissing was a surprise – naïvely I had not expected any difference, but of course the piss comes out through the Prince Albert hole as well: it's no problem to cover the hole with a finger so as not to make a mess and it reminds me I'm a slave.

Questions from a Respectful slave to his New Master

1. Sir, what facilities do you have for training? Is there a training room? Will the training commence as soon as i arrive?
2. Sir, what gear will you wear while you are training me, Sir?
3. Sir, what gear will you require me to wear while i am being trained? Naked, leather, rubber, sports, military, rope harness, etc?
4. Sir, will i be required to arrive wearing any particular gear?
5. Sir, if allowed, how will i piss and eat?
6. Sir, if allowed, in what circumstances will i sleep?
    alone / with you, Sir
    in bondage / free
7. Sir, if i disobey orders or displease, how will i be punished?
8. Sir, if i wish to please you especially, is there anything in particular which turns you on, Sir?
9. Sir, do you approve of:
    alcohol y/n   grass y/n   poppers y/n
    LSD y/n   MDA y/n   ethyl chloride y/n
10. Sir, would you indicate (0=no, 5=very much) which (if any) of the following will form part of the training:
    Gas masks ... Gags ... Tit work ... Enemas ... Uniforms ... Rubber ... Shaving ... Catheters ... Verbal abuse ... Domestic chores ... Piss ... Boot licking ... Dildo/buttplug ... Wrestling ... Cock & ball torture ... Sucking your cock, Sir ... Boot polishing ... Being fucked by you, Sir ... Physical exercise (press-ups, etc) ... Bondage in public ... Immobilise ... Training with a second Master or slave ... Cat/Cane/Tawse/Belt/Whip ... Grease/oil/mud ... Mummification ... Rough massage ... Suspension ...

MORGAN

Anything not listed:

Sir, the following are definitely out so far as i am concerned: rimming, head-shaving, fistfucking, cold, very heavy CP when my cock is soft.

Buttplugs and Boxing

January 1987

Dear Jim, Sir,

Thanks for writing. I was interested by the gear you've got, Sir, and even more so by the training you give the guy, making him stay in uniform overnight with buttplug and tit-clips on underneath and a chastity belt over his shaved cock and balls. I imagine he must feel a total prisoner like that, looking down at his uniform and boots and feeling helpless. How big is the cell he is put into?

It would be interesting to insert an enema tube into him before he is locked up in such a way that he cannot dislodge it. Keep him under observation and when he is firmly asleep very slowly administer the enema. He would wake up at some point to a very peculiar and degrading feeling as he discovered his arse was being filled but he was unable to prevent it or to move against his restraints.

There's a new shape buttplug now on sale: 'doorknob' or 'double doorknob' tells all. It's got the usual plate to stop it going in, then the shaft to grip on, then, instead of the long cone shape, it has a ball shape, or the double one has two balls so it can go in once, then another stretch and you, Sir, can pull it in and out, stretching the sphincter but not totally removing it. Also for long-term use, the single doorknob buttplug doesn't leave a sore spot inside . . . us slaves are getting spoilt!

I've not really done much boxing myself, though the idea of it turns me on greatly. I've enjoyed your boxing story on many occasions after Training, thank you, Sir.

The feeling of a groin protector, laced on tightly; plus flat-soled boxing boots, laced on but strangely not reassuring as you feel the ground underneath through the thin, flat sole which offers only a little spring and protection. The gloves that are your only weapon against the opponent's attack, your hands immobilised inside. My cock easily gets hard thinking how it would be inside that protector cup, enclosed and free to move, yet unable to get any stimulation or satisfaction.

All of this and then the Trainer inserts a buttplug to keep the fighter 'on his toes'; the strain on the arse-hole forces the body into hyper-drive, unable to come, committed to fight.

I've been wrestling, yes; various rules, the most successful was a many-handed fight where it was submissions, fighting naked, cock and ball holds allowed but not hair or punching or eyes or dropping, etc. There were four or five of us. The rule was that after a 'hold' the fight continued from a kneeling start and that he who submitted stayed on the mat to fight the next one; thus the only way off the mat was to win or retire from the session, the winner being the one who was left at the end. This was very nasty as the guy left on the mat was already shagged from previous rounds and was put against a fresh opponent who'd also seen where his weak points were.

Once the guy who stayed on the mat got mad and really went at the other guy hammer and tongs and won his way off, but mostly it was a masochistic way of getting us all to take more and more punishment before inevitably having to retire, more hurt than any of us would normally allow. Another time we tried it where the winner stayed on the mat but that wasn't so good. Almost invariably a man won one round, was then tired and against a fresh opponent who got him to submit, so he was off the mat. Most people had two rounds on and then were off.

Fantasy Training Session

March 1987

I arrived at my Trainer's house, left my pushbike in his garage and changed. I'd ridden there as usual in singlet, tight black cycling shorts, white socks and short brown Doctor Martens boots, fending off the stares and hungry looks from passers-by.

I stripped, cold-douched myself with the nozzle provided in the outside toilet, and changed into my usual training gear. Still the white socks and DMs but with a pair of specially designed leather shorts with a cod-piece pouch on the front of them and a tight lockable belt round the top that was wide enough both to keep the shorts in position and to function as a gym belt and contain the buttplug I usually wore for training.

I was to lock the shorts and place the key into the box that was there for the purpose. Once dropped, the key was irretrievable by me. I greased and inserted the buttplug, slipped into and locked the shorts, cut tight to slip up the crack of my arse so as not to impede any movement like squats or crunchies.

The codpiece on the front had to be removed to fit my cock and balls through the cock-ring sewn in the front of the shorts, then my cock was firmly strapped down, my balls similarly contained and finally the codpiece tightly snapped over. I was now ready to present myself to my Trainer.

I knocked on the Training Room door, then my Trainer opened it and let me in.

'Parade Rest,' he ordered. I presented myself, boots well spread, chest forward, arse out and arms tensed behind my back.

He gripped my pecs, twisted my tits and deftly placed mild tit-clips on my nipples. The inspection continued, my Trainer pinching the slight gut the tight shorts revealed; he checked my arse for the dildo, ramming it home through the shorts and causing me to half lose balance. He kicked my legs wider and rammed the dildo once more.

'Touch your toes ten times, legs apart.' I complied, but bent my legs, which my Trainer noticed.

'Repeat for punishment, ten strokes.' I bent over, the dildo now easily ramming itself further into my guts, yet helped by my Trainer's cane, so far mild and on target on the leather shorts.

'Parade Rest,' again.

'Give me fifty deep knee bends.' I complied, taking care not to touch the tit-clips on my chest, but it was not sufficient. Taking some black boot polish, my Trainer blackened the heels of my boots and ordered me to make sure that the exposed cheeks of my arse touched my boots every time.

He watched the increasing blackness on my arse as I felt the dildo gently resisting on every stroke, then jumping home as I reached the boots and felt the blackness spread over my skin. The set completed, my Trainer then told me to rub the boot polish into my skin and the leather.

He removed the codpiece from the shorts and changed the straps on my balls to a ball-stretcher. A 2½kg weight was attached to a chain attached to the ball-stretcher; if I stood, the chain was long enough for the weight to stay on the floor.

The next exercise was pull-ups; his chinning bar was at just the height that the ball-weight had to be lifted halfway through the power stroke. My Trainer believed in chinning. He ordered three different types of pull-ups: overhand close, underhand close and overhand wide. He allowed me to keep my legs crossed together; this helped retain the buttplug but he always stood behind me with a cat-o'-nine-tails. If there was the slightest hesitation at the point where the power stroke started and the ball-weight began to bite, the cat would crash across my tensed shoulders, firmly ensuring maximum effort.

His method produced excellent results. I soon learnt to coordinate the pain of the power stoke, the latent bite of the tit-clips, the expected pull of the ball-weight and the probable crash of the cat to excellent effect. The muscle pain was negligible for it allowed me to train deeper and deeper into muscle overload, thus producing excellent progress.

The chain was removed and the codpiece strapped up tightly again, continuing to ensure that I did not attempt to play with myself.

The next exercise was push-ups. My Trainer stood 'At Ease', his boots that I'd bulled at the end of the previous session pinning my fingers to the floor, myself propped at the ready position. My Trainer gave me a few preliminary cracks from the cat over my shoulders while he calculated today's target; it was high and my Trainer started hitting me hard with the cat almost as soon as I had begun.

This kept me going well, balancing the pain from my arms with the applied continuous pain on my nipples and the stinging over my shoulders as the cat bit harder into my flesh. I visualised the little knots on the thongs as they hit my tight skin, depressing the hard muscles, momentarily whitening the skin amid a growing redness. I reached the target but he would not let me stop, stepping and crushing my fingers with the nails of his boot soles, applying the cat ever harder and demanding 'Ten More'. I wearily complied, hallucinating completely with the cumulative pain and oxygen debt.

My Trainer led me to the Machine. He had cunningly devised a method of performing the bench-press exercise which still allowed him to be in control. An ordinary flat bench or even a multi-gym bench with fixed press bar only allowed him marginal control. My Trainer had first experimented with the latter: my feet had been strapped to the legs of the Machine and my hands placed on the bar, ready to perform bench presses with my thumbs locked into thumb cuffs welded on to the press bar at a rather wide position. For sure there was no cheating.

The method of control was uncertain. My Trainer had initially linked the tit-clip chain to the press bar, thus ensuring pain at the moment of greatest muscular strain. This was unsatisfactory as, even if the tit-clips did not come off, the pain was too sudden and fierce. A refinement had been to strap the trainee to the bench by his belt, then pull his legs high and wide, exposing the arse for punishment and control.

This had produced satisfactory control, but an extended session produced numb feet, which was undesirable.

Thus my Trainer had designed and built this Machine. It was an adaptation of a leg-curl machine, crossed with a Nautilus bench press and flies machine, inverted. I was to lie on it face downward; the belt of the shorts had fixings which connected with straps on the bench; other straps loosely retained my boots to the leg-curl bar, while I placed my hands on the first press bar. Now enclosed, I could safely perform bench presses, leg curls and flies from the one position.

My Trainer had an excellent aim on my arse. He placed pulse-measuring electrodes on my wrists and breathing apparatus to my face, the gas mask covering my nose and the tube entering my mouth through a wide bite piece. I was breathing oxygen-rich air, could only move the relevant parts of my body, couldn't shout back and was totally exposed for punishment.

My Trainer had been rapidly increasing the weight and the reps he required from me, the progress assisted by the regime of pain and oxygen which transformed the achievement rate. He started with light weights on every session, demanding many reps, then with only brief stops as I was not out of breath, only quivering from muscle exertion. He would change the exercise to another of the three basic exercises possible on the machine, and start me up again with one hard crack from the leather strap he used for encouragement. The punishment was not especially hard in the early stages, but by about the third time round the cumulative effect of many light cracks from the strap, plus the extended muscular effort, began to produce hallucinations again. My Trainer knew this and encouraged it. He would feed me suitable fantasy matter such as mud-wrestling outdoors in a muddy stream wearing boots and a jock strap, pissing over the other wrestler as he lay taking the pain of the hold I had him in; or of entering the boxing ring totally in bondage for the fight: tied inside boots, protector and gloves, committed to winning, his 'boxer's friend' filling his arse – fighters had buttplugs first!

My Trainer kept me in this Machine longest of all the

exercises. I knew if I was pleasing him he kept me there a long time; it pleased him to see his work having good effect on my body, my body which owed so much of its current glory to his efforts in training me.

My Trainer ordered me to remove the Training Shorts. The sweat inside was tremendous. Squats were performed free-standing in boots and an ordinary gym belt. Punishment if the buttplug did not stay properly in place. This was not easy as I had to concentrate not only to control my legs but also my arse. My Trainer watched intently as each power stroke caused a pulse of blood to my already-hard cock, making it bob up and down perkily between my exerting thigh muscles. The rest periods were spent touching my toes with slow but hard punishment from the strap, thus a longer rest meant more beating, now on unprotected skin, giving considerable reason not to lose momentum.

If I dropped the plug it was necessary to perform arse stamina and strengthening exercises. I was to place the buttplug on the floor and then squat down on to it and accept it in my arsehole, fucking myself, then raise up and drop the plug back on to the floor, then sit back down on to the plug for the number of repetitions required.

Now my Trainer demanded crunchies; his version of sit-ups demanded considerable skill as well as muscular effort, but was very pleasurable. He blindfolded me, removed his jockstrap and sat himself on a chair. I lay on the floor between his booted feet, my knees next to his but my boots round his waist, my hands behind my neck. I had to do sit-ups to his well-erect cock. I could not relax back down until I had taken his cock each time deep down my throat till the cock-ring he wore was inside my lips. These were not quick sit-ups: sometimes his cock moved and I could not find it in the dark. Sometimes he would piss into me and I could not release his cock and suffer the danger of spilling his piss.

The sit-ups continued until I had completely sucked him off to his satisfaction. My Trainer would then get up and prepare me for my final exercise. The buttplug would be checked, I would be placed standing in Iron Shoes with weights so heavy I could not move my feet from the widespread position my Trainer placed them in.

On my right hand he put a tennis player's training wrist strap filled with sand, the other hand strapped behind my back held in 'Parade Rest' position by a leather strap round my neck. My Trainer attached a pinprick cock and ball strap with pricks round the ball strap, the cock strap and the strap going round my cock. This last was especially painful as the harder I tried to come the more pain was induced.

My Trainer applied a much more severe set of tit-clips. For lubricant he applied menthol cream, immediately producing fiery stabs of coloured pain from the pinprick strap. I knew I was to wank myself as rapidly as possible. My Trainer assisted the purpose with massive strokes from his strap, covering my back from my knees up to where my hand was tied. I usually came within about ninety seconds from the first strap.

Then, when I was spent, my Trainer ordered me to don a tracksuit, no jock, and to run the three-mile circuit whilst he followed on pushbike. After a cold shower in the corner of the training room, I was dispatched on my pushbike, which felt much harder to pedal . . .

Postscript – December 1990

A further machine that has been brought to my attention as being suitable for pain-enhanced Training is a rowing machine. The type with a centrifugal fan at the front and a computer-type display of effort, strokes per minute and a timer is ideal for solo interval training along the lines of a one-minute workout, at a specific target effort level as indicated on the display, with twenty or twenty-five seconds' recovery time between sets and a one minute break after five sets. This is an excellent single workout as it exercises all the major muscle groups as well as the heart–lung system, as is apparent from the 'shattered' effect on the trainee.

Not so readily apparent is the ease with which a small buttplug can assist heavy training. With the trainee wearing a jock only, a buttplug attached to the rowing seat ensures secure location on the seat and the rowing action requires the arse muscles to be clamped tight.

A pinprick cock-strap (always a good thing to wear under a jock) and tit-clips ensure a high pain threshold so that the pain from the workout is masked until it exceeds the applied pain. This assures a worthwhile session.

To wear a buttplug at a commercial gym, invest in a wrestling leotard – singlet and shorts in one piece.

Finally, consider purchasing a workout timer with a bleep that can be set to different rates per minute. This allows control of the rate at which common exercises are performed. Press-ups are a good one to start on, i.e. one push per bleep.

It's another weapon in the armoury for those who have moved on from 'no pain – no gain' to 'workout till you puke'.

CP Skinhead Rick

April 1987

Skin Rick,

Your letter turned me on but also confused me. You wisely stated that you wanted to be careful because of diseases, then you went on to talk about unsafe sex. I appreciate you're turned on by things you don't want to do casually, so am I, but (with our safety in mind) there's plenty we can do that's not-risky if / when you come here or we meet. There's a soundproof, slightly damp cellar here with a few useful fittings that you might like to explore. Whilst I'm not a real NF skinhead at Chelsea FC, I know a bit of what you like because I too wouldn't really mind being done over by a six-foot-four knife-and-boots skinhead and his mate, being held down by one while the boss pissed over me and made me lick his boots, seat of his jeans, armpits, tattoos and finally, if I was lucky, his cock, while his mate fucked my arse and held me down.

In the real world, though, fantasies are not the same as reality: I want to do real things with real people, but still go to work the next day and all that. I'm into myself going to someone else's place and being done over, by which I mean being tied up, maybe given a joint, made to lick boots, suck cock, being beaten, tit-clips, dildos, masks, rubber . . . And I'm into having someone round here and having a good session together either in my cellar, or with the weight-training bars and bench upstairs – it can get quite heavy weight-training hard with a mate who won't let you stop when you say you want to and if need be there's a belt or two to encourage each other with. Which is worse – the pain from the weights or the pain from the belt? Or me in boots and jeans standing, you naked doing press-ups on the floor between my DMs, and if you start flagging you get belted or caned?

To show how tough you are you take the punishment across the shoulders.

The really best CP scene I've got involved in to date (well, there're two joint best really!): one was me and this other slave both hooded and otherwise naked but tied to each other front to front standing, wrist to wrist, ankle to ankle, ball-stretcher to ball-stretcher with a bit of chain and padlocks, each given six or twelve in turn. I could feel the other guy taking it, feel him bracing, taking the stroke, reeling in the pain, which I shared with him and tried to make him feel good by soothing him as much as I could despite the restraints.

Then we were turned round and it was my turn to be beaten and he was nice to me while I was caned, being careful not to move after the stroke or I'd yank his balls. Afterwards we were separated, the other guy tied to a bench or horse or something, given a belting, and then I licked his bare heated skin; then it was my turn to be belted.

The other good CP scene that happened to me was where the guy stuffed a buttplug up my arse first; the pain from the cane and the pleasure from the buttplug were great – and I've never been marked so much or enjoyed sucking cock between canings so much.

Don't get the impression that I don't enjoy beating the shit out of a guy either: it scares me how much I enjoy it, so long as he's turned on by it too. Someone I wrestled with once insisted that the forfeit for losing was a good belting. That really got us fighting hard and dealing out the belting was great, and made the round after faster to get back at him, etc.

Writing letters is all very well. We must meet. You should phone me. Do you fancy a motorbike ride one night?

Joseph: LA Cop

May 1987

Hi, Joseph,

Thanks for your reply to my ad: I've never advertised in America before and wasn't quite sure what replies to expect.

I'm 30, 5'8" and 148 pounds or so. I live on my own in a house within walking distance of Earl's Court and the leather bars there, etc. I have a lover, Peter, who, like me, has cropped hair; we call it 'skinhead', which I think means circumcised or not in the US. Anyhow, I'm circumcised and also have a Prince Albert ring in my cock.

Being skinheads, we're into boots, tight jeans and T-shirts, though not football ourselves. I work for a television company on outside broadcasts and get to football grounds for work a lot. There the skinhead look is fun: I've had the whole of one end of a crowd yelling 'skinhead . . . skinhead' at me before now. I'll get a photo together of me in skinhead gear for when you write next.

I like gym-training with a mate. I have got a bench and several bars and dumb-bells here which is best — we can organise music and go at a decent pace: too many gyms here are crowded and you end up waiting for a bench or machine for too long; nice though it is to watch the other men training each other. There was a gym I was going to in the East End, at Stratford, that had all sorts, boxers included, training there. Nice to see one guy bullying another to keep him at it, not just doing regular routines but hard ones like underhand pull-ups in combination with barbell curls, really making him go through pain barriers and sweat. Wish I could do that!

There was a sauna there for afters, too; not swish and posh like a US or European sauna but rather squalid and small. It was mind-blowing lying there with these straight hunks talking about the security systems they'd just installed and how their mates could get round them and burgle the places. And everyone wanked off in there or the showers so the atmosphere was great considering it was a straight place.

I'm into leather, SM, CP bondage and so on. I can play Top but prefer to be the slave. I've had quite a few good times in playrooms around the place and also in Amsterdam. I'm into most physical things: outdoor walking, hiking, tenting, as well as the motorbike. Like doing military training outdoors: lots of running, press-ups and marching. Like uniforms: preferably dirty combat gear, and boots – and being made to clean boots too.

My preconceived ideas about an LA cop have more to do with CHIPS and the American gay leather magazines than reality: I hope you're into handcuffs and CP and SM, otherwise you wouldn't have replied to my advert. I'm also into uniforms in a big way, mostly sweaty grubby combat uniforms and heavy, shiny boots.

So, yes, I'll be interested to get a correspondence going, also interested to see you as and when you're over here. And I do like a nice wanky letter. I did have a correspondence going with a guy in the Royal Navy who sent me audio cassettes of him training, and I sent some back of me training: that was quite fun. It works quite well if you set up a cassette recorder while you're training. Once you get it into your mind that you're speaking to me even though I'm not there you can really train hard as you know I'll hear if you stop training or cheat and stop the tape. Try it, maybe? Keep the tape going when you have a wank afterwards and wank aloud?

'The Green Shorts' and Dartmoor

May 1987

Hi, Joseph,

Good to hear you on the phone: it's wonderful to hear voices from the other side of the world!

What have I been up to since? Well, there's a club starting here based on uniforms and partly military; it's called the Green Shorts and it's run by some ex-army men who like CP and training people. They've got access to a farm in the country and are running weekends there for everyone's enjoyment, presumably themselves included. Anyhow, to get admitted you have to be inspected by one of the officers, so I met up with this guy near a park in Tooting: Tooting Bec. He got me there in PT kit, white shorts and trainers, and had me running around soccer goal posts, doing press-ups, crunchies (that's sit-ups with your knees bent too) and running. About ninety minutes of that and I was worn out, but I've been invited to the camp so I'll see what happens there.

I spent one weekend last August in a tent on Dartmoor with a mate who has an ex-army Land Rover, all painted green and black cammo. Spent the whole weekend in boots and mucky DPMs – squaddie-talk for disruptive pattern material, i.e. camouflage. Found a quiet bit of forest, pitched tent. Some messing about that degenerated into a bit of a muddy scrap, chucking leaves, turf, fir cones at each other and throwing each other about and wrestling, boots all over the place, shoving dirt inside each other's uniform and eventually me getting dumped in the stream nearby.

Also went out for a long day walking on the high part of the moor. Started early and walked about eighteen miles taking food and stove and had a good lunch near a brook out of sight of anything. Didn't do anything very heavy but had a good matey wank in the sunshine on the moorland. Then back to the Land Rover for some more disgusting tinned food

MORE AND HARDER

and hordes of bloody midges! Maybe not your scene, but it was a good laugh too.

DPMs and boots feel really great first thing in the morning: damp, cold and sweaty from the day before when your cock's hard and aching for a piss; add to that a warm bum or stinging shoulders, tired stiff muscles and you're close to a masochistic heaven.

I'd love to go on a proper survival course, be made to stay out when it pisses down, get punished out of doors, push-ups or belt/cane, etc., love someone to pace me on a push-bike, or me and others running in combats and boots. I'm not totally inexperienced outdoors myself, can map-read in clear weather: had lots of days out on Dartmoor, etc. I also get a kick from taking someone less experienced than me out then bullying them along to keep them going. Still prefer someone to bully me along though!

In the real world I'm the first to admit that I'm no good at drill or marching and would easily fail a kit inspection but I like the idea of being inspected naked or in shorts that would show a hard-on and not lighten any strokes I might deserve. Being tapped all over by the officer as he inspects me, my having to look front and not wince as he taps my cock, takes it and wanks it nice in his hand while caning me with his other hand, alternately wanking me nice and painful. I'd guess you have far more ideas for punishment detail than I have. There's a barracks opposite a place that I have to visit for work and I've always got a soft spot for some soldier who is cleaning four-ton trucks in full combats and webbing on a Saturday afternoon. I doubt if that's through choice!

Whilst I haven't ever run naked outdoors, the idea of a march outside in boots and socks only, chest out and cock forward, feeling the breeze between my legs and round my arse, being corrected by you, Sir, sharply with a cane if I lag or break step or flag.

Being made to rest and do press-ups on the muddy ground, you checking to see that my cock and balls really touch the ground at the same time as my chest. You keeping my bum down with your muddy heavy boot, rubbing it over my bum and up around my arse. You keeping me doing press-ups by making me do them to your boots, Sir, and caning me on each stroke to keep me at it. Rewarding me by letting me wear my uniform, then sending me to crawl along a muddy brook, keeping down to avoid breaking cover but getting wet and muddy and covered in leaves, etc.

I've been a slave most of the time I've been gay. I started riding a motorbike at 21. I've learnt about handcuffs, gags and getting fucked by heavy guys in leather.

I like bondage, being tied up and turned on and being unable to do anything about it, screaming because I want to come or screaming because I'm turned on and you're putting me through pain and it hurts but it's nice and one bit of me wants more pain and the bit of me that's hurting wants it to stop but I know I'll be sorry if it does stop.

At school I was a cross-country runner. Then I moved to Maidenhead in Berkshire because of my job, and the running club I joined had wrestling as something extra after gym-training. That was straight, but I've enjoyed wrestling with gay people since then. Sometimes to amateur rules but mostly ignoring technical falls and holds and only wrestling for submissions. The people I've come across aren't always my size so oil has got involved. Maybe starting in singlets and briefs, but more recently I've been wrestling with another skinhead who likes to start off in Doctor Martens, jeans and bare chest each, oiling each other up and fighting. It's also fun to wrestle with a pair of handcuffs – it ends when both cuffs are shut . . . that can get quite vicious though.

Grease, Belt and Boot Slave

Colin, New South Wales, Australia

Hi,

I'm aged 31, I'm 5'8" and 10 stone 8. I'm a skinhead: hair cropped Number One or Two once or twice a month. I like boots, tight dirty jeans, tight army green fatigues, leather and so on. I weight-train regularly here at home (I've got bars and a bench here) and then go out for a run afterwards: it ought to be twice a week but in practice I usually only manage Monday nights.

I own a Yamaha FZ600 bike. Unfortunately (to put it mildly) it was nicked about three months ago. Not very nice drawing the curtains and seeing an empty bit of road outside. The bike was locked up with a big chain and padlock as well as the steering lock, etc. It's the start of winter here, rain, wind and drizzle all the time, so rather than buy a new bike now and get it dirty I'm stuck with a car till March or so.

The FZ600 was a racing bike not a dirt bike, but the combination of dirty jeans, boots, filthy leathers and cut-offs on a nice clean white bike was fun! I did a couple of rides on it in leathers with a dollop of grease down the front and arse of my (unlined) leather jeans, rode a good way cock hard and arse squelching inside the leather, found somewhere off the beaten track, parked the bike, had a smoke in a wood on a log, cock in hand through the leather. Nice wanking outdoors but you need grease or something to stop going dry . . .

What dirty jeans have you got? I wear jeans to work so I can wear them in easily: at present I'm on a pair of black Levi's 620s, which are tight leg, bum, etc., and blue 501s which need no description. After they've got well worn, I don't wash them any more so there are lots of pairs of scruffy jeans round the house. One pair that I keep for bike maintenance with grease in the crotch: gets me hard just squeezing into those and the grease has dried hard so needs more putting in every time. No jock of course and all the grease and oil from my hands gets wiped on the legs of the jeans. Put my 14-hole DMs on nice and tight as well; that stops me wanking too quickly and gives a better chance of the bike getting seen to before I get too excited! The grease soon warms up and starts spreading, my hard cock finds its way up from being pointed down the leg to pointing sideways and eventually vertical; the grease first feels warm and then a coolness. The bum of the jeans slips sensually over my arse. I have to find something from a pocket but my cock's there already so I pinch the tip a bit so it stings for a while. Eventually the oil's out of the bike and, while I'm waiting for the last few drips, I take the oil pan inside, tip most of it into an old can for the skip but pour some in each of the four pockets of my jeans, wanking standing legs apart, cock now out through the zip as the warm oil seeps down the tight denim on my legs towards my boots. I get my cock back inside the jeans just in time to come into the accumulated grease oil . . .

I just got nicely soaked this evening: the weather's all changeable at the moment and it looked safe to go out shopping in T-shirt and the 501s that I'd been wearing all day at work, but specifically took the briefs off when I got home as that feels nice . . . Anyhow, the weather decided to change from sunny to thunderstorm whilst I was browsing in the newsagents so I was stranded ten minutes from home. Only one thing for it: once you're wet the rain doesn't matter any more and wet I got: T-shirt sticking to me like shit to a blanket and jeans tightening up like a noose. All good fun and not too cold either so I got home feeling just fine and randy.

My friends who go to bike rallies say that it does all happen there: kids staked out on the ground, a tent peg and rope at each hand or leg, jeans undone and cock out and kicked around by the bystanders' boots, beer and lager tipped over the guy if not outright pissing over him. It all sounds much too good to miss, but I don't seem to get on these rallies any more . . .

Other little 'discovery' which maybe you'll be interested in is about cock-rings: someone said to try going to sleep with a tight-fitting one on, so I did and it was great: went to sleep disinterested and soft. Woke up in the middle of the night with a raging hard-on and the cock-ring hurting like crazy and the only thing to do was . . . and even then it was a while before I could get the cock-ring off. The secret, I'm told, is to make sure it's a tight-fitting ring otherwise it falls off as you go to sleep. The next thing is to wear it all the time.

Sir,
Since typing that bit of the letter I've changed into greasy jeans, greasy oily DPM cammo jacket and dirty army boots. I've got a can of oil and poured it over my chest, stood up and let it soak all over my body, getting faster as it warms up and dripping down the cammo trousers round my cock-ring and balls. Just now my cock hurts real hard as the ring bites and stops my cock getting bigger.

I've got a greased buttplug and sat on it feeling the point go up my arse, feeling the stretch, then it went in good. Cock even harder. Wish there was someone here to belt me proper. Good hard belting with a heavy leather belt. Bet you've got some good belts; you say you're into 'brutal CP'. What does that mean? Someone strapped me down tight and gave me just a dozen with a heavy stitched leather tawse/strap that really hurt bad for a week. That was good.

Do you do CP outdoors? I like that, tied to a tree or gate or something, greased up, plugged with a dildo, maybe gagged or hooded, and beaten hard and pissed over. Tell me, Sir, what sort of beatings you give, what you use, where you do it, fast, slow, tied up or free, please, Sir? Tell me please, Sir, what you like to do with grease, Sir, how long you leave it on, what sort of grease, what sort of gear?

Grease, belt and boot slave.

Skinhead Party

September 1987

I went to Peter's council flat in Peckham on Friday evening directly after work. After I'd stripped off my bike leathers and work jeans Peter gave me a leather hood and told me to put it on for a surprise. When I was stripped naked except for the hood, Peter took me into his sitting room, sat me down and got me licking his boots. But they weren't one of the usual pairs of Doctor Martens: these had big chunky hard-rubber Commando treads and a big tough toecap. Peter told me to lick the lace holes and count them starting from the toe end. I counted – not only were these army-type Commando boots but they had twenty holes. Fantastic!

Peter said I'd got to be prepared for the skinhead party the following night. He guided me across the flat to the bathroom, stood me facing the bath and started putting a cold lotion on my chest and then all over my body – armpits, arse, legs and all. It smelt funny and felt cool but I didn't know what it was and it wasn't a conversational situation.

He left me there standing for a few minutes and then returned, got me on my knees, removed the hood and cropped my head hair down to a very short Number One.

I could see the white lotion all over me and two big bottles but without my glasses I couldn't identify them. 'Immac – hair remover,' said Peter. 'All your hair will wash off in the shower leaving you as smooth as a baby's bum all over.'

And I was. That was the smoothest I had been since before puberty. Pretty soon the itching started but Peter knew the treatment for that – lots of talcum powder.

Out from the shower, Peter also had a pair of the 20-hole Ranger boots for me so we looked a pair. We had dinner, both wearing our new boots, tight skinhead jeans, Fred Perry shirts and braces.

Without hair, my skin felt super-sensitive. Jeans and shirt

cloth felt more sensual than usual, cock and balls naked against the denim, chest and tits unprotected from dark-blue Fred Perry shirt. Peter was also Immac-smooth so we cuddled close that night – skin to skin, pun intended!

The party was on Saturday night in Northampton. Brian is in the process of selling a house of flats he's had as an investment. The tenants are all out now and he expected to hand the keys over to the new owner the following week so it was ideal for a Gay Skinhead Nucleus party. Most of the skinheads that Peter and I know from the Shoreditch pub were there. Most of them have nicknames which got used as we were all 'family' and also it got over the problem of distinguishing between the many Peters or Nicks.

My Peter ('Dolly') is Secretary of GSN partly because he has a Commodore computer and can do the newsletters and mailing list but also because his business sells rubber clothing and does body piercing, which is quite in demand.

The house was a typical rented-flats place, lot of tiny single bedrooms with knackered Yale locks on the doors. All the bedding and furnishings had gone, leaving just the communal settees and kitchen table, etc. No carpet so two dozen pairs of Doctor Martens and other boots made quite a row on the bare boards and stairs. Several stereos going in different rooms with unrelated music.

Peter and I were in our new 20-hole Ranger boots which no one else had yet got. Lots of cruising conversation openings possible: 'How much?' 'Where did he get them from?' as well as the obvious interest in licking them. My head hair was nothing special being only a Number One when several of the others had had Zeros but the Immac treatment was appreciated.

I spent most of the early part of the party drinking from the bowl of punch in the kitchen while Peter flitted from group to group paying social calls; he kept returning to get another can of lager. He seemed amused that I preferred the punch. Nibbles were being reheated in the oven – someone was a baker so there was a huge supply of yeast goods.

I kept clear of the bathroom on this occasion but it was noticeable that most skins' jeans were getting damp. There must have been a piss-scene somewhere but I'm not into that with Peter so didn't take part. The yard was another possible location.

Time came to go to bed. Peter's jeans were also damp and we slept together in a single bed with our jeans and new boots still on.

Next morning everyone eventually staggered down for tea and breakfast – I'd got a socking hangover but was advised not to have the tea. The reason was that it had been made with piss. It was explained to me that piss is sterile and infection-free and that boiling it would make absolutely certain but still I didn't want to try it. Then they told me that this had been one of the ingredients in the punch . . . So that was why Peter was so amused that I was refusing clean cans of lager.

Greasing and Blackballing

December 1987

Hi, Colin, thanks for your letter. I guessed it was from you and didn't open it till evening and after training, then putting on dirty cammo trousers and boots and an unwashed singlet, so I really enjoyed the letter, thank you, Sir. Like you say, there's a culture difference between us, though I'd rather say that it's amazing that we are on the same planet and no one should forget it. End of politics, but it's minus two degrees centigrade outside here tonight and your writing that you've never had a pair of jeans is pretty mind-blowing. I didn't go out for a run – I sprained my knee in September and, whilst I'm not hobbling any more, I've been limiting my weight-training to a set that doesn't stress my knee, i.e. sitting mostly or pull-ups and press-ups.

You say you never wear jeans so I guess you must be heavily into shorts all day – I'd be interested to hear about it; also what work do you do?

The whole idea of never getting into long trousers is amazing, particularly here on a bitterly cold night when just getting into shorts earlier tonight to do my training was a little bit cold. Shorts make me feel randy just because there's so little protecting my cock from the world: just a thin bit of material, or not even that if I wear shorts without a jock. Outside that's really living dangerously: going out to a pub in town, one erection and I've got a problem.

Please tell me what happens if you get randy at work: here I grin and point my cock down my jeans' leg and hope it doesn't show. I guess I'll have that problem when I think of your letter at work tomorrow. Usually have to wait till I get home to have a wank and let it out. Nice waiting though.

There's a pair of tight leather briefs I've got which are greased inside but don't let out the grease; even if they did, it wouldn't show through the denim. I'll wear those just to make sure I'm good and randy all day, so when I get home I can wank good and hard re-reading your letter, Sir.

I'll put the greased briefs on and make sure my cock's tucked down so it's painful when I get a hard-on. I'll feel my cock hard and rubbing against the greased leather, unable to get fully hard because it's trapped but getting more and more turned on the more it tries. Finding myself rubbing the workshop bench with my cock to try to bring it off; discreetly at first, maybe less so later. Cock softening for a bit if I'm distracted by work, then going hard again unexpectedly later as the greasy squelchy feeling gets the better of it.

While I'm writing and before I wank off for the second time tonight, I'd better reply to your questions, Sir. Cropping hair to Number One means that the cutters are set to '1' which is supposed to be a week's growth only, about 1cm, Number Two would be 2cm, etc. 14-hole DM = Doctor Marten boot with 14 holes each side, i.e. 28 per boot total. Most street skinheads wear 10-, 14- or 20-hole DMs: what are yours? DMs are always uncomfortable to wear till they're old: piss in the boots and then wear them for a hard day and they'll get much better. My best house DIY gear is either DMs and shorts and singlet (summer) or DMs and an army overall (winter). Tightly laced boots and a pair of shorts that show off cock and bum on me and whoever I'm decorating with is great, each liking looking at the other and knowing the other likes looking too: frequent wank stops.

Skinheads: I wrote a bit in an old German rubber magazine that explains about skinheads. If you haven't got that, I can send a copy next time.

Blackballing. I don't know much about that directly. An ex-army friend (Coldstream Guards I think) said that when he was on guard duty there was a particular uniform made of heavy material (that showed nothing through) that was used for Punishments. One of which was tying a rope round his balls, the other end of which was secured either to boots or ankles and adjusted so that when standing to 'Attention' a light pull occurred; however, when marching a severe pull was exerted alternately . . .

My Hell's Angel friends here go in for ball-greasing,

usually on new recruits who aren't fully initiated: at the meet before a run the new guy is held down and his cock, balls and arse, as well as the seat of his jeans and maybe his armpits, are greased. Obviously this is only a start, but the guy's then aware for the whole of the run (weekend, race-meet or whatever) where he stands. He'll probably be running around for the Members for the weekend and if he fucks up on something there'll be more grease or piss or oil. Most Angels I know/have known wear two pairs of jeans, the inner pair often either greased leather or filthy denim.

What sort of football shorts have you greased up, Sir? I've got a pair of rugger shorts that I like for training (English rugger shorts with button flies and pockets that you just can't reach your cock with – different from Aussie Rules shorts; I've always liked the look of them but never yet been able to get any: do you fancy a swap? I take 28″ waist).

GREASE, BELT AND BOOT slave

Skinhead New Year Party

January 1988

We had a party on New Year's Eve, organised by word of mouth around GSN members and by going round likely-looking lads at gay pubs and bars and giving them invites. About 30 or 40 skinheads and degenerates ('degens') turned up to postman Danny's high-rise council flat in southeast London, mostly bringing a bottle. A good trick of Peter's: organising a party at someone else's flat!

Two had spent the previous night in police cells for some reason or other and were much into being kicked around and abused. One of these was getting more and more used by quite a lot of people to his own and our enjoyment!

There was a fuck-room going, though everyone I have anything to do with was only doing safe sex and I wasn't in on the drugs except alcohol. After the midnight celebrations the real party got going – yes, even degens celebrate New Year with the chimes of Big Ben from the radio.

Bernie, on acid, was seized by two others and taken into the fuck-room and was next seen crawling out of there licking another skinhead's boots as he walked over to the bathroom. Bernie's clothes were unaccountably wet after that; and he was often on the floor in the main room where the party and music was, going round the boots, licking them almost unasked.

There was quite a lot of roughing up going on in the fuck-room. Like holding a skin down on the floor and making him lick boots, spitting on him, kicking his bum till he cries out for mercy then kicking in the balls and at his hard cock, kicking him all over so he doesn't know where it's coming from next, all the time held down by Doctor Marten soles on his wrists or fingers, some skins seeing to him: shoving fingers through holes already in his jeans and up his arse, others kicking and abusing.

Others were had up against the wall, roughed up arms

behind the back, forced down to lick boots, cock or arse. There was one heavy belting, the guy (I think it was his birthday, and not his sixth or twelfth either) was forced on the ground, head held between two boots, arms and legs with a skinhead or two on each and his jeans hauled down to expose his arse, which got soundly beaten by his friends in rotation with a studded belt. I reckon the memory of that lasted well into 1988.

The good thing about Doctor Marten boots is that you can kick fuck out of someone and get quite heavy without really doing any damage: my Commando boots which have more sturdy soles and Vibram-like treads, steel toecaps, etc. are too dangerous for much kicking, though they're good if you kick with the instep not the toe.

Thailand

April 1988

Dear Mario and Joachim,

Peter and I went to Thailand in March for two weeks. It is a lovely country, quite different from Europe, and the people are very tolerant and friendly. The Thais have no worries about two men together: they all do it, it seems. Similarly, women's lib is a very new, foreign phenomenon. We visited Bangkok, Chiang Mai (an old capital city in North Thailand) and Phuket Island with the beaches in the south. I think the Thais are busy ruining Phuket by building large concrete hotels on almost every beach there.

There were other disadvantages, not the least being the heat (36 degrees day and 27 night) and we both got food poisoning either from the diet of crab, tiger prawns, lobster, etc. or the cloudy tap water they probably used to wash the salad.

The whole country was very photogenic: I have a large album of pictures in the making just now as we visited quite a few temples and palaces from Bangkok and Chiang Mai, though it's very easy to get an overdose of temples, like visiting only the churches in Europe. The contrast between the poverty and crude agriculture in the villages, and the splendour and art in the temples is extreme.

We did visit Patpong, the red-light district of Bangkok but found it unpleasant because you cannot just sit and watch a show: you are expected to watch the show for a short while, select a go-go dancer that you like, buy him a drink and then go upstairs with him for the business (massage and more). There is no social cruising like there is in Amsterdam. Even walking the streets is unpleasant as every block has people harassing you, offering massage, go-go bars and so on. It must be great if you want, and must have, a boy for an hour or day or night (I've heard of people getting excellent escorts who show them the temples, etc.) but not a place to see a tasty show with your own friend.

Some time ago I started in a small way 'collecting' SM pictures after I came across the guy who does the published 'Sam' drawings. I bought a couple of pictures that he'd done already and asked him to do one specifically for me and the collecting started there. Now my bedroom walls are covered with original pictures: it is fun working with an artist to make a fantasy 'right' on paper and much more involvement than buying in a gallery: I've done that on occasion, too – antique prints or Tom of Finland.

West Berlin

July 1988

Peter was admitted to St Bartholomew's hospital when we returned from Thailand and was diagnosed as HIV positive. He has been getting involved with self-help groups for people with AIDS. It seems that the outlook may not be as bleak as the newspapers make out. There is a new drug called AZT which he may be well enough to start taking shortly.

For a holiday from all of this Peter and I flew to Berlin with Dave (Peter's previous lover) and his lover Tim. Very interesting city; the atmosphere is quite different from, say, Amsterdam, and of course there is the Wall and the East. But all the stucco and mouldings everywhere recalling the Weimar Republic and before were fascinating.

Alas, the airline lost Peter's baggage, and he also got a fever and had to spend almost all our time there in the hotel bedroom and has had to be admitted to hospital again back here. But is now home and getting well again quickly. I've started dreaming up erotic fiction stories instead of actually having sex.

So Berlin was not a total success. I would like to go there again – but I'm not sure Peter will want to.

The Earls Court Leather Bar

October 1988

I went to the leather bar last Saturday night in 20-hole toecapped black Doctor Martens, yellow laces; a pair of old US green cotton fatigues, a check shirt that is a couple of sizes too small so it's torn under the arms, and over that a disco harness going down into the greens and my dirty leather bike jacket with two sets of cut-offs. The underneath cut-off is filthy and with a few studs around the collar; the top cut-off has a five-pointed star on the back and lots of biker badges and patches on the front. The US greens have been modified by tightening up the arse and the legs so they hang right if my cock is hanging out of the flies, and hang tight when it's inside . . . Zip done up but waist button open.

I had a scotch and two pints of plain water before I left the house, walked to the pub, weather wet and windy all the way. Ordered my lager and stood in the light near one of the toilet entrances. Lot of interest but not from anyone I liked. One guy came over and asked me if I had any acid for sale: I certainly hadn't; I keep well away from drugs. He'd just come out from Rochester nick Wednesday of last week; three months, not sure what for. He said he'd been kicked about a bit, which he didn't like as he couldn't kick the screws back. Not been fucked there, he said.

I sent him off to the door where the dealers sometimes hang about, got another lager and went back to posing. I'd seen a group of skinheads come in and wanted to see if anything was doing. It wasn't, but a guy in a combat jacket with the parachute flap hanging unbuttoned down behind him, dark red wellies and a one-piece black rubber suit was also moving into range. He stood closer to the toilet door than I did and then went in. When he came out again there was piss all down the front of his rubber one-piece suit. I moved over and started talking. He was going on to the leather club at King's Cross to meet someone there and I had arranged to go walking on the Sunday so we swapped numbers only. He'll be there again and so will I – one in the savings account for a rainy day! He said I must be wanting to piss, which was true. He had me stand there in the crowd of the pub facing him and with my boots spread apart. He said piss and I had to piss until he said stop. He was pinching my cock through the greens and putting his finger at the piss hole making it even more difficult to piss. One leg of the fatigues went dark green as my piss ran down into my boot. When I couldn't stop on command he flicked my cock with his finger making me jump. When I stopped he scrunched my cock over to point the other way and ordered me to piss again, making the other boot and side of the trousers pissy. When I'd finished he hauled me against him using the harness and rubbed my warm wet greens against his rubber-covered legs staining them and really turning me on further.

We drank and talked a bit and he went off. A leather biker guy who had long Angel hair, leather jeans jacket, looked as if he'd put his clean gear on for the gay pub and would wear Angel gear in the right company, had been watching this but he wouldn't come to talk. I cruised around a bit more, lots of looks but not from anyone I liked the look of. The skinheads were busy among themselves, and although I wasn't ignored, I didn't want to join their group. I had a bit of a chat with a mate who was also there cruising. Then to the toilet before going out into the cold. Wet greens are great but bloody cold in a gale. Had a piss and found I was followed by a guy who had the back seam of his jeans unstitched, and dirty as well. He'd got a buttplug inside it which I was able to manipulate for his pleasure. He'd had that in since 8 p.m. and it was now after 11 p.m. I'll try that next time – either with the harness or with a pair of open-arsed jeans.

On the way out I saw the off-duty Angel standing on the pavement outside. He followed me as I went off home and he got in a large white van and sat in the driver's seat without moving off. I should have gone and talked then, but didn't ... and regretted it, but by the time I had walked back he had gone. I shouldn't hesitate like that ... dammit.

So that was my Saturday out.

Devil's Punch Bowl

May 1989

Hi, mate,

Thanks for your reply to my advert in the Australian paper. It really turned me on! I enjoy sexy letters – and at least writing and reading wanky letters is definitely safe sex!

I read your letter at about 2000 hours on my bed having stripped off my work 501 jeans (I'm breaking in a new pair just now that haven't been washed ever so far, and I've been wearing them for a month at work). Rain pouring down outside (though it's supposed to be spring!), the temperature outside's about 4 degrees C and in here my thermostat's set to 24 degrees. I read your letter stripped off, cock in hand. I've since put on a grubby pair of olive drab army mechanics overalls – with pockets right through, meant for accessing trouser pockets, but I'm not wearing trousers underneath – and a pair of 14-hole 'Ranger' pattern combat boots laced fairly tight.

We're into similar things – perhaps I'm more into the army/uniform/boots turn-on than you say in your letter: wearing heavy boots and shorts really turns me on. I'm also quite into cropped hair – mine was cropped to Number One two weeks ago and it feels great just now. CP really turns me on too, though I have to be in the right mood for it, build up to it, etc., but if everything's going fine I like a lot of it, marks, bruises for a fortnight, etc.

My main excuse for not signing up with the TA (Territorial Army) has been that I have to work some weekends and I can't commit myself much in advance for that reason. However, there's also a certain amount of lack of getting on with it, possibly because I have at times been getting around as a slave quite enough without having army discipline and commitments as well. I'll be interested to hear what you've got up

MORE AND HARDER

to in the Army Reserve. I suppose you are less likely to get frozen solid outdoors than we are in the UK.

My favourite form of humiliation outdoors is probably boots and shorts and then drinking a load of beer and not being allowed to the toilet – although in this country it's more practicable (warmer) to wear jeans and be forced to piss those. My army cammo combat trousers have also been pissed in many times . . .

A variation is with boots and army-greens. I'm told this happens to soldiers who get back late from drinking and they're kept in the guard room at 'Attention' till all can see that they've pissed from the lines of darker green down the fatigues. I suppose a belting follows rather than be reported.

I wish I could be the skinhead you take out on your bike to humiliate and fuck rotten and rough. You'd have to use your greater height and your belt to make me submit. And even I don't go around with the arse seam of my jeans slit open, so you'd better slit it with your knife. Maybe when you're in the UK . . . I used to have motorbikes. At present I'm riding my mate's Suzuki GSX750 because mine was stolen eighteen months ago and it's been cheaper to have the one bike between the two of us. I've ridden bikes to the Alps and beyond as well as round the UK and to rallies and Hell's Angel meets and gay bikers' rallies. All good reason for wearing leathers and/or filthy denims and of course boots.

Last summer, a biker friend and I went out for a ride two-up on his bike; his name's Hans and he happens to be German. I have a lockable ball-weight that is made of turned stainless steel and locked on with security screws, so when he turned up at my place I locked that on his balls, stretching them pleasantly when sitting and the weight pulling on them when he walked. I wore my lockable leather jacket which the leather company made for me rather nicely. It's a classic biker's leather jacket adapted so that there are concealed ways of locking it; there are ten padlocks to secure it, all with the same key.

There are locks on the collar (a nice thick collar made of tawse-like leather), the main zip, the belt and on each of the pockets so that the wearer has to ask to be allowed to smoke and get at his own keys or wallet. The chest pockets have been modified so that there is no lining and they access the tits. And inside the sleeves there are wrist straps that are also lockable then concealed by the sleeve.

On the back, he has added three D-rings that look innocent (or punk) enough, but are strategically placed at the collar, middle of the back and at the waist and are useful as fixing points for bondage. Inside, the jacket is reinforced with leather straps so that pulling on any of the D-rings or other fixings strains the straps not the jacket leather which isn't strong enough for that. The internal straps can continue as an arse and cock strap that goes through the legs to keep a dildo in place. All of this is invisible to a passer-by or petrol station attendant, burger bar waiter, etc.

Under the jacket was my new stitched leather harness intended for long-term wear and chastity. There is a jock secured by lacing and a lot of eyelets. My cock is strapped inside the jock and tied up by the Prince Albert ring. There are also ball straps. This is great as the harness is tight on the body; turns me on rotten yet my cock can't even move. Frustrating.

So we left on his bike. I drove and he rode pillion which is domination enough – being made to ride pillion on your own bike. Every time I braked his balls got crushed between us. I rode us to a safe piece of countryside, the Devil's Punch Bowl; we parked and descended into the woods. He stripped me down to the harness and boots, tied me to a log and messed me about, tortured me with holly, stream muck and leaves. Then I locked the jacket on him and spread-eagled him to a tree that had fallen across a stream, mucked up the denim shorts he was wearing and made his balls hurt by pulling them and torturing them with holly, mud and cold water. I stuck holly inside his shorts front and back, left it a little while, and then started belting him hard across the arse, the holly and belting making him scream, sob and moan into the leather hood. I wanked him off eventually using stream muck as lubricant, safe-fucking his arse through my harness, his shorts and the holly. I came inside the harness, he in the stream.

The postscript is that we tidied up and rode back on the bike and then he went off home but he 'forgot' he was wearing the ball-weight. As it was then 0200 hours he had to wear it to work all the next day and arrange to be released the next night!

Wimbledon Common

May 1989

I went for a training session Wednesday last week with my running partner, Togie; he's in the Royal Marine Reserve. We run together on an occasional basis round Wimbledon Common near here. He's into much the same as I am – PT, combat uniforms, combat boots, CP – but he's a bit older than me. Togie's favourite CP fantasy is a Borstal Tawse punishment administered with him holding me down across a refectory table, my trousers wetted to make the stripes bite harder, and the strokes administered slowly by a Master with a long (24-inch) leather Tawse. Then I hold him down and he takes the same as he put me through. I have had the long Tawse over a table, but there was no way to hold me down and I took only twenty. Quite different from a cane; rips through you like hot wire.

I said we'd meet at a bridge over a stream after dark. I cycled there – that's about thirty minutes including a long hill up – cut the lights on my bike and rode through the park along the path to meet him. We both stripped totally naked except for boots. He was wearing UK army DMS boots which have a chevron pattern rubber sole – DMS means direct-moulded sole. I hid the bike and the clothes I'd cycled in and started running in my 20-hole combat boots.

There are lots of paths there so getting lost wasn't a problem. We ran for forty-five minutes including a hill upwards that is about three-quarters of a mile long. I had great fun making him suffer up that by not stopping, keeping the pace just fast enough for him to be able to keep going, relaxing it enough when he started flagging too much and picking up again almost immediately. All the tricks from my competitive cross-country days except I didn't make him drop. Obviously we splashed straight through puddles, mud and water going all over. It was raining anyhow and we didn't care about the wet; anyhow, nice to feel the cold slap of it amongst the wind between the legs. Wind on the chest, legs moving freely with big fucking boots on the end of them splashing anywhere. Cool up the arse with a slight trickle of sweat and rain down the crack. Easy to finger each other. Nice place to fix the eyes on. Cock and balls bouncing in the breeze, starting big and bouncy, soon shrivelling up.

Up the top of the hill there's a golf course. We kept on running when we reached the top of the hill and a few minutes later stopped for some press-ups (3 × 20) and burpees (3 × 20) in the mud. I pushed him down in the mud and got a couple of bootprints on him: one on the middle of his back and another right across his arse. He printed me too. That was nice thereafter because I was leading from behind, chasing him to keep him going, and the sight of his bare arse and back with muddy boot marks on it was great. His front looked good, too; there's something very gruesome and humiliating in a nice sexual way about a dirty, muddy man's front without any shorts to break the vertical lines of sweat, mud and rain pouring down from his hair to his legs. And the thought that I'd made him that humiliated, that primitive, turned me on nicely.

More running across the golf course, the lights of London tingeing the clouds and the rainy mist orange, the wind cooling us, the boots tramping sure-footedly and softly on the grass. Back down on another path, this time with branches (and holly branches some of them) across the path. Covered over by branches and so darker, stumbling, but saved by the boots. Faster, too, except for some muddy paths, unexpectedly sucking the boots in. And back to the bridge over the stream.

I collected a couple of stiff twigs, bent him over and gave him twelve across the arse, holding him by his shrivelled cock and balls, and then he did me too, twelve. Mutual toughening up. I gave him his shirt back but not his shorts and sent him running back to where his car was parked on the edge of the playing fields, so he had to choose his moment to break cover and unlock the car. He likes that, especially if he's not expecting it (and it's in a safe-ish place to do it, obviously). I pulled my combat trousers up over my boots, collecting more mud inside; they were cold, clammy and wet but felt great. Ditto T-shirt and I cycled back home, one hill up, one hill down, and greased a buttplug, squatted on my training bench and wanked hard into my DPM trousers . . . again.

That all happened last Wednesday, although I would have preferred if it had been me being Trained and paced up the hill.

I hope this letter hasn't given the wrong idea – I do very much prefer to be humiliated, used, abused, fucked (safely), but it doesn't often work out like that, particularly with men my own age. More often it happens as me and a mate do each other over for our mutual enjoyment. Most of the purely slave scenes I've got into have been with Masters significantly older than me; still good sex, but a different kick. I also haven't said much about bootlicking – but I do like that too, and the ex-soldiers and officers I know here have got me well trained in that art!

I don't cruise bars very much – mainly because it doesn't work for me; adverts and letters seem much better. My gay friends are almost all 'out' and mainly into some form of SM; if I go to the bars with my mate Peter (it's his bike), we'll bump into someone or other we know. Peter's far more into bars and piss than I am, and he's been known to have a piss scene there and then in the bar!

When I placed the advert I had a couple of ideas about how to make the correspondence interesting, as well as writing about what turns us on, which seem to agree with what you're into:

1. We could exchange audio cassettes – maybe next time you're wanking after training or after a couple of days without sex you could record me an audio cassette about what turns you on as you wank, the best scenes you've had in boots, or about a good CP scene you've had. Or maybe you could go out in the bush or a mud hole and record a fantasy there about what'd be a good scene for us. Where you'd tie me up, what you'd beat me with (and let me hear it). Say what boots you're wearing, tramp

around in them so I can hear the sound of them on the ground, squelch them in the mud and then tell me on the cassette how you clean them. Put a cock-ring on before you start just to make things zing!

Or tape a real CP session with your slave if you happen to be able to.

If there's any space at the end of the tape then is there a gay radio station near you? I'd also be fascinated to hear what they broadcast – there's nothing like that here. And I will do one for you in return.

2. We could exchange used shorts or jocks or Speedos (I'm 28″ waist, 38″ chest but 'small' T-shirts fit me best!). There are some tasty-looking Aussie Rules rugger shorts currently advertised, those ones with the lace up front! Would you like a UK Gay Pride T-shirt?
3. And there're photos: I would like to see photos of you in your torn jeans or boots and shorts, with your cock and balls hanging out. You could also put a muddy footprint on the paper of your letter to me after you've written it.

Peter W: RIP

July 1989

I'm writing this whilst Peter is still in hospital, almost a fortnight after he'd been declared unable to benefit from further treatment. It's typical of the way he fought his illness that he's still fighting on, hope against hope.

Peter didn't like obituaries in the Newsletter: since recovering from his first hospitalisation, he's been desktop publishing the Newsletter from his home; indeed, the day before I took him last into hospital, delirious and frightened with dehydration, we'd both attended the Newsletter group meeting at the centre. Even on that last admission, he got out of the wheelchair we'd used to get from the car and he walked through the door into Spurgeon Ward.

His skinhead attitude was to get on with living. He was unlucky: he contracted 'flu eighteen months or so ago, so it would be easy to say that he neglected to look after himself; the other side of that statement is that he was too busy burning life's candle at both ends to bother with something like 'flu that he rarely got and usually quickly recovered from. The Peter we knew and loved would not be told to do anything; he did what he wanted to.

This time the 'flu dragged on. We booked a holiday to somewhere hot, Thailand, to get away from it all. Peter spent the second week of what could have been an idyllic holiday amidst the white sands and palm trees limping between the bed and the toilet suffering with bad diarrhoea.

Back in his flat in Peckham and on weekends away Peter and I tried to pretend there wasn't a problem. He wasn't eating much. We both had decided not to be HIV-tested unless there was a reason or a treatment available; although we both knew quite a lot about HIV/AIDS, we dreaded it so much that it wasn't mentioned. Live Acidophilus yoghurts, relaxation, etc. seemed to help a bit and we persevered with those.

Peter was eventually HIV-tested, and was indeed HIV positive. It was a blow. He'd always said he didn't expect to live beyond the age of 40, and in some ways I couldn't conceive of the Peter I knew in a ripe old age. But like everyone else, he had hoped that he would be young for ever and that he could 'get away with it' and not catch AIDS. He talked of the rapid progress in research, every new week bringing new knowledge to the medics. He hoped to hang on in there until there was a cure for him.

1988 Gay Pride came shortly after this. Peter went along, on his own, to join in the celebrations. 'Sing if you're glad to be gay' now had a new, bitter taste on Tom Robinson's latest version. Peter saw the others and was amazed that they were happy and looked as if there was nothing wrong with them. His hope began to resurface despite his symptoms and his fears.

Another holiday, to Berlin with friends, was planned and Peter doggedly packed his bags not to let us down. That was important; recently he has had the attitude that he mustn't be a burden to his friends, even though it would cause him pain. He would not take the decision to cancel a holiday. It was always I who had to cancel, as I knew the trip would cause him too much pain. The number of tablets Peter needed to carry around was beginning to increase: he'd had Acyclovir for ages, now there were Ketaconazole and multivitamins as well. Peter packed his day's supply of these in his hand baggage; the rest went in the suitcase.

His luck was out again when our luggage arrived on the carousel in Berlin and his wasn't there. The airline later admitted it had gone to Bombay. We bought some Acyclovir locally, discovering the true cost of maintaining a patient. Despite this, he spent this holiday, too, commuting between the toilet, the washbasin (washing) and the bed.

Back in London, I took him into hospital on his motorbike and we cried publicly in each other's arms when he was told he would be admitted 'for tests'. He always saw straight through doctors' euphemisms. He didn't expect to come out of there alive. He fulfilled the biker's dream and told me I could have his bike when he died.

By that weekend he was hallucinating on intravenous antibiotics, very lonely and very scared. They diagnosed Salmonella septicaemia, moved him into a room on his own for isolation and he thought he was there to die, out of sight of the other patients.

Meanwhile I was talking to his friends and mine. Jimmy Sommerville was still singing 'Don't leave me this way' and Pet Shop Boys were singing 'You were always on my mind'. Friends convinced me that he could recover, that there would be a quality of life that would be worth the struggle. I convinced Peter and he was discharged rapidly and we all rallied round him at his home, his tablets now increased to include two antibiotics to be taken at different times of the day from his other tablets.

He was persuaded to change the STD clinic to a local one. Unknown, small and very, very friendly and proficient. I made him walk there to prove that he could. The first consultant was peeved but it was for Peter's quality of life that we made the change. The tablets' regime was rationalised. AZT was mentioned, not as 'You're too ill to benefit even from AZT' but as a hope for the future: 'Your blood's getting so much better, keep up the effort and you'll be able to benefit from AZT very shortly.' Peter started going out to do his own shopping again and contacted a Support Group.

Our first visit there was a complete surprise. In panic Peter had stopped smoking, drinking or enjoying himself. People with AIDS were drinking, smoking, living life to the full, maybe while they could, but who knows what's going to happen tomorrow? There was a similarity with the West Berlin atmosphere ('enjoy yourself tonight, the bomb may go off tomorrow') that Peter had been too ill to appreciate directly.

AZT became appropriate. Peter made the decision after finding out the facts. The same day that he started on AZT he returned to work, still as a computer engineer, on light duties. Soon he was fully back at work, was again running his own rubberwear business and dramatically brightening up the

Newsletter. He gained weight, confidence and enjoyment in life. We had an enjoyable holiday in Gran Canaria over the time of the first World AIDS Day. Peter really felt sad waiting for the minibus back to the airport. Peter could work, play, eat, drink and even smoke as he wanted to. Peter could coexist with the AIDS virus.

We had Christmas Day together and alone. He said it would be the last. He gave me a set of silver-plated knives and forks. Peter said he'd always wanted a set like that for himself. We had Boxing Days with the respective families.

But Peter's luck was out. He had a skin problem which baffled the dermatologists: psoriasis. They didn't dare to treat it because the treatments are basically immuno-suppressive. We had another holiday in March, to Dubai, under the care of Peter's previous lover who is teaching there. Peter was worried going through Immigration and Customs: the quantity of prescription drugs he now had to carry was getting obvious and it wasn't at all clear what the United Arab Emirates' attitude to a tourist carrying a quantity of AZT would be.

There were moments of real happiness on that holiday and also real peace. Perhaps alcohol-induced but also with relief at getting away from the grind of hospital appointments. But the symptoms of skin breakdown increased relentlessly and by the time we returned home Peter was having trouble walking properly. He still went to work, was still the organisational lynchpin around which the Newsletter revolved and still ran his business.

A career opportunity came my way. Peter was adamant for me not to neglect my life by spending too much of my time and effort with him. It was a great thought, impossible for me to fully implement. Later he told me off for over-visiting him in hospital and, though he really appreciated my staying overnight in his hospital bed with him, he also dismissed me for 'nights off' with my caring friends.

The pain of walking increased. Peter drove everywhere, insistent on retaining his independence and mobility. I cancelled a holiday to Cornwall that would have been too painful for us both. Peter was very upset because his frailty was now stopping us from doing things we wanted to do. Two days after that decision I took him into Spurgeon Ward. Despite the pain he insisted on walking in. He walked out, much stronger, ten or so days later, specifically in time for the next Newsletter editorial meeting.

Sadly, Erythromycin, which had given him an almost miraculous remission, didn't go on working for him. Other dermatological drugs, the hot weather and the strain of one, two, three, four or even five hospital appointments a week with different clinics all took their toll. His business, the Newsletter and the hot dinner for me when I arrived at his place on Friday evening – shattered after a week's work – all continued.

The weekend before Peter's final admission, we'd done DIY around my house and then gone to the newly opened Centre for the Newsletter meeting. Peter insisted that I stay through the meeting. He admired the plants, the wall coverings and the new television. He had a cigarette, and then another, on the bench outside St Cuthbert's church and we looked at the blue sky, the leaves on the trees and the growing red and orange tinges of the sunset. Not many times had Peter felt at peace with the world, but this was one of them.

The next day I phoned him in the morning at his flat: he seemed OK. That evening I phoned but it seemed the phone line was faulty. In fact Peter had the microphone to his ear, had picked up the handset the wrong way around. This happened several times before panic set in. I telephoned his HIV consultant, went immediately to his flat, got him to hospital and comforted him. I was taken to one side and warned by the consultant, and then had to leave Peter, dehydrated by the weather and psoriasis but in good hands. One couldn't ask for better care than that at Spurgeon Ward.

He kept needing reassurance that he was getting better. It was now a year since his HIV diagnosis and he was wondering how much more was in store for him. We gave him reassurance and he fought on, winning another battle against Pseudomonas septicaemia. The psoriasis did not abate and his kidneys had been irrevocably damaged by dehydration.

Even after all this history, when Peter was told that there was no more treatment available, because of his kidney damage, he defied us all by living and laughing on despite all hopes, fears and predictions.

I asked him if he was afraid of dying. 'That's simple,' he said. 'You go into the room, put on their clothes and walk on out of the other door.'

His funeral service that I organised in St Cuthbert's was well attended by skinheads, a skinhead organist and his mate page-turning, many rubbermen and our families.

Mark Goes to Jail, Part I

August 1989

So Hans and Roger put me on the bus at New York to Scranton. I was under the impression that Scranton was about thirty miles north of NYC (somewhere near West Point Military Academy) and I spent the first hour of the journey wondering if I was on the right bus. I hadn't meant to have any sex on this trip anyhow; it was meant to be a relaxing holiday but RMR-Togie had phoned up Roger and at breakfast the next day Hans and Roger asked me whether I wanted to be sent off to see this Ian that I'd heard so much about.

My first reaction was 'no' – everything I'd heard about him said 'heavy' and I didn't think I was in the mood. However, people that I respect had always come back having had a great time under his care. I had heard that he was in the US army and spent a lot of his time teaching soldiers how to deal with capture by the enemy and subsequent interrogation and prisoner-of-war (POW or PW) situations. Hans had, in addition, been building up his reputation by saying to me when I complained about overnight bondage being too uncomfortable, 'Ian wouldn't let you out of this . . .'

So it was with some fear that I put down the phone, having arranged to unexpectedly drop in on him. Fear and 'oh shit what have I got myself into this time'. He sounded just the sort who would hurt and hurt a lot. Totally 'professional' on the phone, asked all the right sort of questions in the sort of way that made me give all the answers that I meant rather than the shy and unadventurous answers that I would give if clear in the head. 'Which would you rather sleep in, a bed at the house or behind a prison-cell door on wooden slats?' And I enthusiastically opted for the second one.

This was spinning through my head for the twenty-four

hours between arranging the meeting and the bus journey. Besides this, once Hans and Roger knew that I definitely was going, the winding-up shifted up several gears. That evening Roger, who knows Ian very well, phoned him from the restaurant where we were eating, put me straight on, and I had to say what I wanted to do — to which I said lots of PT, press-ups, sit-ups, etc. There were other questions and details. Roger took over the conversation and I went back to Hans. I worried what he was telling Ian because Roger had seen me in London the day after one of the heaviest CP scenes I have ever had: I went to someone as a skinhead going for Borstal punishment, twenty strokes of the 24-inch tawse. My backside certainly looked like a Rembrandt after that.

Back on the coach I was the only male amongst about half a dozen crumblies or blue tits. I started talking to the one opposite me who seemed as charmed by the 20-hole combat boots with the butch indented rubber soles as the NATO green sweater and olive-green Fred Perry (skinhead) T-shirt I was wearing. And I'd cropped my hair to Number One before leaving London three days previously. I told her I was going to join some friends to go camping in the forest around Scranton. She said I'd enjoy that.

The journey was through what was for me spectacular country; the Delaware River gap, for instance, was just huge country with immense forested hillsides and a big basin beyond. There was a steep hill that took over ten minutes at 55 m.p.h. as a steady grind upwards. The coach eventually arrived at Scranton and my fears about not being recognised were proved groundless. Ian turned out to be an obviously fit and strong man of the thin and muscular type. He got me in his car and explained the form: I was there to talk about tramways, the hobby that his wife knew about. He would introduce me to her, she would probably chat about her family and their never having made it to England and then he would take me upstairs to see his handcuff collection whilst she made the dinner.

The handcuff collection was fascinating — I tried several times to think of a way-out type of handcuff to see if it wasn't there but never managed to find one. He got me to point out a favourite and before I knew where I was they were on my hands and snapped safely shut in a very expert manner. You can get scared when someone does that so efficiently that there is no point in resisting.

He also showed me a proof copy of one of my stories that I had sent him as magazine editor, although I hadn't been aware to whom I was writing as he had used a pseudonym.

Ian warned me about his wife's cooking – it was almost an SM experience in itself, he said. She had wild ideas about flavouring and the food was liable to be either burnt or not warm at all. In the event she was very pleasant, if a little dotty and preoccupied with medical matters; the baked beans had vinegar on them and were half-hot and half-cold. If I wanted to produce that effect I don't think I could do it!

After dinner he talked to me more about what limits and so on and I dug myself further into the shit . . . although I did say that I haven't been in the mood for heavy CP recently. His reply was to the effect that 'But you don't mind painful bondage, do you?' And I agreed. So it was agreed I was there for a night of old-fashioned prison discipline and PT.

We got into his car, me still chatting away like a songbird, and he drove off. His wife's parting comment was something like 'I do hope you'll be comfortable, we do like our guests to be comfortable.' He stopped at a shopping plaza, handed me some leg-irons and old-fashioned handcuffs, just the sort I had said were my best for being strung up in because they didn't cut. Whilst I put them on he explained that I was going up to 'The Stockade' blindfolded. The method of blindfolding so as not to arouse suspicion should the car be stopped was a set of party eye things that were black cups over my eyes and, to disguise those, a pair of punk dark glasses. I continued rabbiting on nervously despite these precautions.

After some miles, evidently uphill, he stopped the car; he got out, leaving me with my hands cuffed behind my back. He took some things out of the boot of the car and opened a front door. Then I heard very little more except a dog barking in the far distance. I opened my side car window to hear better my surroundings. I think he'd said on the way up that the track that we were now in the middle of was a fifty-acre site halfway up a mountain and there was a vertical cliff downwards on one side and forest on the other. He returned and, in a totally different voice, gave me a real military bollocking on the lines of: 'Who told you you could open that window?'

'No one said I couldn't.'

'From now on you only do what you are told to. Wind it back up again.' He locked a metal collar around my neck and went away again.

He left me there for a further time listening to the noises of the trees, the far-off dog and some chain-clanking sounds from within the house that sounded like fun! When he came back again he opened the car door, rushed me out and hustled me in double-quick time along a path, over some grass, and into a house. I still couldn't see but could hear all the different sounds that my boots made on the gravel and the floor.

I'd been told that there was a prison cell in his basement and it wasn't a surprise when he said, 'There're some steps downwards now, one false move and you'll break your neck.' Sometimes when I've been tied up and hustled into a cellar it's been done to make sure that I don't fall down the steps. This guy positively pushed me so that I went too far, scared myself with the void I felt and by what he'd said, with the only steadying being possible through my hands that were cuffed behind my back and being propelled onwards by himself. I guess I felt very dependent on him just then.

Somehow I made it down the stairs and felt hard cement floor underfoot. He ordered me to stand with my legs as far apart as the leg-irons would let me, my hands still irrevocably behind my back. The metal collar around my neck was attached to a heavy chain which pulled to my right. I did not have a lot of freedom.

Standing behind me he removed the blindfolds and I could see a grey cinder block wall with some white lines painted on it: a vertical white line and four other lines which corresponded to the extremes of an 'X' at about the places where hands and feet would go on the wall for a very extreme spread-eagle. Just now the top two 'X' marks kept flicking in and out of the inherent blind spots on my eyes. Apart from that the wall was quite bare, as was the floor. There was my shadow thrown against it by a single bright light and also his shadow, larger than mine and evidently wearing uniform trousers and boots.

I thought of cinema scenes with the prisoner being interrogated with a bright light in his face so that his captors could see him perfectly and he could not see anything but the bright light.

My fear level increased.

'Whilst you are here you will only speak when you are spoken to. You will begin every sentence with "Sir" and finish every sentence with "Sir". Do you understand?' And I said only 'Yes, Sir' which was wrong. An English officer demands only 'Yes, Sir' from subordinates; that is what I say when I'm on automatic response, as I was here. There was a stream of abuse about the English and I was warned that I would be either beaten thoroughly or zapped with a cattle prod or worse if I did not obey orders.

'The command "Wall" means that you place your nose against the white line on the wall and your boots, feet apart, against the wall. No other parts of your body touch the wall. You do not move. You do not move from that position unless you are ordered to do so. Understood?'

'Sir, yes, Sir,' I said deliberately, having to think to make sure I didn't fuck up again.

'WALL.' And I clanked towards the wall, found the white line and slightly fell towards it, hurting my nose against the rough cinder block surface, simultaneously shuffling my boots so that the toecaps both touched the wall.

He grabbed one of my boots and started to unshackle them, then he undid the handcuffs.

'Remember that at all times you will be secured. There is eleven foot of chain on that collar and that is all the freedom you are allowed: eleven foot.'

'Sir, yes, Sir.'

'STRIP.'

And I fumbled and clanked with my belt, jeans and boots

until they were in a heap on the floor next to me. My shirt, I took over my shoulders and on to the chain attaching me to the right. I was back, nose and toes against the wall, naked.

'Another mistake. It is possible to feed the shirt through the collar and off over your head. Do it.'

'Sir, yes, Sir.'

When my shirt was also on the floor I went back against the wall with my hands at my sides.

'If you are permitted to have your hands free they should be behind your neck, fingers interlocked with your elbows back behind your shoulders. DO IT.'

He replaced the cold leg-irons on my feet and the handcuffs on my hands where they now were, behind my neck.

'Take two steps backwards.' I did. 'Open your mouth.' I did, and for the first time since arriving there I could see him as he came in front of me to look inside my mouth. He was now wearing full woodland camouflage battle-dress uniform, cap, shirt, trousers, boots, all in good turnout and properly ironed and tucked in. His name and 'US Army' were on patches on his chest and there were some patches on his arms and quite enough chevrons on his shoulders to command respect, in addition to his being several inches taller than me and in boots, compared to me naked, feet flat on the cement floor.

'Open your mouth,' and I did. He searched inside it, the rough skin of his finger probing under my tongue and inside my cheeks, searching for materials of escape. Next he searched my hair, short-cropped though it was, behind my ears, my armpits, around my cock, gathering my balls in a sac in one hand and pulling threateningly while he looked underneath my cock.

'Bend over' was the next order, and I saw him putting on heavy black rubber gauntlets. He checked between my arse cheeks and then started inside, two fingers, four fingers probing inside my guts for anything at all that might have been planted there by me to attempt to escape from this prison. I saw stars mingling with the partial view of his boots that I had from my bent-over position, hands still interlocked behind my neck, legs straining to maintain balance against the searching rubber hands up my arse.

He finished as efficiently as he had started, ordered me back upright, removed the irons and handed me some green BDUs.

'Put on your prison uniform and your boots. Your number is one seven five.'

I wasn't expecting this to fit, but it was spectacularly badly fitting, shirt too tight and trousers within an ace of falling down at all times. 'Lack of turnout is lack of self-respect' had been laboriously drummed into me from basic training onwards and both the poor fit and the insecurity of having to hold the trousers up myself, no belt allowed, took yet more control away from me. This Interrogation Officer knew his stuff. My worries on the bus were justified . . .

He replaced the leg-irons now over my boots, cuffed my hands behind my back. I fucked up again by not returning them to the behind-the-neck position and this drew renewed threats from him. I could still see and was taken a few paces to my right, still with the same chain attached to the iron collar around my neck. The cinder block wall with the white marks on it that I had been staring at since the blindfold was removed led to a cell. The cell door was open and in the few moments while I was being walked into the cell I could see that the door was hinged at one side from top to bottom, the moving part was a good six feet wide and eight feet high with an obscured part where the lock was. Obscured, that is from the inmate's side.

He had me stand in the cell doorway. The cell consisted of a wooden plank bed on one side, a piss can, a bare wall on my right with more white paint spread-eagled on it like on the wall outside; the whole cell was illuminated by the single bright light from outside which cast intense shadows of the cell bars and on him, my tormentor, and myself, legs and hands spread in the 'Submit to search' position.

He closed the door behind me with a convincing clank. Images of prison movies came into my head. The Birdman in Alcatraz for year after year after year. The calendar on screen flicking through the days and months far faster than for him inside, yet conveying the heart-rending hopelessness of long-term incarceration in 'humane' imprisonment. The Southern States with iron slavery for the blacks and jails like this for the whites. And he'd only just shut the door on me.

Mind wandering like this, I hadn't been paying attention to Orders and I fucked up yet again: my elbows were wandering forwards and it was noticed. I held them back, parallel to my shoulders, and the strain of it gradually increased on my back. He was doing things outside the cell and I evidently couldn't get away with anything. I wondered what he would do next with me, how else he would demonstrate his complete power over me. I started thinking what would be the worst possible thing he could do, or would do. Heavy CP I supposed. My mind going off like that stopped keeping my elbows in place and he came towards the door and opened it, ordering me to put my hands through the cell door bars towards him. He unlocked the handcuffs, made me push my hands through the bars so that most of my arms were now outside the cell, my arms going through different gaps in the bars at about shoulder width apart. He again cuffed my hands. I shuffled back against the cell door, feeling its cold and slightly flaking, rusty strength, still standing legs apart as ordered; I also got more relief standing like that, able to slightly shift weight from side to side and front to back.

He left, banged the door shut and turned the light out. My eyes adjusted from the harsh single light to the almost total dark and my ears to the complete quiet. In time (how long?), I thought I could see something – a shade of light and dark against the cell wall, but it disappeared as fast as I thought I could see anything. Gathering dusk outside perhaps.

Eyes useless, my ears took charge. The dog that I'd heard barking was still at it. Then he stopped too, quiet for the night. I thought I heard something making noises inside, a field mouse or something. Then a definite flying noise. A bat maybe? Bat and mouse? Who knows? I kept quieter than both of them and was then convinced that there was someone else in the cellar with me, also breathing so quiet so as not to be heard. Somehow I didn't want to make any noise to let my terroriser know that I was there or that he was having any effect on me. If there was someone there, was he friend or foe? If he wasn't in the cell that I was in, where was he? Bat noises again. At least my body didn't hurt – or did it? Come to think of it, my feet weren't too happy about standing still for long, but nothing too bad really. Best not to think about it.

There were also noises from upstairs: he was moving around. And a compressor or fan or something. Fridge or heating or air con. But basically no sound, no light, no smell except something that was like a damp-proofing liquid or cement sealer. My cock got a bit of a hard-on for some reason. Something I could still do perhaps, despite total subjugation. That made the loose trousers shift and feel as though they might fall down. For some reason I resisted that. Perhaps he would have liked to return and find his prisoner with his trousers around his ankles? I didn't know and once they had fallen it was irrevocable, no way to hoist them up again. He'd searched me once, he might play with me using those rubber gloves again, me fettered to the iron cell door with my arse presented like that must look fairly attractive to a guard . . .

How long was this for? No way to tell. When he returned (he did return . . .) a dim light went on first and then the bright one. I saw all the shadows exactly, yes absolutely exactly, as they had been the moment that the light had been switched off. I hadn't been able to move at all for all that time. Nothing really hurt.

He uncuffed my hands. I wasn't sure whether to thank him or not so I didn't because I hadn't been spoken to. And while thinking about that, my hands had not gone to behind my neck, where they should have gone by default. He told me I'd fucked up and he was keeping a tab on all of these fuck-ups.

Me still standing, legs as far apart as the chain would allow, hands now interlocked behind my neck, he unlocked the cell door and ordered me out.

'Right, you say you're good at PT, now's your chance to prove it and maybe redeem some of those fuck-ups you've accumulated.' I shuffled out backwards, still maintaining the position ordered.

'Do you know the position "Front Leaning Rest"?'

'Yes, Sir.'

'You're forgetting something.'

'Sir, yes, Sir. Sir, beg pardon, Sir.'

'Do you know the position "Front Leaning Rest"?'

'Sir, yes, Sir.'

'Then get down to it ... NOW. When doing press-ups that is position ONE. There are two other positions, position TWO is the fully down position, not touching the floor but one inch above it.'

Just as I was discovering that 'front leaning rest' was anything but restful, he ordered 'TWO'. This was certainly not restful, but then it wasn't called 'rest', and anyhow my experience of American army positions called 'rest' was that they are exactly the opposite. 'At Ease' is similarly misnamed so I should have been warned.

'There is a third position which is halfway between positions one and two: THREE.'

Worst of the lot this, I'd reckon on being able to do fifty press-ups straight off, properly, i.e. good style, back straight, elbows locking in the up position and straight against the ground but just above it in the down position. However, these take-position-and-stay exercises caught me unawares, knackering my muscles before I was even started.

'ONE.' And then he ordered twenty press-ups. I was sagging by the twentieth and was shaking when I was in position One, the misnamed 'front leaning rest', receiving xenophobic abuse about Limeys.

He put me through a series of sets of press-ups and then ordering me between ONE, TWO and THREE. Shagged, muscles quaking and sweatily out of breath I soon started getting confused between what the hell I was supposed to do for each number, and chalking up more and more fuck-up points. He was really enjoying making me fuck-up more and more, and it was getting so easy as I was getting more and more confused, scared by his threats and simply shagged from the exertions of the fatigues he was putting me through.

He had me stand up next. My hands went to my sides and I'd scored again. At his rebuke they flew behind my neck. He handed me two iron bars about an inch each in diameter and a foot long.

'The three positions for this exercise are as follows: ONE, both bars straight above your head. TWO, both bars straight out in front of you and THREE, both bars out at your sides, arms outstretched.' He'd said it so fast and once only that I'd no chance, still suffering from the previous lot. I got it wrong before we started and only learnt which position was which by trial and error.

'Just remember,' he said, 'you will be punished for each mistake unless you redeem them. I'm not punishing you now; you will be punished in the forest tomorrow when we know how much you deserve.' Cunning that. If he'd been punishing me as I made fuck-ups it might have spurred me on at the time. By amassing punishment debits I was making for myself one helluva big beating or one very big fatigue session to work all the punishment debits off. And presumably the night to think about it.

Standing like that, iron collar still on chain pulling me one way sideways, hands engaged holding these bars that felt heavier each time round the positions that he ordered, I started to neglect the uniform I was wearing. The trousers started slipping down round my bum, the shirt started riding up and soon he was deriding me for looking a shambles, being a physical wreck unable to even lift simple bars and for constantly hitting the wrong positions when ordered about.

He'd got me totally jabbering, submissive to his commands and quaking at the prospect of the forest tomorrow. He wheeled me back into the cell again, standing against the now clanked-shut door, legs fettered together, the chain this time passing through the bars of the cell door, my arms as before also passing through the bars. But now he attached a chain to the handcuffs' chain, telling me to put my hands up to my neck. I, now submissive, like a fool did so and even helped them up a bit higher when ordered. He chained them to a loop on the iron collar, locked securely with a chunky feeling padlock. Out went the lights and down came the silence.

MORE AND HARDER

Not too bad I thought, at least I'm back in this cell and not being ordered about, being confused and bollocked. The uniform was pleasantly sweaty, going cold now. Feeling OK didn't last long at all. The exercise drill had loosened up my muscles, my shoulders included, and now the stasis was tightening them up again. With that process came an element that so far my torturer had not particularly dealt out.

PAIN.

He'd left me before with at least the freedom to move my legs if required. This time that was absent. I couldn't move the vertical bars up and down because of the lock plate. I couldn't twist or lean back or forwards. I could lift my hands slightly closer to my neck; a gamble this because it was a bit more painful short term but long term it allowed me a little relief when I relaxed and let the chain, rather than my muscles, hold my arms. And all the time the pain was increasing as my newly exercised (i.e. loosened-up) muscles tightened up of their own accord. This wasn't sharp corporal punishment type pain; it was long, slow and insidious. Nothing would relieve it to any great extent; most of the times when I thought I'd got any relief this turned out to be illusory, false dawns that only presaged worse pain.

Soon – how soon, what time this took place over I don't know – all my reserve had gone and I was twisting and turning the small amount the chains would permit, my hands gnawing at each other in agony, my eyes screwed up, hallucinating on the pain I felt searing my shoulders. I didn't even notice he'd put on the small light and was outside the cell gloating at my discomfort. Tripping on pain I'm not sure what or whether it came out of my mouth at all. Vivid colours coursed through my head; the bits of me not directly in pain were also hyper-sensitive and my head waved in the air feeling a cooling breeze on my cropped hair.

And something was turning me on. Helplessness or tripping on pain or my total dependency?

'STATE YOUR NUMBER' in menacing military drawl ripped through what was left of my consciousness. I struggled with what was passing for reality. He had assigned me a number a long time ago. It was three digits. First digit was 1.

The first convict he'd had there was probably number 100 or 101. Silly to start with prisoner number 1; it would have given that prisoner a false sense of importance. I think the rest was 82.

'Sir, one eight two, Sir.'

'Wrong again, one seven five.'

How had that happened? Surely I can still remember numbers. And why 182 anyhow?

'Since you made such a mess of the last lot of PT, I will let you choose the next exercise you will do and the Target.'

'Sir, sit-ups, Sir. Sir, fifty, Sir.'

The moment the last 'Sir' left my lips I knew I'd made a mistake. That was my normal target in normal circumstances. Could I do that many after this punishing yet absurdly simple and non-marking, non-scarring bondage position? He allowed me to specify the type of sit-ups. As I was almost certainly going to pay for a shortfall on the Target I might as well enjoy the view beforehand as I was being offered the choice. Or was this another competently laid trap? My favourite type of sit-up starts with my back on the floor, knees bent, with calves on a small chair and a helper sitting over my calves holding them down. I get a great view of the helper – Ian in boots and full battle dress uniform – and each sit-up has the incentive of aiming for his cock and my elbows connect with his knees to establish a valid repetition. I guess the view from his end's not bad either: prisoner straining and paining away in collar, hand and leg-irons, working his way to a beating.

The catch was that when I didn't make the fifty reps without a break, there was more and worse of the cell-door torture to come, for failing to make the target. There turned out to be another cell, similar to the first and next to it. The door on this was slightly different and it wasn't necessary to chain my hands to the collar: they were looped through the bars over the lock plate and just cuffed there. It wasn't necessary to chain the feet to anything, although the leg-irons remained in place.

Yet again it didn't feel at all bad initially, but inexorably I was taken to screaming cringing agony. The pain came from the height of the lock plate, which was the lowest that my arms could go, but which meant that I was straining almost on tiptoe to minimise the pain. So damnably simple and so fucking painful.

I wasn't taking notice of the light going on and off and him coming and watching his tormented prisoner. I don't know how long it lasted; he didn't speak or touch (or if he did I didn't notice it). Some of the time I was turned on, some of it I was scared, some time just quiet and enduring it, taking the pain and letting it sear through me, obscuring all else. Cathartic screams came after that and then the onset of crying. He never took me further than that . . .

He released me from this latest horror, my hands still cuffed behind my back but relatively mobile. Chucked a blanket through the bars and told me to lie on the bed. He shortened the chain to the iron collar so that I could lie down but without much choice of position, my hands still behind my back. This looked like sleep time – or if it wasn't I was going to try to anyhow. With some difficulty I manoeuvred the blanket over the majority of my body and stretched out. The bed, of course, let alone the blanket, wasn't long enough to stretch out fully. I relaxed as much as possible considering the circumstances . . .

'STATE YOUR NUMBER.' Was I dreaming or was this for real? It had sounded like a public address system announcement – there wasn't anyone in the cell and the light was off.

'STATE YOUR NUMBER IMMEDIATELY,' sounded again, more urgently.

'Sir, one seven five, Sir.'

Nothing more came over the PA, but shortly the lights went on and he clunked down the stairs into the cellar-jail, unlocked the cell door and entered my cell. I was lying face down as being the least uncomfortable way of sleeping. He placed one boot up on the board bed, by my mouth, and ordered me to lick it. Meanwhile he roughly undid my BDU trousers, exposing my arse and my three-quarters-hard cock. This he repointed downwards, against the bare boards. I started humping the boards, trying for some relief. His response was to start smacking my arse, first with his bare hands and then with his own leather belt. Those neither stopped my hard-on nor my boot-licking tongue. He seemed to enjoy this and soon had his own cock out and was wanking that thoroughly with the hand that wasn't beating my arse.

'You want to piss?'

'Sir, yes, please, Sir.'

He started to unlock the chain that secured me and pulled on it so that I had to get on my feet and start walking, following him. He took me out of the cell and up the cellar ladder that I had stumbled down, totally blindfolded, earlier. This led up to a small porch and then outdoors. I couldn't see much in the darkness outside but he evidently knew where he was taking me. Next I found myself pushed against a tree, one hand uncuffed, pulled round the tree trunk, and then swiftly cuffed again so that I was secured to the tree. The same happened to my chain between my boots. This was surprisingly uncomfortable because my centre of gravity was quite wrong.

He got the shirt out of my trousers, undid the buttons and pulled it up to my neck, exposing my back. He unbuttoned the flies and got my cock out through the hole.

'Piss now,' came the order. I didn't or couldn't and a smart crack of his belt whipped across my shoulders.

'Piss now,' he repeated. Still I couldn't and he dealt me two blows in quick succession.

'You owe me a dozen for your lack of performance at PT and now you're adding to it. You won't get the first dozen until you've pissed. Now get on with it.' I can't remember how many times he went through the cycle of ordering me to piss, beating me, which made it impossible to relax, then punishing me for disobedience, but the end result was that I had to lose control of my piss and pissed, not voluntarily but through sheer animal panic or fright, totally losing control and breaking down.

Then the punishment for the failed PT started; I counted out the strokes as they smote through my already tenderised back. I didn't care, I was past caring, just counting out the punishment and taking it.

The dozen was up. He left me there, hand- and leg-ironed to the tree, black night and rustling forest noises swathing back into my consciousness.

And it was less than twelve hours since I had arrived there . . .

TA BFT

November 1989

Hi, John,

Answering all the ads in the gay magazine that had any sort of 'army' or 'uniform' mention in them has produced a guy from Wiltshire who does TA there and consequently has all the kit. He's been getting me to go to somewhere in Wiltshire in full combat kit and rucksack and has been putting me through the Territorial Army Basic Fitness Test (TA BFT) that they all have to pass once a year to stay in the service and also to get paid Bounty.

This consists of a mile-and-a-half run which he does in boots, greens and a sweat top, and his time (I think he's in the 40–45 age band) is better than fifteen minutes. My time is supposed to be better than nine minutes, and to make it more fun he has had me in DPM combat kit: DPM trousers and jacket, boots, carrying either his webbing with all the stuff in the pouches (knife, water, rations, gas mask, etc.) or my own rucksack similarly laden. I've been averaging eleven minutes twenty or thirty seconds and as he is into CP there is a penalty to be paid for being outside the nine minutes' target time. Also a load of press-ups to be done, and he always seems to choose a particularly muddy patch for me to face down in.

The good bit (not that running hard and getting caned aren't good; perhaps I mean 'the ecstatic bit') came when he found my water bottle, removed my 'Benny' hat and tipped a bit of water over my hair and down the inside of my neck, me standing to attention. If I'd have had the energy to come just then I think I would have done! Hot and sweaty inside: the trickle of cold water was ecstasy!

His other training exercise was a speed march in Nuclear Biological and Chemical protection kit. I have had a gas mask for a while (doesn't everyone?); the military call them 'respirators'. I bought an NBC top and trousers a while back and was very disappointed when they arrived. I'd been expecting a rubberised and black overall, whereas it turned out to be green cloth with a nasty charcoal lining that leaves black bits everywhere and irritates the skin. Basically I didn't know what to do with it.

What you have to do is put the respirator on in nine seconds from receiving the order, which ain't easy getting it out of the pouch on the webbing and then putting the NBC suit on over the combat kit. That makes you very hot (and we did this just after the BFT run so I was dripping already) and bulky. Speed-marching is faster than marching at the double but not quite running. And still in time. I found it impossible to keep in step with him, which, considering the situation, led to punishment press-ups and more caning. Also speed-marching wearing the respirator meant breathing was a struggle and a couple of times I got into a panic because my lungs had to work so hard to get any oxygen. I think that was more head-panicking rather than any real danger, but it felt jolly real at the time!

After ten or fifteen minutes of that I was totally jabbering and out of it (great!). Being drilled around by him doing almost anything he said, usually wrong, made things worse and it ended up in a bit of woods with me getting caned still in the gas mask (he wouldn't let me take that off) but with my arse exposed to his cane. He said the steam coming off the inside of my DPM trousers looked great . . .

Start of a New Decade: New Year 1990

March 1990

Sir:

Thanks for writing. I had a good time over New Year: the TA guy in Wiltshire has a friend on the Isle of Man and it was arranged for me to go there the Thursday after Christmas. The Orders were to travel (via Heathrow, it's a one-hour flight) in DPM combat kit, rucksack and boots. I've never done that before through an airport and I was very apprehensive as to what the security searching mob would make of it, not to mention the armed policemen who are all over the place. Apart from a funny look from one evidently retired and wealthy Manx person, there was absolutely no notice taken at all. In a way I was most disappointed!

So I arrived at Ronaldsway Airport and while I was waiting to reclaim my rucksack this man comes up to me and discreetly says in my ear, 'I'll be waiting in the café for you.' After I collected the rucksack and found him, he took me outside to the car park and got me to empty my pockets of keys, ticket, wallet, cash, etc. He weighed my rucksack and added a 5kg-scale weight to make it up to 22kg. Handed me an envelope and a 1:50,000 map, got into his car and drove off.

The envelope contained Orders which visually informed me where north was and gave two grid references, a 'you are here' one and a place to get to. It said I would be timed. Fortunately(?) it was a pleasant day with the sun shining lightly so off I set. Six and a half miles later, and 550 feet higher on the map, I walked into his farm; that had taken two hours twelve minutes, and I was quite nicely warm! The Orders said to ring the doorbell and wait in the shed by the farm gates – this turned out to be a full farmyard although he doesn't run the farm now. He came out with a Hexamine stove, water and a tea/coffee brew kit and left me to get on with myself. Later he brought out some hot soup and some bread and butter – a reward for not setting the barn on fire I think! That done, he removed my rucksack and jacket, gave me some wellies and farm overalls and pointed me at a ditch that needed digging out. Not being used to digging, that was hard, although messing about in water, mud and a stream brought out the kid in me! He had me do some PT in the barn again then, sent me out for another timed run around his field – grassed over but it's amazing how muddy the stock make it. And then a nice warm bath and a bit of civilisation by the coal fire in the house.

He used to work for some posh regiment and has been all over the place with them, jumping out of helicopters into the sea at night and things like that. Known as 'The Fox' and a jolly good bloke with it, too. I suppose you don't do all that sort of stuff for real if you're a prat. He gets a kick out of supervising me doing what he is now too old to do.

New Year's Eve I said I wanted to see in outdoors with a campfire and champagne. So we recced the top of Snafell (601m) on his big motorbike. (All the island seems motorbike mad!) Snafell's the highest mountain on the island, and the most practical way of finding the summit at midnight was going to be to follow the mountain railway track, which was not in use for the winter.

New Year's Eve came and we got togged up to go out. Not too wet but it was windy. As we drove there we went up into the clouds and car-visibility got to be about ten yards! We finally made it to where the road meets the railway, parked the car (leaving the keys in the boot in case of mishap) and set off in the thick cloud up the railway. A torch didn't help and it was better to go on in the dark, just able to make out the rails by sight and once in a while an overhead wire pole, but basically feeling along the rails with boots.

This was fine until I fell into a ditch – the drainage culverts were faced with stone and the rails went directly over them without what you would call a bridge . . . From then on the walk got more exciting – you had to test the ground before you trusted it. We made it to the top after counting these culverts, and walked back one culvert to make the stove, have the champagne and some tinned stew. Timing-wise it really worked out well, so that we started on the champagne at pretty well the beginning of the New Year, i.e. midnight.

After some photos, we abandoned the rubbish, wondering what the plate-layers would make of a bottle of champagne and some petrol station champagne glasses up there when they find them in the spring. Then we felt our way back down, dodging most of the culverts. It felt much less distance on the way back not striking out into the 'unknown'. So that's how we saw the New Year and New Decade in. He also chucked me out of the car in clouds for a daytime hike with day rucksack, map and now compass and was sitting brewing tea when I emerged at the bottom of a valley at the rendez-vous (RV). We did that sort of thing several times and each time he pulled the trick of having made himself invisible until I'd walked past him. Neat!

Next hike he sent me to climb a good calf-knackering 600 feet up a valley of magnetic rock, knowing that by trusting the compass I would be deflected into a particularly wet area at the top. Some of the military certainly know how to exploit masochists!

Christening My New Boots

April 1990

Sir:

My fantasy army identity now includes a realistic serial number, 24207516, which can be shouted out in one breath, or abbreviated to '516.

I wish I'd been here to see you cleaning up after your mud training; that sounds like 'good clean fun'! River mud in particular is often very fine so that it is impossible to get it out of kit. There was a guy I met before Christmas who promised me he was into mud, so I turned up after dark one winter night in full DPM kit and a pair of new hi-leg army boots that I wanted to christen.

We set off from his village, no torch, into some woodlands and then down a fairly steeply sloping pasture with a pond at the bottom. Chatting away happily and then all of a sudden we were in mud up to our waists. It was great – no option about it: one step forwards did it, and the canny sod had had me in front of him so I found it quite innocently! The waterproofing on my DPM kit held out for five minutes or so whilst we wrestled around with each other, mud down the front of each other's shirt/jacket and some in the armpits as well. Opened the fly zips and let it in there, all gooey and slightly rough. Great on the balls and a little bit on the arsehole to make it pucker. Struggling around in the stuff kept us fairly warm – once in it you had to really pull the arm or leg hard to move it. And getting back out was only possible by a humiliating crawl with the hands clawing at the mud.

We did some grab-arse mock wrestling on the edge of it so that we both ended up well in it. Pissed over each other, wanking the mud, piss and whatever else nicely until we more or less spunked. It was a bit difficult to feel much spunk among the mud, but it felt good until we cooled down and had to tramp home a couple of miles, the kit heavy and clinging, boots laden with mud whatever we did. And we spent ages and ages hosepiping each other off outside his place. This was at about five degrees C and I was totally frozen by the time we had got enough mud off to start stripping off to get inside. Cold showers are the least of it!

My boots were well christened anyhow, and didn't actually take that much shining to get them back up to standard. These ones make Doctor Martens seem like toys. I've worn them well in now and they feel just great. And walking or marching in them they have a 'go faster' quality which speeds me up walking on level pavement. I think it's that the rubber grips very surely and the sole is curved so that the sole stays in contact for longer than with a flat sole. It works anyhow. I can't wait for summer and boots 'n' shorts weather.

Grease, belt and boot slave

Mark Goes to Jail, Part II

August 1990

Newark Airport, NJ 16/7/90 en route Scranton, Pa. – Denver, Co.
Fresh #1 haircut (which gets a lot of attention).

I've just had a great week – you've read 'Mark Goes to Jail' by now; well, this was the same guy, different scenario! He met me at his local airport off the puddle-jumper flight from Newark, took me home and (apart from another SM meal from his wife) we had a long, long chat – including why I was shit scared of going back. He showed me the galley proofs of 'Mark Goes to Jail' for the magazine, out soon. Spent that night (and all others) in handcuffs, but on a normal bed. Last night, my last night before flying out, I was secured by a pair of 1849 transport cuffs that were much heavier castings than modern cuffs and the insides felt well used and smooth . . .

Next day, after some shopping, first trip to the Stockade – the place where the Jail is. Played around with high-security leather hoods but nothing particularly intense. Confidence building.

Thursday after dinner we went back for real. I had on the lockable stainless steel ball-weight and he hooded me as we started on the half-mile track up to the Stockade. Found myself in the cell in the living room and he was showing me off to the two lodgers who house-sit there. They are both builders, one into outlaw/rebel SM, the other an ex-army motor-sergeant (28) who claimed, I was told later, he had never been in handcuffs or locked in the cells there – though he must have done guard duty in the army. He wanted *me* (or my body!) and was talked into allowing hood and cuffs on himself (extra humiliating for an ex-sergeant) and once locked inside the cell we had an amazing slave-to-slave scene.

His body felt great and we wrestled, arm wrestled, massaged, punched each other. My cock was hard the whole time and his certainly was too. This sounds like bullshit but he really did have one of those big, thick and long American cocks that you see in videos and never normally encounter. He kept his dog tags, boots and BDU cap on all the time, and all night!

In the middle of the night we started up again, and he rubbed himself off against me, coming between our stomachs, which was deliciously messy; then he woke the Stockade, rattling the cell bars demanding to be let out. I called him a 'wimp', which I later denied but was belted for because he didn't deny it when SIR asked him directly. Prisoners should stick together . . . He left the next morning for a weekend of cruising on the gay campsite in the next county with his reputation for not being into bondage shattered.

SIR served me breakfast the next morning. 'Grits', a US cereal rather worse than semolina, in a dog bowl, made with water rather than milk and then left to go cold. Very nutritious, though.

Left in cell alone for a couple of hours then allowed out for some shackled manual work.

Disaster started to strike. Phone calls came successively that Roger was in casualty in a New Jersey hospital after a motorbike accident on the way to the Stockade. By Sunday, word had come through that he would be OK, which was a great relief. Also the other slave couldn't make it. That left one other slave to arrive. SIR put me into a leather sleepsack with one of the leather hoods installed with the sound headset modification that I had worked out back in London. Totally immobile and controlled, the experience was of floating and total suspension of my own choice. You can't ignore or shut out sound and if there is little other sensory input you become overwhelmed by the forced musical appreciation.

The hood remained and I was taken, heavily shackled, and placed naked in one of the (cold) cells in the Jail downstairs. That hood only just allows breathing so complaining about the cold was out of the question. A while later I was allowed a sleeping bag for warmth. A lot later (2300ish)

MORE AND HARDER

I heard the other slave's Interrogation begin; remember to ask me to demonstrate the proper use of a nightstick against the windpipe some time. The other slave was in shit because he had been recaptured after escaping a month ago. He was searched by SIR, and another handcuff key was found in his boot. I couldn't see, but I think that he spent a long time during that interrogation up against the wall, nose, hands and boots strictly spread-eagled on painted white lines on the cinder block wall.

There *is* something magic about painted lines: there are red lines at Newark International Airport immigration desks. The procedure is that a lot of people wait in one queue until directed to wait on a red line, two paces back from a clerk who is dealing with one traveller already. So you wait a couple of minutes behind this red line on the floor, not permitted to cross it until summoned by the immigration officer. You feel controlled by the inhuman and unyielding nature of a line.

There was a lot of shouting, threats, denials by the other prisoner, and then begging. There wasn't any really heavy beating or anything like that, although the nightstick seems just as effective and the other prisoner was certainly not 'At Ease'. He was eventually bundled into the other cell, still ordered to maintain a spread-eagle at the paint marks on that cell wall, whilst I was removed to the cell upstairs.

In the course of time, the other prisoner arrived, still shaking from heavy threats. I had been told to let him find me in the cell (rather than jumping on him as I had done the ex-army sergeant). We had a good night, both in shackles, despite an inadequate blanket to share between us. He wasn't sure if I was a 'mate' or a 'stooge' and we were both cross-interrogated next day about whether he was planning to escape. That got heavy with threats – made more real by SIR handing the station cattle prod through the bars and encouraging us to test it on ourselves. Neither of us had learnt the 'stick together and say nothing' rule; we *had* been talking about how to pick the handcuff locks and SIR sensed it, and could very well have got us to admit it because we started dribbling little titbits out. By the next night we had coalesced far more.

The other prisoner was well into civil prison scenes – he had a prison shirt with MCF 865 across the shoulders. I got on well with him: the rest of the weekend there were various indoor and outdoor scenes – me cooking tethered by an eight-foot chain and iron collar, the other prisoner (Jamrag) getting acquainted with various heavy hoods, body sacks, etc. Americans are very fond of little electric night-lights around their apartments so that it is never truly dark inside at night. I think that may be one reason why (to generalise) they are more readily frightened by hoods.

The Stockade now had a jail-cat. Definitely a 'Top-Cat', who used his claws. I found it delightful. There is a cute set of watercolours from, I think, Changi jail. Singapore International Airport is on the same site and perpetuates the name of a notorious Japanese WWII prisoner-of-war camp. Three of the watercolours show kittens in cute gambolling play and the fourth is a stark picture of a steaming hot-pot. There are big philosophical attractions to the prisoner of a cat that *can* go as it pleases, that *can* play in or out of the cell, unlike the prisoner. And the knack of playing blindfolded with a mobile animal, anticipating its movements and finding it without sight was a challenge. Later on SIR faced his two prisoners off in a hooded wrestling match on a sheet of polythene on the grass outside and this skill came in very useful. Although the other prisoner wasn't blindfolded in any way, I had him submitting repeatedly in some fairly classic and painful wrestling pins.

The other prisoner wasn't so keen on the four-legged cat. Prisoner-to-prisoner rapport was increased by my sleeping nearest the bars to intercept the cat before he leapt on the other prisoner, who would shout and scream but was otherwise restrained from defending himself. SIR found this most entertaining and I was amazed at a slave who would happily take far more and heavier pain than I can, yet couldn't take an unexpected slight touch or paw!

Saturday night we spent chained wrist to wrist, ankle to ankle, which is worse than individual cuffs and irons, even sleeping cuffs behind the back, because you can't sleep on your side – among other restrictions.

On Saturday I had been taken out in the car whilst the other slave was stewing in a cell; I had been dropped at the foot of the hill leading to the Stockade and given seventeen minutes to report back. Not easy as it was hot, humid and uphill. The threat of the belt and/or cattle prod spurred me on. On Sunday morning I was extracted from the cell, re-permitted my only, but by now stinking, T-shirt and shorts and given thirty-two minutes for the return trip, to include purchasing and bringing back the *New York Times*, a real heavyweight among newspapers. So nice not to have an aimless, pointless task!

To SIR's chagrin I made the two miles and 700 foot of altitude each way well within the time set and this time had the presence of mind to report myself back formally. MCF 865 hadn't heard '516 do that before and as he was hooded, spread-eagled and under some pain in the main room it seemed to keep him turned on even further!

There was also another metal collar and arms-up-behind-the-neck scene whilst the other prisoner did the washing-up after brunch. He started taking his time and I started calling him (not SIR) names like 'maggot', 'fuck-head' and many more. Yelling assuages the pain just a bit. Screaming therapy? He seemed to answer to 'Jamrag' most happily and that name has, er, sort of stuck, if that's not an inappropriate word . . .

Subsequently I did clothes pegs on 'Jamrag'. SIR was very complimentary about my technique of not using a lot of pegs but of putting them where they count. Jamrag and I had already had a conversation along the lines of 'you get real nice pain from another slave' and that's particularly true of clothes pegs.

Subjects for future thought at the Stockade SM University:

You get the best pain from another slave.
You only get really heavy pain from another slave (rather than brutality).
Pain from another slave is real economical because he

doesn't bother with pain that doesn't count, that is only distracting.

Discuss!

Part-way through the scene when Jamrag was well flying on clothes-peg pain, I left him for a minute or two and busied myself with things on the table, then said to him, 'You know that ring in my cock,' and he nodded or something. 'D'you know how it got there?' and whilst he was about to reply, placed a clothes peg right on the tip of his cock. He screamed terrifically! And was almost immediately furious with himself for being taken in at such an apparently obvious trick!

Finally, SIR blindfolded and strung up each of us in turn, with the other one watching, handcuffed, from the cell. There followed an incredible CP and punching scene. The effect is almost impossible to describe because by then us two prisoners were so closely attuned to each other that watching the other one take it was almost as intense as being there because we could identify with the other and could feel with or for the other as he was put through it.

I think there is a slave-to-slave effect similar to the much vaunted (and almost as much misunderstood) Stockholm effect, whereby a captive becomes very attached to his captor. The effect was first documented with some terrorists' hostages who got very attached to their captors in the 1970s. It takes some time to develop and people often attribute it to captivities that are far too short in duration (less than twelve hours for example). What I ended up feeling about Jamrag seems to me to have been similar in depth. There is also the change in perception caused by having got to know each other first by the animal senses not by (human) words, so that we knew each other physically and instinctively before we knew each other intellectually.

Can't wait for it to resume . . .

CP Fantasy: The Tawse

I've had a very good advert running – it reads: *Tawse – does the word Tawse make your heart race? Ex-Approved School recidivist, now 30s, gives and takes the Tawse.* I've had lots of replies although many of them haven't been too good. But I've received a couple of good beatings, the best a Master in Hastings. He ordered me to visit him as a skinhead hooligan coming for Punishment by the Tawse. He said he had two 24-inch Tawses and one 18-inch Tawse. I drove down wearing tight thin dirty white jeans, nothing under, sleeveless T-shirt and 20-hole Ranger boots – they're a commando hi-leg combat boot, steel toecaps and chunky soles. I polished them up the night before.

The door was on the latch and I was to let myself in, lock it and bring the key up to his flat. He was waiting in a dimly lit room: leather jacket, white officer's shirt and tie, leather jeans and tall leather boots with sharp spurs in them, his handcuffs in one hand and a cane in the other. He ordered me to lick his boots and he had me crawling around on the floor for a short while. Then he handcuffed me and also put leg-irons on my feet and ordered me to stretch my hands and legs apart and bend over the big table he had.

He tipped a cupful of cold water over my arse, which startled me, and tightened the jeans up. He took aim, and the first stroke of his twin-tailed Tawse cracked across my tight arse. I took six all on the same spot and with a wait between them so I felt them all. He just waited while the pain sunk into me and then administered the next stroke.

He gave me twenty in all – three sets of six, slowly, and two rapid fire at the end. It hurt a lot at the time but didn't bruise that much. It was the first time I'd been there and he wouldn't go any further. But I'm going back for more, and if you want to come too that'll be OK. We can go either as Borstal boys or as soldiers or as skinheads, he doesn't mind.

I've not heard of Paul from Greenwich, but please fix it

up for a Monday night and tell me where to go and in what uniform and I'll be Punished with you, mate. I'll make sure you take your Punishment properly and don't have to be punished further for screaming or moving. I'd like to fix you in the straps on his horse or hold you down, and you do the same to me, if this Paul will let us do that. I'd like to piss into your boots before you're Punished and you piss into mine so I feel my mate's piss in my boots between the strokes of Pain on my arse. Handcuffed and strapped over this guy's Punishment horse, naked except for my boots and they've got my mate's piss in them and I'm taking strokes of the Tawse or the Cane . . .

After we've both been punished I'll make your cock feel good and make you spunk into the seat of your army greens so that when you sit down in them the hot stripe on your arse will feel your spunk cooling it.

Dartmoor Hiking

I was out hiking on Dartmoor with Keith; he is a Sub (Lieutenant) in the Royal Naval Reserve but prefers to be an army or Royal Marine Sergeant for hiking and backpacking.

We had intended to camp out overnight but the weather really was a bit specialist – i.e. wet – and we both wimped out, which means we took the non-macho option of sleeping at his flat. Next morning there was thick mist but we still got out for some more hiking. The moor was really ghostly with less than fifty feet of visibility. We navigated by compass bearings and found the places we intended to visit but rather slower! It is very satisfying when you see your target looming out of the mist in front of you exactly in line with the direction that the compass is indicating! Keith has decided to chuck the tart he was with and settle on being gay, which may be a bit limited in provincial Plymouth.

Mark Goes to Jail, Part III

November 1990

35,000 feet en route Scranton, Pa. to Miami, Fl.

Sir, Keith, SIR; whoops, Sarge, that should have been Sarge, Keith, Sarge.

I'm on my way back from a really good four days. I turned up at Scranton 1800 Friday. SIR collected me from the airport, leaving 'Jamrag' and a diplomat (Mike, on home leave from darkest, deepest Central Africa) in separate cells at the Stockade. SIR's assistant Sean was monitoring the two of them: Mike was in a cold cell downstairs, which now has closed-circuit television monitoring with sound; Jamrag was in a warmer one upstairs. Mike had already undergone an initial interrogation and had revealed a date of birth and agreed that he was a diplomat. He had been put in a cell together with Jamrag but nothing further had come out. The cattle prod had also been used on him and his resistance to that seemed good. Both were wearing US woodland camouflage BDU trousers, boots (with laces . . .), olive-green T-shirts and full leather hoods with nose and mouth holes only.

When I arrived I was kitted out the same as Mike and instructed not to speak – or it was the cattle prod. I was then put in the cell with Jamrag as if I was Mike, the diplomat. Jamrag was told to get as much information out of me as he could. When it became clear that I wasn't going to speak, Jamrag was given fifteen minutes to make me speak or it would be the cattle prod for him.

Sarge, you'll remember that on previous visits to the Stockade, Jamrag and I had got quite close. On this trip, SIR had invited him to the Stockade and let me know. SIR and I had decided not to tell Jamrag that I would be there so I would be a surprise. Despite several phone calls, I'd not let on but had told Jamrag he was in for a 'treat' which he had guessed as Mike. I had convinced him that I was on holiday in Key West. I got him to promise to phone me on Sunday when he had 'escaped' and returned to New York so we could wank it out together ... SIR said that Jamrag had been convinced and was feeling well-guilty at not meeting me when I was over on the US side of the Atlantic.

Sarge, so once in the cell, Jamrag starts sympathising with me (as Mike) about the cattle prod, etc., and touching me up. I make as though my thighs and bum are real sore, and ten out of fifteen minutes into things, still not speaking at all, I make as if I have fainted and do a stage drop into the other corner of the cell away from Jamrag. He panicked immediately. SIR came in, squeezed a ball, got a reaction and left. Jamrag then made a decision not to cause me any more pain: possibly doing what I'd reminded him of when we spoke on the phone – stick together with any other prisoners you may meet. SIR intervened and got the hood off me. Jamrag identified me as Roger, another New Yorker, the same one who had sent me to the Stockade in the first place. SIR had me standing eye to eye with Jamrag as he removed Jamrag's hood. You're always bleary-eyed coming out of one of those and he couldn't believe his eyes at all! A real 'magic moment'! Despite the remaining handcuffs and leg-irons we hugged each other well and truly.

For us, Sarge, nothing else happened that evening. We had a disgusting (but nutritious) meal from two dog bowls: cold beef stew. We slept together, each in cuffs, one sleeping bag shared. Apart from when the Stockade's cat apparently slipped through the cell bars and Jamrag jumped two feet into the air, screaming. The four-legged cat still scares him far more than the other cat – one scares, the other scars him. Well, it doesn't actually and it's a matter of honour with SIR to inflict pain to the limit and more, and not leave any marks. Not that that makes the pain from the cat any easier to bear!

Meanwhile Mike was undergoing more Diplomatic Service hostage training (unofficial). He was told to write a list of all personnel he had worked with in Nairobi, and he had been found out as having given the wrong date of birth. The cattle prod becoming ineffective, SIR used a ball crusher. I dunno how he spent the night – us upstairs heard him tossing and turning a lot. Reckon it was his hands cuffed behind his back and the stress of the situation he was in.

First thing next morning, Mike was brought upstairs. He couldn't piss (too frightened?) and was given a morning whipping with the cat-o'-nine-tails across the shoulders. I think this was just to harass him. Jamrag and I watched spellbound from inside the upstairs cell. Mike then had to write the list of personnel again, and was left in his cell downstairs to identify six who had 'exploitable weaknesses'. I was left 'At Ease' but in cuffs upstairs whilst SIR and Jamrag went out shopping. Sean dozed, watching me upstairs, and Mike on the CCTV monitor, but he never dozed enough for me to creep to the stun gun left out on a table: I wanted to fire it and scare the shit out of him as he woke up . . . drat!

Sarge, I was still in the same place when they returned and was then hooded with the heavy duty hood – double-skinned leather and tightly laced. Small nose holes only. The others seem to panic in that – tee-hee! Hands still behind, I was taken to a cell downstairs. Mike is still in cell number two. An hour or so later the hood is getting to me and I flick the cuffs round to the front, undo the hood and lie down much more comfortably. The CCTV monitoring was working. Just after I thought I had got away with it, SIR is down the stairs and has me up ordered against the far wall of the cell where he rehoods me and applies the bastard metal collar with the cuffs attached to it by short chains. Hands behind my back again and now attached to the collar. Ouch!

Jamrag takes a whipping upstairs and, through the hood, I hear Mike in the next-door cell, wanking off to that. Next a tabletop is set up in the cellar outside the cells, one end on the ground, the other set up on bricks or a box, so the thing is at an incline. Mike is ordered to strip, and after some preliminary questions in his cell, is strapped to the tabletop.

The hood comes off me too, and Jamrag, armed with the stun gun, is stationed outside the cell door to keep me quiet. It is an interesting question whether he would have used it on me, seeing as how it scares him shitless to think about it . . . Sean assists SIR attaching electrodes to Mike, wired to a hand magneto. Ball crusher and cattle prod to hand, SIR interrogates Mike about his High School. Suddenly it emerges that Mike is in very bad luck as SIR had been to the same one and knows all the geography so Mike can't bullshit. There are also lots of questions that SIR can ask him that Mike just can't remember – the situation he's in didn't really help him relax and remember!

After he's fucked up several times and the effect of the magneto is beginning to confuse him, SIR steps up the pressure and demands that all questions require a response within five seconds or there is an automatic jolt from the cattle prod. 'Don't know' doesn't count as a response either. Additionally, all of Mike's sentences must begin with 'SIR' and end with 'SIR'. He gets pretty confused about things and questions get muddled very easily if he starts thinking or trying to make things up. Mike is now answering questions automatically and without thinking. If he knows an answer, he says it. If he doesn't, he gets zapped. Simple. Suddenly SIR switches to questioning him about the personnel where he worked and about theirs and Mike's careers. It turns out that Mike used to be a cop; when he's asked why he left he breaks out crying. SIR switches to psychotherapy mode and is very, very supportive. Mike says he wants to go on. Asked about Nairobi he says he can't answer for 'legal, moral and ethical reasons'. SIR asks which one. 'Legal.' ZAP. 'I'd have accepted "moral" but not "legal"!'

By now I'm in agony – two hours with my hands up my back and Jamrag intercedes to have me let out. Mike joins the merry crowd to recover. He (and the rest of us) have learnt three things: one – everyone has a weakness; two, there are other people into what he's into, they're not crazies but are intelligent and self-respecting people; three, not to be ashamed of being gay, and to be proud of himself – he took a lot and SIR described his cattle prod performance as 'world class'.

A bit later I am back, handcuffed, in the cell downstairs and Mike is sent down to rough me up a bit further. The rest watch. Initially I let him do me over but SIR tells me to fight back and Mike is very surprised that the tricks from his police training – the pressure points, etc. – have very little effect. It's possible to ignore pain. However, the fighting is in danger of getting out of hand and as he hasn't overpowered me I get him to agree to call it quits before one of us gets hurt. I like to think we respect each other just that bit more after that brawl.

Jamrag has bought some dog treats when he was out shopping with SIR. There is a choice of cheese or liver flavour but it is agreed that they are both disgusting. That doesn't stop them appearing at meal times and the rule at the Stockade seems to be that you don't get any lunch until you've finished your breakfast.

And then on Sunday SIR requires a newspaper again. It being November we have admired the stars and the clear crisp night sky. By morning it is frosty and running down to fetch the paper wearing skimpy shorts and singlet causes some slight flutter to the church-going Sunday-morning straights delivering their kids to Sunday school. Nice clear view to the other side of the big valley – on the way down. On the way up my breath makes big clouds of steam! Anyhow, the time is satisfactory and the best I can manage as it happens. I don't think SIR ever read the paper.

Later that day the US army physical-readiness test is staged again: Jamrag's getting better; all my scores are improved and my press-up score is now at 100 per cent and the main worry is what will happen if my performance deteriorates at the next showing . . .

Night-Run Training

by Private 24207516

Got on the train Thursday night, new Number Two cropped hair, polished boots, tracksuit bottoms and sweatshirt over a rugger shirt, also my DPM rucksack containing, among other things, a flask of hot chocolate for the return journey.

Train was late of course and I was at the extreme front of the train so had to walk the entire length of the platform as instructed so that all the commuters dispersed before I reached the car park. Received an unexpectedly warm 'Good evening' from the unusually smart and young ticket collector. I wondered how often real soldiers arrive there late after dark for fun in the forest.

Located my man's car; the rear door was open; I got in and stripped under a blanket to boots and that subdued urban camouflage cap of mine with 'my' number 24207516 on the back. Laid out a pair of clean white gloves that he'd demanded I bring and then I put on his blindfold under the blanket. Waited and had counted to ninety when the tailgate was opened and the blanket whipped off revealing me and letting in the cold night air.

He shouted, 'Number!' and I replied, '24207516,' in one breath. He replaced the blanket and drove off. Two right turns and one left, about three and a half miles including one petrol station that he stopped to refill at. My distance calculation was proved spot on later.

When he stopped again he removed the blanket and had me get out and stand for inspection. He was wearing a beret and army uniform and was frighteningly imposing, shouting next to me while I stood all but naked at attention. Then he gave me the white gloves to put on, and taped them on with parcel tape, checked the white football socks that I was wearing and taped them up, then gave me a rucksack containing four house bricks to wear. He removed the blindfold and showed me a route map, ruining my night vision with a torch on white paper.

We were in a road turn-off in a forest; there was a trail laid through the forest to my destination. I would be equipped with a hand torch, the map, and was to complete the course without climbing any gates, of which there were three, or getting any dirt on the white socks or white gloves. At the finish there would be some yellow polythene laid out and I was to do a number of press-ups equal to the time I thought I had taken to complete the course, after which the timing would cease and there would be an assessment (and if necessary punishment for) time taken, correct number of press-ups and the state of the white items.

Final imposition was that there were three roads to cross. He would be at each place and I was to stop, report and ask permission to cross on each occasion.

The run turned out to be OK; I'd been training for it. His bricks worried me more through the rucksack, making a friction blister on my back. The forest was nice and dark and, it being a wet and windy night, there were a number of muddy puddles to negotiate. Also a suspicious number of branches right in the centre of the path, maybe due to natural causes, but he had walked the route to lay out markers at the most significant junctions so I thought that at least one, conveniently located near a particularly muddy puddle, had been laid to prejudice the clean white gloves and socks.

Running at night and naked is fun. So is rolling under obstacles; being naked the mud soon dries and isn't cooling like on clothing. So I enjoyed myself. Crossing the roads he had me stand and report a couple of times till I was shouting enough and he gave me a nice hard swipe from a crop as I passed.

At the end I was outside the time he had allowed and got the number of press-ups wrong at twenty-eight. There was a bit of minor dirt on the white items but not much. His punishment consisted of an equal number of strokes from a Tawse and sit-ups on the mud, and a rerun back to the starting point. This was now downhill, not so easy and I fell once, slipping on a muddy rut. The torch batteries were now giving out (was that part of his plan too?) but I was getting more confident and accustomed to the terrain so I was only using the torch intermittently.

Back at the starting place he ordered, 'Five one six to stand in the position of "Attention!"' and wank off whilst he watched. It's difficult to keep the other hand still but he was watching and using his crop to remind me. After that I got the tracksuit trousers back on and was driven back to the station.

On the train back I enjoyed my hot chocolate and the delightful sensation of the mud caking inside the rugger shorts I was wearing under the tracksuit.

Mark's Two-month US Holiday

July–September 1991

'The Stockade'

The trip started off with what was billed as a three-way birthday party: my 35th, Jamrag his 40th and Ian his 60th, all within a fortnight of the US's July 4th celebrations; this was the excuse for a long bash at Ian's screenhouse in the Pocono mountains.

Ian met me at Scranton airport and we went back to his place in Forty-Fort. A night in the 1849 transport handcuffs ensued, together with the traditional threats that my sleeping arrangements would get worse nightly.

A danger of being an itinerant and otherwise unemployed traveller seems to be that hitherto sound structures crumble, paint flakes off and timber deliveries materialise! Not to worry. I had been running an ad in a London gay paper: *Muscular skinhead (34) wearing boots, shorts and belt seeks foreman to keep him sweating filling skips, digging, etc.* I'd also been reading a book about the Nazis using slave labour to build a tunnel through the Alps to Yugoslavia so I was already moving into that fantasy world.

'The Stockade' turned out to be in imminent danger of collapse due to the basement cinder block walls moving. Ian's proposed remedy was to manually dig out the earth from the outside, prop up the house whilst the wall was reinstated and then fill back the outside. Slave labour was proposed, a supply of which was expected for the party. Digging in irons as had happened for the digging of the artesian well was ruled out because of the damage and cleaning required to the irons. I said I'd work naked except for boots. Bear in mind that the temperature was around 85 degrees and the humidity similar.

Ian struck the first sod with the pick. It immediately became obvious that to be shovelling dirt whilst he was picking was not on. He does revel in the description of 'psychopathic maniac' after all! The first day, despite as many taunts about Radon, heart attack, and digging with a slow ramp so that the stretcher-bearers could extract him when he keeled over, we shifted thirty barrowloads of soil. Fortunately he allowed some degree of delegation as to where it should end up, but there is now another hill 'elsewhere in the forest' as they say in opera stage directions!

This went on all weekend. Twenty barrowloads and a lunch at various assorted diners worked OK. Together with preparations for the party, proofreading of the next issue of the magazine and incidental tourist visits, e.g. to Scranton's 'Steamtown', Ian also contacted a friend and I was interviewed by the chief engineer of a local television channel. He had me in mind as an engineer on a satellite news-gathering truck. That could have been fun, living at the Stockade.

On the Tuesday, Sean arrived from Burbank, Ca. I'm not quite sure how it happened but Ian had been engineering a wrestling match (fight would be a better word) between us. Another arrival was an SM novice (but experienced street fighter) called Mikey who Ian had also got in tow. I've heard of Sean through RMR-Togie here in London, he also runs an SM bulletin board computer in LA and Ian's been referring to him since they first met last summer.

I think the first fight was with each of us wearing iron collars. Sean's was connected to his hands by short chains; I was wearing Peerless handcuffs (that cut if you pulled against them) and my collar was attached by a chain to the post in the kitchen.

We went at each other good and proper. Sean turned out to be strong despite his 'skinny git' appearance. But he was susceptible on the stamina front. Hurting him was to no avail: if I pulled on one of his chains, he'd ignore it and administer a corresponding level of pain that I was unable to deal with. The only solution was to tire him out and then get him in a submission hold. The rest of them there, who weren't exactly refereeing normally, kept slowing things down which allowed him respite. As I remember it I got him to submit or it was stopped, and the judges' committee changed from giving the round to me to making it a draw.

There was another 'round' in the upstairs (wooden-lined) cell. I think we were each wearing no-eyes hoods, boots and handcuffs only. I know that cell quite well and was eventually able to get him by going round the back of him very fast. But by this time our elbows were well scratched and bleeding and things were wisely terminated. As the winner I was allowed the choice of what Sean's forfeit should be – should he do me over, should I get done over or what? I asked that he do over Mikey, which threw the cat among the pigeons a bit but I wanted to see how Sean performed on others. They had a good first session. For the rest of the night, which Sean and I spent together in that upstairs cell with one sleeping bag only, there was a wary accommodation between us.

Ian let us out for working party in the morning: more digging. Sean was put to work under the deck (one of the advantages of digging out manually was that the deck hasn't had to be dismantled) and the situation was intended to make a pleasing tableau for Jamrag and his Trainer, due that morning. Holiday traffic being what it is they arrived in time to see the even more alarming sight of me being cold-water hosed down in the garden and Sean filthy and grazed from his exertions.

Jamrag was scheduled for immediate detention in the downstairs cell under closed-circuit television and sound observation. He revels in it and poses in irons, e.g. lying against the back wall in maximum view of the camera! What he didn't know but might have overheard was that there was a large clock with a sweep second hand also in the camera's shot and the CCTV was being recorded with a form of 'burnt in timecode' for use in a later interrogation. Various events happened to him, including a period of leaving him well alone. I was sent down to order him about doing some prisoner PT. Finally he was brought upstairs, strapped down to the old door that seems to serve as an interrogation slab, electrodes were applied and questions were asked. Unfortunately Jamrag's mind was working on the 'if I never knew it I can't tell you' principle and it was obvious that the situation was neither a turn-on nor a fantasy for him. Perhaps he's learning that principle as an interrogation resistance strategy.

He went back down to the cell. Sometime Sean was strung up 'parrot perch' fashion (i.e. handcuffs and leg-irons on, metal bar through his knees and elbows with him bent double so that it fitted) and left for a while, ostensibly ignored but in reality the centre of attention. Late at night I persuaded him to cane me out on the deck. To my surprise his caning turned me on and a moment after he'd administered the set I'd requested/authorised I was wanting more and my cock was back hard again.

Sometime or other I was put in a chastity jock and left down in the cellar cell with Jamrag. I'd got the idea of fighting him for the sleeping bag; same game as with Sean I suppose. Jamrag wasn't really into this and it ended up with me feeding Ian with the line that Jamrag was trying to escape because he'd removed one of the padlocks from the chastity jock. Ian found enough evidence in the cell, i.e. a key; where it came from I dunno. Jamrag maintained that it was planted, and was very unhappy at being placed in the isolation cell as there was not enough room behind the solid iron door to lie down satisfactorily. In the UK it would be called an 'oubliette', word derived from the French for 'to forget'.

I spent that night, and all subsequent nights, in chains on the cement floor of the cell. I got to like the solitude in contrast to the daytime mêlée and competitive slavery. Sean later called it a 'three-ring circus'. One morning Mikey played the prison fantasy mind-fuck to perfection. Early on he brought me down a mug of coffee, saying he'd been told not to, but he felt sorry for me and thought I must be thirsty. If Ian found out he'd done it, Mikey would be in for it. So I had to conceal the mug. The mind-fuck was that the coffee was absolutely disgusting. Not mildly unappetising or oddly presented, but gut-retchingly awful. Jamrag and his Trainer have honed the deliberately unappetising cold grits-style breakfast with normal ingredients presented in unusual combinations, but you don't actually retch on them. And I was supposed to conceal this good turn he'd supposedly done me. In the event Ian's early morning cell search didn't turn up the item . . .

Digging went on outside at a surprisingly fast rate. We got eight feet down in one place and weren't far off it elsewhere. Jamrag's Trainer, being overweight and patently not used to manual work, was the butt of a lot of jokes about 'the Management', most of which he parried in style.

Togie turned up from London late and jet-lagged one night. Roger, who'd brought him from Newark, was wearing a disgustingly tasty pair of khaki shorts and his rowing has brought his muscles out nicely. There was immediate competition between Sean and me to tie Roger up. I got him first attached by the steel plate knight-in-armour-like helmet that Togie had brought in from London. No other bondage was necessary although I think I had him in handcuffs to stop mischief. And played with a cane on his backside and, unprotected by those military-looking shorts, his thighs.

After a rest Sean had him on a bondage board bound tight and hard in what I call the grasshopper position. That's where you are placed face down on the board; you start by kneeling and then bend forwards to put your elbows on the board too, pretty well touching your knees. Tied down in that position your arse cheeks are spread nicely and also your tits are ready to take clips and weights. The arms and legs go numb quite quickly and you may have to be helped to stand when you are released. Can be fun.

Sunday lunchtime presents and a cake appeared. Ian even smiled when blowing out his six candles! He unwrapped his presents and announced that Jamrag's present was one of the Wilkes Barre Jail solid iron doors – if he could transport it to the jail that he and his Trainer are constructing in his Trainer's basement. Me not having managed to find accomplices to physically overpower and imprison Ian, I announced that my present to him (apart from the bit of glass I'd brought when I first arrived on his birthday) would be made available to him if he took the cell keys and went downstairs into a cell of his choice, locked himself inside and chucked the keys out and waited. This caused some consternation and Ian extracted the maximum theatrical capital from the situation, trying to entice Jamrag to take his place for him. After about twenty minutes hoo-ha he sets off down the basement steps, his pick in hand in case he needed to dig his way out, he said. He looked to me like the grim reaper going off to work!

After a little wait, I went downstairs, having put the word around that as the rest of them hadn't been much help in getting Ian in the cell, they couldn't be there as a 'gallery'. When I got down there he'd fucked up the lights and the camera and probably also the intercom so it was essentially a private transaction. I did an interrogation scene on him, based on some recondite tramcar information that he could be expected to know – but seemed not to. He was nice enough to say that I did OK on him. I certainly got him to the laughing and then the slightly shaking stage. Ian has certainly taught us a lot of tricks and he's a good teacher as well as an excellent Top.

That done, we each went upstairs. I think Ian went for a rest. I was wandering around like a foreskin at a bar mitzvah. Eventually I struck a deal with Sean: he'd stake me out on the grass, no DEET insect repellent, and each application of DEET would 'cost' two jolts from the cattle prod. That was fun. I was out there long enough to be surprised that I was a little red from the sun.

Staking out was one of the activities that was last done on me when I was on a run with some Hell's Angels when I first had a motorbike. It's a curious feeling: you can't move, obviously, and yet the tension from five pegs and ropes (arms, feet and balls) soon seems to ease. You can't swat flies or (worse) the creepy crawlies that come up from underneath. After the initial turn-on there's a period of boredom unless those tying you up take advantage of your vulnerability.

This time it rained. This should have been a welcome respite from 85-degree direct sun, and indeed it was. But there's something unexpectedly heavy about being tied up outside in the rain, particularly spread-eagled where you are wide open. I wasn't especially cold, but I was almost scared. Roland, back in London, worked it out: there's an instinct to seek shelter and that was thwarted.

The cattle prod hurt more in the wet – and DEET wasn't so necessary in the rain anyhow – the rain stopped and the sun came out again. Eventually I was untied, muddy underneath and hosed down outside again.

I also ran up and down to the petrol station a couple of times – once at dusk, with fireflies dancing in the forest, and again in the morning to fetch the Sunday *New York Times*. No one ran with me though . . .

People left on the Sunday. There was a lot of talking and thinking going on. Roger, Togie, Sean and myself stayed the night. The digging hadn't been completed and Ian was worried about how to finish it. Last thing we did on Monday before leaving for New York was to remove the cell doors from the walls down there so that he could bring in an ordinary construction crew if necessary to complete the job.

This, however, completed a train of thought of mine: when I had found myself giving Ian his present down there, I had done a double take when I found myself with the keys to those cells in my hand, unlocking Ian. I'd been fantasising about him as the mega-Top since the original 'Mark Goes to Jail' escapade. I'd carried on with the matter in hand but been quite down about seeing that fantasy crumble, and taking down the doors was the last straw. I told Ian I'd only be back there when the jail part was rebuilt differently, and I didn't want to know what it was going to be like until I'm down there next. And also the next time, I'd prefer a lot more of the jail cell and military PT fantasy that was the original turn-on for me there rather than the three-ring circus antics upstairs.

Roger, Togie and I had a long chat in Roger's car on the way back to his place at Monroe, NY and we thought we made sense of a lot of what had gone on that weekend.

We took Togie to Newark airport and it was sad to see him go. Immensely friendly though everyone was, I was on my own from now onwards . . . and the attempt to capture Ian had shown that, even among friends, I was in some ways still on my own. There was no immediate problem though; Roger and his lover Ricky wanted to take me to a bondage demonstration, so we went into the Village to shop and eat beforehand. Stomping around the Village in boots and lederhosen attracted a bit of attention. We eventually had a salad in a restaurant, but Roger and I each wimped out of the bondage demo, much to Ricky's disappointment, and we went back to Monroe after a few more drinks.

Next day, my birthday, we spent an interesting midday holding deck lumber in position whilst the guy's carpenter and triathlon T-shirt-wearing assistant constructed the deck.

After dinner with Jamrag at his Club restaurant in New York City, the enormity of the trip in front of me made itself evident. I spent some time fretting about things and was quite turned on by the prospect of the guy in South Holland, Illinois: if any part of the adventure was going to be the big fantasy sex trip this would be it – a PTI (PT Instructor) into SM and bondage. I'd hastily slotted Chicago into the schedule after Clive in London had pointed out this guy advertising in *Jail Master* magazine who was a physiotherapist with private workout equipment at his place.

South Holland, Ill. – City of Churches

We got into Tim's Chevvy van and drove a mile or so to the back of an industrial plaza. I made a joke about 'So this is where you knock me over the head, dump me out the back of the van, and make off with all my documents and valuables?'

He cruised up and down the back of the units checking – no one there. Stopped and got me to go into the carpeted back of the van, handed me a can of beer, got me to strip my shirt off, handcuffed me and handed me my letter to him and told me to read it back to him. He pulled a video camcorder out and I turned my back. I protested 'no face on video' but I think he kept it going under the front seat while I finished reading. Then he had me strip shoes and jeans off – the van had dark glass in all the windows except the front – he then leg-cuffed me and padlocked a chain round my waist. Duct-tape over my eyes then a sock or something in my mouth which he duct-taped shut as well. Then a black cloth bag over my head. A bit of touching up and a lot of intense tickling and massage.

Then he secured the waist chain, handcuffs and leg-cuffs to the van, cuffs round my balls to a dog lead by his driving seat. Music on and he drove off. He had checked that I was OK by means of nods and grunts. His main line, though, was 'What do you want to happen this weekend?' to which he supplied the answer, 'Anything you want – isn't that right?' and I grunted or whatever in assent. The other question was 'Who's in charge?' or 'Am I in charge now?' both of which he wanted grunts to the effect of 'You are, Sir'.

The leg and handcuffs bit rather more than I would like . . . and the road was bumpy and his cornering seemed severe. The stereo was of OK quality!

He stopped again and came into the back of the van again where I was. This time the touching-up included threatening me with a gun – at my hands, legs, body, arse and eventually at my head and mouth. I froze. It was certainly cold (i.e. metal not plastic), the barrel was hollow and had the bit of metal on the top of the barrel that you point at whatever you want to kill. I can't see any reason for having a gun in the gun box of your van if it's not loaded, but at least with me he didn't play around with the safety catch.

Yip, I was scared.

And I was also obviously and incorrigibly turned on.

Next stop he placed a drawstring trash bag over my head and duct-taped it securely in position. I know from gas-mask games that I can count to 120 before major panic sets in. At 90 I either started acting or panicking for real; at 93 he let me out.

Whilst I was inside the bag with it crackling and billowing increasingly fast and furiously, he introduced a new torture – swiping the soles of my feet heel to toe with a sharp instrument. It's excruciating.

'Who's in control?'

'You are, Sir.' Swipe along foot. 'Yeeow!'

'Are you going to do what I say?'

'Yes, Sir.' Swipe along foot. 'Yeeow!' again.

Back in his garage, he released me from the fixing points on the van but kept me cuffed, tightened the chain now from my balls to my ankles and had me move about to order.

Again on video. Maybe it's the humiliation of being made to perform knowing that he'll be wanking off to it later that I hate about video?

It became apparent that tickling was just a prelude for his major kink: foot torture. He taught me to hold my feet out stretched ready, and he inflicted more swipes if they moved. Also to beg 'Please, Sir, tickle my feet.'

When he'd tortured me enough he unwrapped my head, arms and legs, and I found myself staring again at the video camera with its red light on. He got me dressed again, then took me from the garage into the house merely handcuffed and disguised, presumably so that the neighbours couldn't see. A few glasses of chilled water, stripped off again and cuffed hands and feet once more. Then the blindfold and he got me downstairs into his basement – which was carpeted and the air conditioning had got it very chilly. He had me crawl on the floor, pulling me by a chain on the cuffs. I crawled off the carpet on to a wooden floor. It turned out to be a cage, as he first padlocked the gate shut, then screwed four screws in using an electric screwdriver. Apparently a previous prisoner had escaped.

He had me check it for getting out: seemed difficult, all solid. My first impressions were that the cage was small: I couldn't stretch anything out straight. The base and top were three-quarters or one-inch wood and the bars of similar diameter dowel. Only one showed any prospect of even rotating and they were close together so that a wrist could peek through but not an ankle or elbow. I suppose the bars might have broken with some major effort.

Then he moved the cuffs so I was spread-eagled on my back, cuffed to screw-eyes on the base of the cage. This seemed conclusive. Then he started foot tickling and foot torture in earnest. I was still blindfolded with duct-tape, more over my mouth. After lots on my feet, he moved to my armpits. I don't usually 'allow' Tops to do that as my armpits are very sensitive which of course he revelled in. I eventually screamed 'Fuck off' at him, and he stopped. At least he wasn't a total maniac. It was obvious to both of us that we were each enjoying the fantasy scene.

He stopped, asked me what the problem was and then resumed, including punishing me with some pretty hefty foot swipes for foul and abusive language. Second time round he gets to my armpits again and I scream 'Fuck off' again. That was it, the tape came off my mouth and although I was still secured in the cage by cuffs – hands and feet – he started a conversation. He talked about leaving me in the cage overnight – for me that wasn't on: I couldn't stretch my legs out of the cage. He left me in the dark for half an hour or so.

At this stage I wasn't sure if a psychopathic murderer was dealing with me or not. Scary, but what I was after. Not what I'd gone there for – I'd sent him my 'Fantasy Training' SM gym story and had been hoping for things like that. He played with me some more when he returned. Swapped me to a massage/examination table. And also had me massage him. Made me think of him more as a nice guy. He made me cold: ugh! It was already cold enough due to his overenthusiastic air conditioning.

More tickling – 'Who's in control?' 'You, Sir.'

Then he put me in a whirlpool bath to warm me up – an industrial or hospital one made from stainless steel.

A sandwich, then sat down in cuffs to watch a movie video. I fell asleep! Sleeping arrangements were me in cuffs on the floor downstairs – it's done out as reception room for his patients – and him upstairs. He locked me in though – with access to a bathroom. Middle of the night I was wide awake again, upset about the video mainly.

Next morning he blindfolded, hooded and taped me up again. Wrapped me in a sleeping bag to make me too hot. Then severe tickling and feet swipes, etc. Therapeutic hot packs and ice packs on my shoulders and the trash bag over my head again. I quite deliberately faked it this time: the day before had been too real. This time it wasn't so scary, I knew more about him. Then he undid me and rolled himself up mummy-style in the sleeping bags and I played with him, i.e. 'switched', although I still had cuffs on.

We went out to Stacey's for brunch, an eat-as-much-as-you-can joint. Then to some woods. I think this was a first-time scene. He leg-ironed me to a tree. Took some video –

no face. And led me by the balls, naked and barefoot through the woods. Lots of mosquitoes. Not a turn-on. At least it wasn't running naked through a shopping mall, which was one of his ideas, or sending me in shopping wearing over-skimpy shorts like he'd done with someone else.

Back to his place, did some PT – I'd explained I'd really come for enforced and monitored PT. He cuffed me to his stair-climber machine, and told me to work it.

Slept upstairs at liberty in the same bed, both exhausted. Even if I hadn't gone the full distance, we'd done a lot.

Next morning, he hooded and spread-eagled me to the bed, tickled, heavy massaged and foot-swiped me. Tied a polythene bag over my cock. I hadn't come since in the woods at Ian's and was quite randy – but not enough to come humping the bed only.

Final scene was him – in leg-irons – under me, each with bags on cocks, me humping and fucking on top of him. I'm not sure if he came, or just nearly did.

'McDonald's breakfast; reluctantly he let me snapshoot him, then on the coach for O'Hare. I'm writing this three days later and I can't make my own mind up about him: he's a fool to play with guns. No American I spoke to later disagreed with that: guns kill. A week later the story broke of the Milwaukee serial killer. But this guy Tim was challenging because he thinks for himself; he was doing what turns him on not what he's been taught: he isn't part of any of the orthodoxies. He's the sort of person whom I particularly like to meet.

Charleston, South Carolina

I flew to Charleston, South Carolina with a stopover at Charlotte, NC where a USMC guy not in uniform stared me (wearing brown BDU shirt) like fuck; I blew it by not being sufficiently cool, but we at least had a few words, him en route for Parris Island. I guess he was an officer – sports polo shirt and black rugger shorts over massive thighs and calves. At Charleston he shouldered his two sea-bags plus a carry-on cabin bag and a uniform suit-carrier. There were two others in USMC uniform; they'd been off for two weeks' leave to somewhere in North Dakota. Cute kids, their first long leave after a year in the USMC.

Whilst I waited at Charleston, there was another USMC guy in uniform returning after his first home leave after his first six months. Luggage trolley with his bags on it and his mirror-finish boots carefully and proudly placed on top. He was phoning Mom whilst I phoned Clive, who was looking after my affairs in London and Ian in Pennsylvania.

Went to Dave's house via a tour of Old Charleston, bits of which I remembered from visiting there in 1967 with my parents. Pretty, but it was 95 degrees and 95 per cent humidity.

He got me doing PT – press-ups, sit-ups, leg-raises. To Order. Nicely. I closed my eyes and had a good time. He kept me motivated reasonably far. Kept me in position for a five or ten count after each set, parade rest in between exercises. Naked. 190 press-ups, 35/35/35 sit-ups and either 50 or 60 leg-raises. Heavy duty.

He cooked fresh tuna steak on the gas barbecue afterwards and we had the meal in his formal dining room, him clothed, me still naked and sweaty. His house is pretty with nice polished wood floors and carpets. Another overenthusiastic air conditioning plant and whether it was the hot/cold games in South Holland or jet-lag or face-fucking, I was beginning to have a sore throat.

Next day, more PT first thing, nice fresh-fruit breakfast, then he went to work. I got a taxi to Patriots' Point and spent the day looking round a submarine, a frigate and an aircraft carrier. I was looking for the brig on the carrier and had given up; however, just before it was time to leave I happened across a sign that said 'To the Brig. Five decks down'. The brig turned out to be newly painted, unlike most of the rest of the ship; I guess it's been used in a movie.

Back to Dave's – I got the black cab driver to take me on a tour of Charleston and the ghettos. I was annoyed as Dave hadn't told me about the Old Exchange building which has a visitable dungeon. Then I ran to the seafront and back a couple of miles. I'd hoped that the thunder that had been threatening would have loosed itself for a run in a downpour, but no such luck. However, my shirt was soaked through with sweat by the end of the first block from the humidity.

Merced, Yosemite and San Francisco

Next morning off to the West Coast. I had a window seat on the 737, my favourite type of plane. In-flight hospitality in hand, I watched the great panorama of the continental US unfold five miles below, finally reaching the Pacific cloud and landing at San Francisco.

RMR-Togie had advised me to hire a car for San Francisco to Merced rather than fly ('Keep your options open'), so I hit the San Mateo Bay Bridge in a Buick Century, hopelessly American: underpowered and overbodied and too much air conditioning.

I found Mick's place in Merced a couple of hours later, scores of cats and dogs in a farmyard outside his place. He wasn't going to be able to take a truck up camping in Yosemite as we'd corresponded about, which was a big disappointment, and sex didn't work either, partly due to my sore throat. He was very hospitable though, and saw to it that I was comfortable sleeping in his camouflage-material-lined playroom amongst the chains and cuffs.

Next day I took the Buick up to Yosemite, following the Merced River through the foothills. Spectacular drive up to Glacier Point, the overhang 3200 feet above the Yosemite Valley floor, a spectacular view achieved only at the cost of petrol! It seemed cheating but I was strangely unwilling to get back in the car and leave. Lust for mountains is a strange thing.

One night in San Francisco: my shortest stay anywhere. This was a last-minute arrangement both because of not camping in Merced and because Togie and I had met Robert in Berlin the weekend before I had left for the US. There in Berlin I'd been increasingly conscious that skinhead image only means fascist to the Germans — there were no gay skinheads or red skins like there are in the UK. So me and Robert, who's black, getting cute together in the gay bars freaked out the locals especially in medium-nice restaurants on the Ku'damm! Anyhow, one night in SF turned out not to be enough. I never saw Alcatraz and I was surprised how pleasant the San Francisco city was – it wasn't just another NYC or LA.

Robert and his lover took me out to a busy, dressy, cruisy Italian restaurant on Castro Street. A big culture shock from happy redneck Merced, backpacking Yosemite or suburban Chicago. And there were Gay Pride flags everywhere! Not just on the gay commercial establishments but on private houses in residential areas. I was impressed and a bit humbled by that.

We stayed up late – I crashed asleep – they had to go to work and me to the airport next day. I killed some time in the morning in the local parks and ended up meeting some degens and skinheads. Their idea of skinhead was rather lax on either the shortness of the hair or the type of boot and a couple of them weren't exactly teenagers either. Forty-year-old 'don't care attitude' guys on skateboards were menacing on the sidewalks.

Tucson, Arizona

Scott met me in Tucson – it was only six weeks since he'd been in the UK and we'd gone on touring Devon and Cornwall together. For the first time since leaving Roger and Ricky eight flights previously, I was with a face I knew already. And from this point onwards in the trip I wasn't 'blind-dating' any more, so less of a strain.

Sunday morning packed up Scott's pickup for camping in the Chiricahua Mountains east of Tucson. We made it up dirt roads to Rustlers Park campground, at 8500 feet. Pitched the tent next to the pickup for free as there was a faded sign saying 'No water' and a smaller one saying that signs of bears had been seen in the area.

Rustlers Park was up in the pines and cedars again, higher

MORE AND HARDER

than Yosemite and drier. Nice and cool. Climate a bit like England or Wales on a pleasant August day. These mountains were the Indians' hiding places in the last century when the white men were invading the plains. Because of the Indians' presence, these forests were not felled for the mining or smelting or railroads. Where forests were felled, the soil eroded leaving barren rock.

We hiked ('took a trail') to Saddleback Pass. On the north side there were spectacular lichens and maybe virgin forest, certainly forest untended for fifty to a hundred years so there were fallen trees decaying where they lay.

Picnic lunch at a great place, looking out over the sweltering plain below. Back to the campground, only two or three miles but that was OK. We sussed the campground spring – there was plenty of clean water but it wasn't connected to the tap system. We assumed the lack of water was keeping the other people away: our only neighbours were an Indian family in a camper van – he was wearing a battered desert camouflage hat, woodland camouflage trousers and an 'I went to Iraq' T-shirt.

We had a great fire that night. Local wood and some mesquite Scott had brought up from Tucson. Steak, marinated chicken legs, peppers, salad, fruit, two sorts of beer. And looking at the pine trees disappear into the night as the sky went red and then dark blue with stars through the branches, sparks going up from our fire. Walking away from the fire into the blackness was eerie, seeing the firelight throw through the trees. And the utter quiet of the forest.

We huddled together in the tent overnight. The food was in the icebox in the metal bear-proof container but we were awakened at first light by the drinks cooler being chucked about by a bear. Unsure what to do we kept super-quiet and the bear got bored, not having managed to open the cooler. We found out later that noise usually scares bears off and that not long before at this place a bear had broken a car windscreen trying to get inside.

There was a wonderful dawn chorus sounding together with the light breeze in the trees.

Despite this, we decided to change the plans and look to

camp elsewhere the next night. Slowly and reluctantly, we broke camp. Another hard-to-leave place. Drove back down the dirt tracks and to the other end of the Chiricahua range to the National Monument with spectacular volcanic rock formations. Trails abound, fortunately few other tourists.

A mile or so into the trail, between quick sharp showers, light wind storms and the usual sunshine, the urge came on me to get my shorts off. Hiking a short way in boots only was great, wind between the thighs, balls swinging! Scott did likewise and we found a rock cleft to pose against, then jacked off into the void. The shorts went back on but in some ways the rest of that trail was an anti-climax: now sated and jaded it was more difficult to enthuse about pretty rocks. And what about all the might-have-beens, hiking balls tethered to rucksack, tugged along in a chain gang by those in front, etc.!

Friday, I went in to Scott's work at the radio station while Scott was on air. A skinhead, Jim, turned up in the studio. After lunch he cropped my hair to a Zero, Scott's to a Number Four. Jim moved from LA to Tucson and seems to work on the fringes of the music business.

One night in Tucson we went to a gay bar, me in newly cropped hair, tank top with lederhosen and boots. Scott said I looked like a porn star! Skin Jim was there with his girl Rachel, the first time he'd been in a gay bar. I spent all night talking music (The Jam, Stiff Little Fingers, Cockney Rejects, etc.) with him. He advised us of a shop in Benson, Az. which has an antique handcuff collection.

Leaving Tucson next day was a wrench.

Casper, Wyoming

Allan met me at Casper Airport, Wyoming, and we visited a couple of lesbian friends of his there on the way back to Glenrock. He had got very organised for the backpack trip – everything out and ready, meal and snack packs made up and labelled for us each for every day out. We packed the rucksacks and found that loads of things wouldn't fit; we

MORE AND HARDER

discarded the third set of mess pans, etc. Got the packs down to about 45 pounds each, which was still quite heavy enough.

Next morning, we set out at 6 a.m. across the Wyoming prairie roads. There really isn't anywhere like it: all you can see is the road, a barbed wire fence either side, a two-wire power line stretching to the horizon in each direction, and a mountain range fifty or sixty miles away. Maybe a pair of antelope once in a while, and the practised (bored?) eye starts to be able to trace the track of a long-defunct railroad after an hour or so of travelling.

Casper is just under 5280 feet high and its population is in excess of that. The only other town we went through all day with population exceeding its elevation was Riverton, and most of the towns were of population 4 or 25 or maybe 500 – that'd be a big place! And on the horizon was the Wind River Range that we were aiming for. We crossed over to their western side at South Pass – where the Oregon Trail pioneers found a way through back in the 1820s – it's hard to imagine traversing that inhospitable bare dry prairie in a covered wagon.

The mountains were snow-capped, even in July. The Continental Divide is in the centre of the range – in the prairie it's a bit imprecise because there's a large area with no running watercourses. On the Pacific side we stopped at Pinedale, bought a last cool Diet Coke and sandwich for lunch, and turned off the main road. The country suddenly changed to an idyllic wide green valley with a swift flowing river in its base: the glacier melt fed Green River that contributes the greatest flow to the Colorado. There were moose, antelope and deer grazing on the green grass. Imagine encountering that place 170 years ago after the two weeks or more on the trail from the last decent river on the Atlantic side . . . (And what did the Mountain Men do when they did reach it? Felled the trees, trapped the beavers for their pelts and overgrazed the prairie . . .)

Squaretop Mountain, that we were to climb, heads that valley and it eventually came into view. We parked and changed at the trailhead, signed into the wilderness area, and got walking.

Pine forests in a V valley with glacial moraines that form dams creating lakes. Behind them, glacial U valleys with sheer pine-topped sides and soaring high mountain peaks.

We reached a camping place and pitched tent and started to feed ourselves while the insects fed on us. Very quiet, then at sunset there was a brief windstorm, then quiet overnight. We awoke in deep shade and dew; the insects weren't up yet!

There was a moose feeding in the water a little way along the trail – he let me get real close – they know they're OK when they're in the water.

We'd camped again by the second, higher lake. The trail now climbed at the side of the Green River as it crashed over granite rapids. We were directly below Squaretop and were going round behind it to ascend.

We encountered two brothers each wearing caps with wrestling logos on them. They looked intrigued at the scars still showing on my elbows – I should have been more forthright.

Lunchtime we waded the Green River and started up a 1000-foot steep valley side climb. Now over 8000 feet and still carrying 44 pounds plus water, the blood began to pump and the view through the trees of the mountains and creek tumbling down opposite changed by the minute.

We finally gained the top of the ridge and descended 50 foot or so to Granite Lake below, height 9550 feet, and made camp in the pine trees by a creek there. Allan went fishing and we had four tasty trout for dinner. Squaretop Mountain towers directly out of Granite Lake, and the shoulder of Granite Peak that we'd ascended a previous year rises the other side.

Next day, all clear and bright and, with daypacks only, we make for Squaretop. No trail – it's a scramble, and the route Allan had intended to use was still snow-covered. Fantastic alpine high meadows and rocky brook side flowers in bloom. We made it to the top, via several minor peaks en route. A view of the Beaver Park and Green River valley from beyond the trailhead campground and car park, including the two lakes, the rapids, the rest of the valley right up to the glaciers opposite Gannett peak at 13,375 feet the second highest point in Wyoming.

We could see the usual afternoon clouds rolling in, and set about exploring the square top of the peak – actually it was a boulder field and quite dodgy going. The views all round were great, another, inaccessible, valley the other side, and a col going off further into the mountains that we didn't take.

It thundered, as if to chase us down off the top and we scrambled down an alternate route that was fairly hairy without ropes. Lots of loose rocks.

We cooked and watched the clouds above – it started raining and we turned in. Rain all night and it kept going till nine the next morning. The green grass has to come from somewhere! And when the sun came out the forest colours were newly washed and twinkling with raindrops.

We set off for home back down the slippery trail: twelve miles. Back in Pinedale I booked us into a motel and we found a great diner – the Wrangler. It had local pickups outside and the food was ace, not just that night (anything's great after backpack cooking!) but the breakfast next day was the best too.

I bought a branding iron at a roadside stall. Allan said it was a cattle rustler's brand intended to modify existing brands.

Back to Casper, sunset over the prairie; Glenrock, unpacking and packing again. And another painful departure having shared a good time together.

I landed at sunny downtown Burbank with some trepidation. Would it work out with Sean or not?

Sunny downtown Burbank, California

California after Wyoming was a culture jolt: style, haircuts, smog, heat, lots of people, closed-in horizons etc.

Sean took me to his place, 'Rancho de Chaos', which looked normal enough from the outside, hand- and leg-ironed me in his back yard and put on a leather hood with nose and mouth holes, no eyes. That stayed on for three nights, didn't come off at all. He walked me gently into a metal cage and tied me tight to the sides of it. Administered my buttplug and strapped that in tight. Everything was tight. My arms were bound tight. I couldn't move nothing. And he wanked me off mercilessly and put me to sleep, still shackled, inside the cage which was now horizontal.

What happened while that hood was on? I can't really recount a blow by blow story and I'm not sure I want to. He certainly never did anything twice. I kept up with my teeth brushing and he fed me pizza at night, the taste of which stayed around the hood for the rest of my use of it, and breakfast was pancakes and butter. The same every day. I didn't complain but I think he was trying to get me to.

He had repaired a PC for someone and whilst they were reloading the hard disc he had me suspended somehow in a parachute harness, legs not on the ground (and still hooded) for the afternoon. I hallucinated like crazy all the time! I felt very odd balance-wise when he let me down.

He's an amateur radio ham. He was operating a couple of times when his gay ham group had scheduled transmissions but ionospheric conditions weren't very impressive. He did have a Morse conversation with someone north of San Francisco though, but didn't go into any details about his 'house guest'.

And there was an episode with me sitting as if impaled on a sawhorse and a workout on his bench press machine. And he watched a porn video that I couldn't see.

Took a phone call from Ian in Pennsylvania! And talked about Larry, a blind friend of Sean's; in the hood I could particularly relate to him. Later Sean introduced us.

Sean had seen an item on CNN about transporting prisoners by air – wearing belly chains, leg-irons, handcuffs and chained together. He had me in the kitchen like that.

The third day with the hood I woke and it was like people describe having a migraine: flashing dark blue and bright orange. I baled out and asked him to take it off, but I still didn't want to see his playroom/bedroom. No great problems taking it off: I could see normally and the flashing went immediately; the mechanism that fills in the gaps in sight when you blink didn't work immediately but that soon got OK in an hour.

The place wasn't quite as I'd imagined it either – the layout didn't quite fit my imagined layout. He kept me in leg-irons so I didn't get too mobile!

Psychologically, it seemed as though the three days had been one super-long night. In a way I'd lost three days. I kept getting the day of the week wrong. Whilst I was hooded but 'off-duty', i.e. not in a very serious bondage or SM situation, I was thinking that Sean was the most wonderful person I'd met, was thinking of moving in with him, relocating to Burbank. As he wanted to move out of LA we were considering the mechanics and logistics and finances of setting up together in North California. A bit like the 'Stockholm Effect' but a lot more subtle.

We went out for a good brunch and I immediately re-fell in love with LA. Visited the office of a leather magazine. That night he got the cat out and whipped my shoulders. Tied hands above my head on tiptoe, balls tied to the ground so I was taut. Another thing I've never 'allowed' a Top to do to me before. I didn't expect it, didn't know what to expect, but it shows how well we were getting on that I was relaxed enough to take most of what he wanted to dish out, and like it; and then start worrying about it later.

I had an amazing night of dreams and nightmares afterwards, sleeping on the bed with Sean but still wearing leg-irons. It was like having stirred up all the meat and vegetable soups of my recent past life and watching it all settle again.

Sean and I seem to share one fantasy – that of being strapped down for a severe punishment session that we can't stop. He described it as the big dark black door at the end of the corridor.

The time came to leave, and I think we were both surprised how comfortable we'd got in each other's company. I still hadn't seen the inside of Sean's bedroom/playroom: I joked that there was probably a model railway in there that he kept very quiet about!

Toronto

Metropolitan Toronto came over as very provincial and clean compared to LA. Like visiting Edinburgh direct from London. Derek had arrived there back from London, where he also has a house and does his musicology for half the year. He was able to fill me in on the London Gay Sadomasochists' tenth anniversary party which I'd missed in July. Seems it went fine. In Toronto we went to the Black Creek pioneer village – great, except it had no jail! I know Canada wasn't Australia but were the founding Canadians really that well behaved? We also went out to some of the amazing number of gay bars and clubs in the gay area of downtown Toronto. The leather disco was a disappointment: hardly anyone in leather, mostly disco shorts and denim!

New York wrestling

I spent a pleasant weekend with an ex-college wrestler, now a lawyer but still fighting-fit. We parted after another special breakfast and I checked in for the return flight. I was actually very touched to see the green patchwork of England from 35,000 feet as we saw the early-morning mist over the Malvern Hills. Arrival at Heathrow was uneventful and by 1130 the next day I was signing on at the Unemployment office . . .

Corporal Punishment in Wales and London

March 1992

Next weekend away is to a 200-year-old stone cottage in North Wales near Snowdon. It is owned by an ex-army guy my age. I've been there once before. The deal is a day of slave labour: cottage maintenance, clearing rubble and preparing firewood and night-time orienteering including buttplugs and whipping. Last visit, another gale and rain weekend, my night-time route included a ruined cottage where the guy was waiting for me to report. He ordered me doing pull-ups from the wooden beams and lashed me with a junior cat for encouragement. Had me sit bare-arsed on a stone window ledge to freeze my bum before a caning and then safe-fucked me with my head out of the cottage window in the wind and rain, butt exposed to him inside for a lashing and a fucking. Made me piss my combat trousers before he waved me on my way to the next RV and checkpoint.

I'm writing this with a hot red bum having returned from a CP session yesterday – with a guy my own age, another Peter, also into working out and fitness, and heavily into giving and taking CP. It turns out his nickname is 'Stripe-yer-bum' Peter, which is a help as there are so many Peters around! We had an ace time; he knows what he wants and knows what it's like to take it, and gave me a really good time. Mainly with Lochgelly Tawse, cane and my own thick double-weight leather strap.

We started in military fatigues and tank tops, taking six each, then twelve, turn and turn about with lots of rubbing of sore, hot bums between sets; taking advantage of the adrenalin rush after each set and the cycle of aggression and whacked-outedness. After twelve you're out of resistance, just accepting it, when it's great to be massaged and manipulated and wanked; then your aggression returns, you're feeling high, you want to get your own back, make him hurt too, then massage him; then you relax and somehow or other your body edges toward a bum-presented position that invites further CP to keep the cycle going; or an excuse is found to 'even things up' or 'see if you can take it'.

I didn't keep count but I'm sore and he's even sorer! His Tawse has the ends burnt so they are hardened and leave tasty-looking red marks where the end has bitten that persist after the other marks have faded; they are also a turn-on to look at! Borstal Tawse – given a choice, that's the one I choose!

Camerone '92 – Légion Étrangère

May 1992

Well, I didn't get off to the US again this weekend as planned: instead Togie (my Royal Marine Reserve friend) and I got invitations to the French Foreign Legion's commemoration of their victory in the Camerone in 1842: one of the most 'sacred' events in their annual calendar.

We arrived at Marseilles airport after the most bumpy landing I have ever experienced in a 737: the mistral wind was blowing full-force. We hired a little car and drove towards Marseilles and Aubagne, the Légion Étrangère's main headquarters which moved there from Algeria thirty years ago. We saw our first *képi blanc* in the back of a Légion truck on the *autoroute*.

There was a minor incident in Aubagne centre when two little old ladies drove into the back of our car; fortunately little damage and my French managed to ensure no consequences. We drank a *café* in the town square in the hot sun, relaxing and marvelling at the wonders of flying due south from rainy London.

For accommodation, we were directed to the Hôtel de la Gare, and on asking there it turned out to be full. Just as we were leaving – it was a bar with rooms above – we were advised by a moustached gentleman that we would have to go to Marseilles, it's the Camerone, he said. We replied (well, I did, Togie doesn't speak French) that that was why we were in Aubagne, and we got talking. He said he was a colonel from the Légion, had served as a *parachutiste* in *Algerie* (that's the 1er REP who rebelled and the regiment was dispersed) and was now working for the intelligence services. We showed the invitation that Togie had and wanted to know if I would get in as well. He said it was easy – if they won't let you in at the gate, then the wall is easy to climb, less than a metre high! Climbing walls of military establishments sounded like a way to get into trouble so I asked him if there was any other way. He phoned the office and after some to-do got my name added to the list.

He was also looking for a place for the night and we had a list of hotels, so he phoned around and we booked places in a nearby hotel in Gemenos, the next village. Then we bought him some drinks, other *anciens* (retired *légionnaires*) arrived and soon even Togie was chatting in broken French.

The hotel was delightful: a small family hotel and *magnifique* restaurant with all the right certificates on the wall. We split, for a *douche* before dinner but, when we came down, the Colonel had taken a taxi back to the town, the hotel were convinced that he would be back; after a wait we sat down to a good dinner.

I had a hangover the next morning. Eau Source-Badoit helped but it was still a struggle to get into the white shirt, tie and grey trousers that Togie and I had decided upon as suitable for the occasion. He drove us off towards Aubagne. There was a traffic jam and we parked and walked the rest of the way, watching an increasing number of *légionnaires* and others doing the same.

The gate inspected our passes and we ended up on a grassy bank overlooking the parade ground. On the way in my hangover had received two jolts – one was from the enormous boots that the Police Militaire were wearing, the other was a visceral thrill as a unit of 2REP Légion paras marched past us at about two metres distance in perfect order towards the parade ground. Not a hard-on thrill but a rush from controlled, disciplined and proud masculinity on show. Even if we got no further (because of the ticket problem) the trip had been justified.

But there were no problems – we watched the parade of the relic of Capitaine Danjou's hand, heard the band, stood and sat with the rest of the crowd. A helicopter brought in the French defence minister and some planes flew low overhead. Togie needed to take his AZT and we wondered if he was the first to take this at the Légion HQ.

Togie was getting more gung-ho about photography and wandered off down to the edges of the parade ground for better views. After the ceremony was over we wandered around snapshooting the 'fauna' as you may imagine. Then there was the *kermesse*: stalls selling souvenirs, a couple of food and wine tents, rides for the kids, etc. and a relaxed holiday atmosphere with a few Police Militaire around and lots of families.

I bought six bottles of Légion rosé wine for 89F, and Togie bought lots of souvenirs including a *képi blanc* to complete his parade uniform. After some more photography we left and stopped at the first bar outside the gate – where we found the 'Colonel' again! He'd also had a good time but now seemed to be in the hands of the bar woman! We chatted a bit more and left.

That night at our hotel, another of the *anciens* from the previous night turned up for his meal so we had company once more. He was a lorry driver and his son was in the Légion although this guy hadn't seen him on this visit.

The hotel wanted to know where our friend the 'Colonel' had got to as he had taken a shower and left with the key, neither paying nor saying anything. Despite my morals saying 'don't rat on your mates', Togie urged me to tell them the name and regiment details he had given us – I guess he'll hear nothing more but maybe it'll enable the hotel to get something from a public relations slush fund at the Légion HQ.

That and another incident in one of the food tents gave us a glimpse of the Légion that was at odds with the PR image that was being projected. We'd been drinking in the tent and wanted to get some food. I approached the Sergent-Chef at the meals window next to the sign saying 50F per tray-meal. He took my 100F and it disappeared into his *képi* and waved to the *légionnaires* behind the serving counter for two meals, *vite* (quick)! It was only later we saw that the official cashier was outside the tent and we should have paid there.

Next day Togie and I went mountain bike cycling on an unspoilt island (Île de Porquerolles) off Hyères, east of Toulon, which we reached after a fine drive through the mountains and past the motor racing circuit where the Bol d'Or motorbike race is run in the autumn. The weather was ace and we cycled to one end of the island and explored a ruined Napoleonic fort and wished that we had brought the Légion uniforms with us for fantasy photographs!

Marseilles was torrential rain next day but we found the army surplus stores – there was one that specialised in US uniforms – and bought some Légion items. And, despite protests from Togie, we trekked to the railway station at lunchtime and were rewarded with the sight of lots of *légionnaires* in walking-out uniform on the platforms and in the snack bar.

So that was that really – also a great meal in a gay restaurant recommended to us by the proprietor of the leather shop and then some more heavy drinking in the recommended gay bar.

When we got back Togie and I were invited to a party in honour of an American (Virginia) cop who was visiting London. All the guests were members of the American Uniform Brotherhood. Togie was wearing his *légionnaire*'s parade uniform that he completed by buying the kepi in Aubagne. I was wearing French combat kit and the boots I bought from the shop in Marseilles – they are very nice big beefy boots to stomp around in but they need to be worn more before they will get comfortable. I think the two of us made a good impression at the party and were certainly different because all the rest were in various American cop uniforms. Nice though those are, they are still cops and I'm not sure that I like fantasising about cops.

Birthday in Switzerland

July 1992

I celebrated my birthday in Switzerland with Otto from Stuttgart: hiking in army boots and lederhosen-shorts up to 2850m from the hotel at the top of the Simplon Pass where we were staying. The Simplon Pass has been an important route since Roman times and a lot of this particular route was laid by them. I had quite a fun time imagining the scene 2000 years ago with toga-wearing Roman soldiers tramping over the same stones and sweaty slaves making the roads. A harsh place to work, though.

This summit is not an especially high one and is not on one of the obvious circular hiking routes so we didn't see anyone else until we retraced our steps back to the nearby col. It was ideal for a birthday whacking, one per year from the belt, three dozen in all, with eyes closed seeing stars and eyes open seeing snowy-capped mountains. Contrary to what you might imagine, lederhosen don't protect you from the sting although the effect is rather to transform the sharp pain from the belt into a stinging like a paddle, spreading the area of impact. And I don't know whether you remember but I 'prefer' the heavy, thick weapons rather than the light, flat ones: truncheon, tawse, cane and belt rather than paddle or slipper.

After the belting and the photography we had some excellent Swiss chocolate, unzipped the fronts of our lederhosen and buddy-jacked off in the sunshine and thin air.

Also had a good bit of high-altitude running training, ran from Simplon-dorf up to the top of the pass where our hotel is located. That was 10km and 500m altitude and took 65 minutes, mostly following the alignment of the old pass-road rather than the most recent high-speed route.

Denver, Colorado

September 1992

Bob met me at the airport with his lover Steven. They drove me downtown in Bob's Compact Jeep which was nicely beat-up and non-shiny; we arrived at Denver's leather bar and I told them a bit about myself.

After a few beers in the bar's patio, we left and they drove into some less well-lit part of the city, stopped and ordered me out of the CJ, hands behind the neck, blindfolded me, cuffed me and jabbed me in the side with something, which by the time I had had time to think, I realised was a stun-gun sparking through my clothes.

Back inside on the rear seat of the CJ they drove around the city again and drove and talked as though the cops had spotted their kidnap and were in pursuit. The bickering between Bob, driving, wanting to go faster to escape and Steven, as passenger, urging Bob to drive not to be noticed and to avoid populated routes was particularly convincing.

They arrived at a bathhouse and propelled me out of the CJ. As they checked me in and booked a leather-equipped playroom, the door-person insisted that their captive had to have a one-month membership, and also made some comment about hoping that there wouldn't be as many screams as that last one they brought here made.

Tied spread-eagled, kicked, punched nicely, belted nastily, stun-gunned intimidatingly, etc.

Then breakfast at Bob's lover Steven's at 2 a.m., then back to Bob's other lover Duncan's for some sleep, three-in-the-bed, me in a new leather straitjacket that smelt just great. I woke with sore shoulders and my cock with a raging hard-on that I couldn't even reach as my hands were tied in the straitjacket. Duncan sucked me off in the semi-dark of the bedroom, enjoying my Prince Albert ring in his mouth and throat.

Duncan turned out to be a 78-year-old who had been a

USAF colonel in WWII in Casablanca and remarkably good fun: he'd sucked me off with his teeth out.

Bob took me to Denver Athletic Club, very well equipped, and we had a good Mile High workout each in the Olympic weights room. He staggered up the stairs afterwards, and (two days later) I've still got a sore stomach from the sit-ups 'comfy chair'.

Bob took me out to a relatively local bar and introduced me to John, who was wearing full leather and chaps. John took me back to his playroom, which was huge and filled with almost every toy a slaveboy could dream about, and put a cat-o'-nine-tails across my back. Near the end he ordered me to count the last twenty out. I double-counted as I was enjoying it so much!

Bob re-appeared having met with Steven; we had a bit of matey CP, I gave him six, he gave me six, etc. Then we bear-hugged and John belted us both. I had an unfair advantage, having been previously warmed up by John.

Next lunchtime, I was back for more, culminating in a jack-off scene: the first for over a week. Finally we all met up for a steak dinner before I had to return to Stapleton Airport, which now felt not so much a transit lounge as a gateway to SM friends in the city.

The Beast of Croydon

October 1992

I'm writing this with a very sore bum from the after-effects of a heavy CP visit last evening. On my return from the US there were several replies to an advertisement I was running in a London gay newspaper that is distributed free through the bars. My ad read: *Squaddie skinhead seeks TA or ex-regular mate (28–38) for two-way CP, initiations and endurance tests indoors and all-weather outdoors.*

The guy I visited was in no way a mate. His letter said, 'Your ad interested me. I deal only in hard men who go into bondage and take a genuine severe thrashing gagged and tied down. I left the army a long time ago; I'm now fifty but don't let that stop you. I'll make you obey. If you're tough enough to accept this challenge contact the above number but don't do so if you can't handle the real thing where I set your limits.' Written in capitals on plain paper with just the phone number and a signature, 'Sir'.

I phoned and arrangements were made to meet. I had to get somewhere and then phone the number again. I chose to pedal cycle; I don't have motor transport and that keeps me fit and ensures that I arrive in a suitable frame of mind rather than wound up from driving or bored from a train journey. On making telephone contact he gave me a street intersection to be at and a time. It turned out to be at the bottom of a hill, a golf course on one side of the road, houses on the other side.

He was equipped with whistle, clipboard and stopwatch and a belt. Initially he took me onto the golf course, told me he was going to start the clock, give me twelve across the arse and when that was completed I was to run up the hill and back down. The timing would include the belting time. His belt hurt. I ran the course six times with the same starting conditions and my time got worse.

He directed me to another street corner: he drove by car;

I cycled. I think all this cloak and dagger stuff was to protect the name of his street address but I guess by now it was unnecessary – any under-cover cop wouldn't have put up with running the course and six dozen from his belt.

Inside in his garage he slapped handcuffs on behind my back, blindfolded and gagged me, led me indoors and upstairs. I never saw his punishment room. Being England I guess it was a bedroom with bed, curtains and carpet, which is a real turn-off to me and is why I had asked to be blindfolded.

He tied me down over a small stool, like an army barracks stool. Or at least that was my fantasy. Hands to the front, stool in my stomach, knees wide spread by the legs but attached with rope. Not much verbal, just 'You know why you're here and now you're going to get it.'

I didn't count, just endured. No hard-on, though I've got one writing about it now and I had a massive wank when I reached home. He told me he was using a cane and then a tawse. He did start slightly gently but it soon got to be full-force. He was aiming for one spot and mostly hit it. His game was to make me scream into the gag and I did. Then you just take it. People say the next stage is you get a hard-on but that doesn't happen with me yet or I haven't gone far enough. It was just pain, pain, pain. All the fantasies about skinhead football hooligans getting the birch fifteen or more years ago, army guys taking CP rather than being on Report, rugger (rugby) club training night discipline, all went through my mind. I tried taking the CP and not reacting, stonewalling, but he got to me. Yelling into the gag also. There was a time I wanted to stop but I tried not to yell that. He might have stopped but in fact continued. It's like a rape scene: there's no point in being tied down and gagged if the guy stops when you shout to stop. It only gets interesting after I want to stop and he won't. That's the bit where I feel the humiliation, my own motivation's gone, and I'm his toy.

This guy did stop. He left me there for I don't know how long then came and untied me without saying anything, took the gag off and offered me the option of staying for a chat. I declined and said I'd rather be on my way but a large mug of coffee would be welcome. He took me back down to the garage, checked I knew my directions, for safety told me to phone him when I got back home, left the coffee and closed the house door.

When I leave something like that there's a fantastic sense of escaping and of freedom. I pedalled like a bat out of hell. It's over twelve miles through suburbia back to my place here and it took fifty-eight minutes. The outgoing trip had been over seventy-five minutes because I was saving myself for his physical training and also allowing a time buffer so as not to be late.

This morning I'm sore on the arse from his flogging, marked quite strongly and it's at the purple and red stage still. No broken skin. And also sore in the legs from twenty-five miles' cycling and hill-running.

Brabant Soldiers Camp '92

Report by BSC#921031067

After a lot of preparation – made more difficult because I didn't quite know what to expect so took everything – the train finally pulled into Eindhoven at 2200 hours late on Friday night. It was misty but not freezing.

Following instructions, I located a *trein-taxi* queue and waited. This system turned out to be a taxi-sharing system and when I showed the driver my destination and he read it back, there was a snigger from the others in the car – I saw why because when we turned into the road the Ladies of the Night were strutting their stuff on the pavement in the fog. Cool occupation.

My destination turned out to be the 'Playpen' safe-sex club which is run by a guy, Rieks. Friday night was a leather-rubber-uniform night.

I was introduced to Rieks and, after changing out of street clothes, helped with stapling inserts into their magazine *Scratch*. Others arrived, including Walter, from the Cologne gay soldiers group (Gay-Soldaten Köln) who had originally passed my enquiry to the Dutch. Rémy, Fred and David, the organisers of the event, arrived and soon there was a large table full of uniforms, boots and webbing being sorted for the next day.

Meanwhile sex was going on downstairs in Playpen's dark areas and some people were drinking at the small bar wearing slave attire. I was getting my ear attuned to the Dutch and German languages.

My kit had been chucked in one of the cells with an iron gate across the front. As things turned out I didn't end up sleeping there but on an army folding bed.

Next morning there was breakfast, we helped clear up the bar, and eventually Rémy and Fred had their hired mini-bus loaded. I travelled with Walter and Wili from Austria, via a snack bar at Eindhoven station. We arrived through Tilburg at the forest site to find the others disappointed that the place was full of school-kids on pushbikes, unlike previously when they'd done the recce. Putting tents up would have to wait until later so as not to attract too much attention.

The Camp officially commenced at 1600 hours at Tilburg station and the mini-bus was there to collect people, all arriving in civilian clothes. In the forest we were struggling with the puzzle of how a frame tent fitted together and transporting equipment, food and water to the proposed site for the Camp.

People arrived, including four from Berlin in a camouflaged Kubelwagon, just as the light was disappearing. The immediate priority was to get the tents up in the remaining light and then to change into combat kit and webbing. There was a mixture of US Woodland Camouflage and Dutch Olive clothing; I was in British DPM. Some of the Dutch were wearing webbing loaded with pioneer spade, water bottle and pouches; I had the UK '58 pattern equivalent.

Some time later, someone called everyone together in the dark in a clearing and the Camp started. Recruits were formed into a line and it was explained that recruits were not to speak unless spoken to by one of David, Rémy or Fred, and we were to reply calling them 'Sir'. Then we were split into three groups.

The squad I was assigned to was four plus Fred, in charge. We ran back to one of the main paths across the forest and he got us marching in step, shouting out numbers as we went; halting, turning, sprinting, etc. We did OK, although there was an anxious moment when only three out of four recruits emerged at the end of a sprint: in the dark Jurgen from Amsterdam had tripped over a post in the ground.

We returned to the clearing and there was some Physical Training and Discipline, by which those in charge meant following orders exactly and not moving out of line when left for a few minutes.

Back at the HQ water was being boiled. My Hexamine stove boiled a small amount of water faster but I didn't get

MORE AND HARDER

any business offering coffee at exorbitant prices. We hadn't been searched so my packet of Mars bars was also useful.

There was some discussion in German and Dutch which seemed to be that the Berlin people were unhappy at being ordered around and the Dutch organisers suspected the Berliners' politics of being right-wing. The squads were rearranged with Ralf from Berlin in charge of the discipline squad (#1=Fred #2=Mark #3=Jeroen and #4 also from Holland), Rémy in charge of the not-so-disciplined squad.

Ralf took us on a tour of the forest, first marching then crawling. This was interesting in the dark. First I used my mini Maglight but I found I only needed quick flashes of it. Finally I stopped using it except when the forest was really thick. Ralf switched people around in the squad so that the #2 and #3 'inside' also had experience at the head and the end of the line. And he was strict with halting and replying with a smart 'Yes, Sir' although to my ear the Dutch never really put much aggression into shouting 'Yes, Sir'.

He halted us and asked if anyone knew which direction the HQ was. No one did. Then he asked for a light for his cigarette and asked if anyone had any water. He took a drink but didn't let us have any. He asked if there were any complaints. None.

Cigarette over, Ralf led us straight ahead, and the camp proved to be right there and he had us in a line again doing press-ups, first together then he pulled each one out of the line for individual instruction. We set off again and I realised I'd not put my torch back in its usual place when called up front to do PT. We searched the clearing but couldn't find it. Later on it fell out of my webbing – I had misplaced it or been set-up. However, for the rest of the evening I was now dependent on Sir's flickers of light up in front for the next run through the trees and PT at the clearing.

Some food was evidently ready – even out of doors, not having eaten properly since lunchtime, this soup/stew tasted disgusting, although I still finished my lot. The office in the tent gave us the honour of receiving our recruit-training booklets including our BSC numbers.

It was now past midnight and we formed up again into

two squads. Us in Skinhead Ralf's squad were given five minutes to escape into the forest and Rémy's squad would pursue us. Faces were blackened, helmets were camouflaged with bits of tree and we set off, crossing the paths and doubling back through the forest. Ralf selected a place, ordered two guys digging, two scavenging for branches.

A small position is built, three of us dug in, #4 roaming. #1, Fred, is laying on the ground; Ralf comes over to him and gets him licking his boots without moving the rest of his body then kicks him a bit. Leaving #1, Ralf comes over to me, lying in the hole #1 had dug, kicks dirt all over me and orders me to stay there and not to go to sleep. He goes to #3 and tells him to make his hole bigger. #3 says there are too many roots, and gets kicked for answering back. #4 is invisible.

Ralf takes #1 out of his position and away to me and #3's left and we don't see or hear any more. Then someone comes close by waving a torch about, no more than two metres from me. I stay put and don't jump him – he goes on further, searching this part of the forest. Twenty minutes later he is still searching this part of the wood and comes by again and although suspicious of my bush, goes past, but turns and gets the light on me. I challenge him and he turns out to be #4.

We get comfortable and talk about what to do next. I reckon that the searchers aren't going to find us – they've had over an hour and we've had no sign of them. #4's worried about what's happened to #1 with Ralf. I've heard no screams! #3 emerges from his hole. We agree to wait twenty minutes till 0230 hours then bug out. Someone has something other than water in his flask. We have an odd conversation. We know we are on the right path home because the cycle path and the horse path running side by side tell you which way you are proceeding along the track.

Back at the Camp HQ there is some nice food and the search group are all back. There is a difference of opinion about Ralf and #1, Fred. Me and Rémy go out to find them. I reckon they are lost – you can't have sex for that long out of doors.

We see a light on a track we haven't marched on so far.

Rémy challenges them with his whistle and by calling Fred. The reply doesn't sound familiar so we hide. In fact it is Ralf and Fred retracing their steps to reclaim Fred's shovel and also to see what happened to the rest of the patrol.

Now, after 0330, we get into our respective tents.

Sunday morning there was some food and we struck camp before the joggers, kids and horse-riders began to swarm. There was some horseplay and some photography but we ended up back at the vehicles. Some people returned to Tilburg and, still wearing uniform, we went into a bar for some beer, to the surprise (and financial delight) of the patron.

Running Steve to Southfields

November 1992

The *Squaddie skinhead seeks mate for tough training* advert that I placed in the UK gay papers while I was in the USA has come up with Steve from Brighton; he is the same age as me but has spent much of his late twenties in one of the UK reserve infantry regiments and is something of a tough nut.

First time he came round here we did some weight-training me bossed him about mostly because he hadn't been pushing iron recently. He'd had his appendix out nine months ago and is just getting back into form.

His thing is military PT and training, even more seriously than me. He turns out to be the only other person apart from RMR-Togie and myself whom I've found to be interested in Légion Étrangère combat uniform, commando training, etc.

Steve's read the usual Légion books and has a set of their lizard pattern combat uniform; that's the pattern the hardhead continue to wear even though it's ancient. He wants to get himself fit for a realistic sentence of *pelote*, a legendary Légion punishment, although neither of us is quite sure exactly what it consists of. He also has a video of Légion commando training, which shows plenty of the sort of unarmed combat attack techniques that are probably best not to try at home, kids! But also some PT and punishment scenes – my current favourite is press-ups from a standing position down to the ground and back up, into shallow sea ... Wearing combat uniform, shirt off, of course. Also pull-ups to the front fender of a jeep, body under the engine. And 50-kilo rucksack punishments: 50 kilos is bloody heavy – it's a danger to the rucksack, never mind the recruit!

After the PT at my place, I ran him across the Thames via Putney Bridge and up Putney Hill to Royal Marine Reserve Togie's at Southfields. Unfortunately for Steve, his out of condition state and his susceptibility to being verbally motivated

MORE AND HARDER

by me resulted in his arriving at Togie's in a jabbering wreck state. (I was most jealous – I want that to be done to me!)

So much of a jabbering wreck that when we left after ten minutes for the run back, only then did Steve realise Togie had called him an 'unfit Pongo' and Steve hadn't even noticed, let alone replied to such an inter-branch insult as regimental honour demands. Steve was furious with himself! Great!

Anyhow, Wednesday this week, after I had spent the day in my photographic darkroom printing the Brabant Camp photographs, I went down to Brighton on the train for the return trip to Steve's. This time we committed ourselves to an hour's training either way; he started on me first, again lightweights, boots, shirt off.

He got me well shagged with knuckle-down press-ups, sit-ups, and then started on rifle drill – he has a plastic toy rifle but it felt like it weighed a ton. And also a medicine ball for catching, taking on the stomach, etc. He also has a light barbell to keep above the head whilst receiving punishment on the shoulders. And some nasty (South American?) torture position lying on the back, and head, legs spread, arms outstretched in the air. Nasty and quickly vicious.

I reckoned the way to get him to feel things was to do aerobic exercises. He'd blitzed me with anaerobic take-a-position-and-hold exercises that are my current weak spot. I got my own back with as much cruelty as I could muster so that he was, like me, unable to hold a coffee mug steady when we finally stopped. I corpsed him with catching the medicine ball, raising it above his head, chucking it back at me, whereupon I would throw it back at him full-force so he got it in the stomach. With that, and others, the strap on the shoulders got the adrenalin going and one sort of pain obscured the other, training further.

Next time: More and Harder. We each reckon we've at last found someone working the same masochistic seam. I wish I had his stubbornness and he wants my strength. He's very into shoulders-and-back CP and wants to take a bull-whipping someday, but in a military context, not a gay SM context.

Lake District in the Snow

December 1992

Steve (stubborn ex-infantry mate) and I had a great weekend in the Lake District. We drove up, camped in the frost at an organised camp site, warmed up in a climbers' pub. Woke up next day to a frost-stiff fly-sheet and frozen condensation inside the tent.

Having started up snow-topped Helvellyn (mountain) with the intention (borne out by 20kg of equipment each Bergan) to camp overnight at a high tarn (lake), we were turned back by high winds and drifting snow on the ridges at about 750m. We booked into a bed and breakfast hotel after icy rain and gale-force winds started even down at lakeside altitude. Fairly mad but not totally? It's amazing how rough the weather is there even at such comparatively low altitudes. The *alpinistes* never believe this.

On the Sunday we had another hike up high, not loaded with overnight camping gear, and enjoyed watching the clouds lift to reveal the mountain tops and high moors. I got Steve doing some shirt-off soldier-PT with rocks held out at arms' length, and doing press-ups with a big rock across his shoulders like on the photo RMR-Togie took of me in Pennsylvania.

Steve and I have been doing 'toughening up' PT on each other, soldier exercises with a leather strap to improve and maintain motivation, usually applied across the shoulders. He does a good line in verbal motivation along the lines of 'Take it – it's only pain'. I get him holding the rifle above his head while I work on his shoulders: 'Let the rifle down and you're out.' The plastic rifle's now laden up to 7 pounds for reality's sake.

We're getting on well together – the Lake District trip was good both because we didn't stop on the hill-climbs but also because I think we each recognised that, although we're each fairly intense and determined at what we do and what we get out of it, we do have a sense of what is too dangerous.

However, on driving back down south he was asking about the POW interrogation techniques that I learnt principally from Ian. Steve put his head into the noose yet again, asking to sample the delights of my cellar at home. A facility which I set up before I realised that I don't like being tied up in my own house, so it has only rarely been used. The previous time was a year ago when a visiting Californian from Laguna Beach inveigled me securely into my own sling and rape-fucked me (safely) very hard, very long and very smile-on-face-for-a-week afterwards!

Steve fell for all the old tricks. He'd never had a pair of handcuffs on so I gave him the key to some size three 'old pattern' Hiatt Darbies round his neck on a thong for confidence. When they were on, I asked if he could get out of them, showed him the position, and he slipped his hand out, silly boy! Out with the slap-on cuffs . . .

Ditto, he'd not experienced a leather hood before so he got a single-skinned one with a nose-piece but no eye-holes.

Access to my cellar is down a cramped ladder made from scaffolding pole. I didn't know Steve can be scared of heights . . . so that was also good for his apprehension. By the time he was on the ground down there, he was shaking good and proper. I haven't previously had the privilege of such a hard case with so little experience before . . .

This was a time-limited exercise so I had to do the quick ones not the long slow ones: hoist clip to cuffs, rope between legs, pull – hands go between legs and try to go up the back. He still can't work out the topology even now, which is great . . .

'Parrot perch' – stick through elbows and knees. Then tip him on his side for a kicking and some of the strap on the shoulders – he won't take it on the bum yet – I reckon I got to get him so sore on the shoulders that he pleads for it on the bum. The equation in his head is shoulders=soldier=man, bum=school=kids and he's a man. That gave me the opportunity to leg-iron him with a leg-iron/spreader bar and to get the slap-ons off before too much damage or marks occurred.

Final exercise was spread-eagled stretched tight, face

against a brick wall, still combat trousers, boots, shirt off. The restraints I have for this are lockable ones and transferring him was a secure operation. He wasn't resisting anyhow.

He wanted to taste the cat – and did. He is usually proud that he neither moves nor makes a sound when hit, but he had to be reminded to shut up.

And I got him mentally attuned to an interrogation fantasy, then used the cat on him a bit, and then asked which door of the car he'd unlocked first. He replied 'The driver's door' unhesitatingly! I reminded him that 'I cannot answer that question' is the only authorised UK reply other than Name-Rank-Number. Steve literally banged his head against the bricks in frustration at his failure.

Getting which door he unlocked second out of him was more difficult – he was prepared to endure the cat but no one had told him that position is also ideal for tickling. He lied, deliberately giving the wrong door, but I pointed out to him this was useless in a three-door car and let him down with the line 'You're a stubborn bastard, Steve, but I think I've made my point.'

Even then I didn't let him see the cellar, taking him instead exactly back to where I got him to put the hood on himself.

It's paid off – he's agog as to what exactly is in the cellar, wants more, and *best of all*, he's got more vicious with me.

For PT I've been running five miles to Mr H, a PTI near Victoria station – this entails a run along the Embankment which is fun because the squads run there also and there's a good, unspoken camaraderie to tune in to.

I think this guy is either an acrobat or a wrestler coach. He's getting me breathing and standing differently – chin up, chest out, stomach in. He tests it with the occasional full-force punch to the gut . . . and he's got me doing loads of variegated sit-ups, legs over the head, etc., using a belt and a heavy stick for motivation.

RMR-Togie has been getting me in his kickboxing hydraulic leg spreader machine. Dunno why, but that position with legs at 140 degrees apart is an almost guaranteed cock hardener as well as a different sort of screaming-cringing-agony.

Potential Brig-Rat

December 1992

Sir,

Thank you for another detailed and arousing letter, Sir, which caused severe jack-off cramp on Monday night after work. I'd done a heavy workout including lots of curls. So please picture your potential brig-rat somewhat bleary-eyed, letter in one hand, cock and balls out through the button flies in the other, coffee brewing in the kitchen with severe cramp in the right bicep straining to jack off but finding fatigue and cramp delaying the climax frustratingly. Intrigued and jealous of prisoner Jean-Pierre's training, wondering what Herr Kommandant used to peak him; was it the stock prod or tickling or simple threats cunningly conveyed? And was the result of getting him ejaculated further truculence or resigned acceptance of the inevitability and immutability of his prisoner status and subservience to Herr Kommandant? And what was the alternative to his forced march/run that made him prefer the latter so much?

And he flew home plugged, which suggests that he spent his prison-time plugged when not being irrigated or fucked or impaled. The impaled position of bondage has always been of interest. I believe it can be done reasonably safely but securely so that the prisoner is able to support his own weight on his feet but is unable to raise himself enough to get the impaling dildo or rod from out of his arse. In a hot climate like Florida, a regular soaking by a fire-hose would wash off the sweat and insects ... and frequent administration of drinks of water would promote a humiliating flow of piss.

Your correspondent did jack off yesterday on receipt of your letter, Sir. In fact three times during the course of the rest of the day, Sir. However, for today and tomorrow he has to abstain as he is booked to appear at Leighton Buzzard railway station (about an hour out of Euston) on Friday at noon for aggravated PT and a workout.

Orders are to travel wearing the minimum clothing: trainers, no socks, track-suit trousers (no jock) and sweat-shirt top. Rucksack to contain gym-belt, buttplug and lube, enema kit. It will also contain a Mars bar, but I'll eat that before leaving the train.

I believe (hope) there will be a physical inspection, then a cross-country run shorts and trainers only – daytime temperatures are around 40 degrees F here – and then gym workout in his garage gym which he says has the equipment salvaged from a bankrupt gym that he used to be involved with. Apparently he has a stable of several trainees and a house-boy who helps him maintain discipline, as well as a friendly relationship with a local farmer who facilitates horse and pony games: 'equine sports' – buggy pulling and rickshaw races, etc. The near-naked running will be on this guy's land apparently. He also has a 'trim-trail' laid out round the property, which I understand to mean a running course with workout stations at intervals. Assault course but very much not so severe. To quote from his initial letter:

Warning:
(a) Minimum training session time four hours.
(b) Fortnightly endurance tests (compulsory) last between 8 and 24 hours, plus bimonthly between 36 and 48 hours.

Preparations for (a) and (b) vary between 20 and 90 minutes, including enema and cold showers given by houseboy.
(c) All training sessions and endurance trials are concluded by a correction period which can be up to several hours. The following visit cannot take place without a reminder at its commencement of what took place during the previous correction period. This is to ensure that errors are properly corrected and mistakes are not repeated.
(d) You will be closely shadowed by me and/or my houseboy during training sessions for immediate (and

then, later, further) punishment – we always carry several CP tools with us. If my houseboy misses an opportunity for punishment in my view, then he gets it, so he doesn't miss much.

Now I hope that this will all happen and that it is not only a fertile imagination on my and his part. I am sceptical because he claims a stable of four others aged in their twenties and, in my experience, few men are conscious of being into such regimes that age, except those who are doing it in the Armed Forces who usually are as unaware of their underlying motivation as they are committed to their machismo and masochism.

And, although three dates have been arranged so far, there have been plausible reasons for cancellation: you would be amused I think by the most recent which was the day after some very heavy rain: 'The canal is in danger of overflowing and we have moved all the household valuables to the upper floor of the house.' Actually it suited me to cancel that time because of a regrettable incident the previous weekend . . .

You will be aware of the 'Operation Spanner' convictions and jail sentences handed out to gay men who were convicted on charges of assault occasioned by consensual and non-hospitalised heavy SM. There was a demonstration ten days ago when an estimated 700 men and women marched in protest. It was amazing that it was so well attended and reported in the press and on television.

After the demo and speeches there was a disco, profits going to the campaign, under the railway arches near London Bridge station. I cycled there, this time wearing combat trousers, boots and genuine army PTI shirt (that none of the gays recognised for what it is . . .) and after enjoying the disco (as much as I ever do, smoky, crowded and noisy places, although I now always wear earplugs to protect my hearing), I cycled the six or seven miles home in fairly heavy rain. Cycling on the pavement along the Thames Embankment and in the dark and with the rain on my glasses, I ran straight into an iron bollard, which stopped me dead.

Shaken, I found all the bits of me still worked although

my left knee (already the dodgy one) had taken the force of the impact. I was hobbling all the next day and taking it easy for the rest of the week.

However, cycling over to RMR-Togie, he scored a lot of points against me by noticing that the crossbar of the frame now has a five-degree dogleg in it. I'd been wondering why the front wheel had to be steered not in line with the frame to go straight ahead. Togie was cock-a-hoop that my free and often-faster than him in his car transport is kaput . . .

I have made a dastardly little box with some electronics in it and a photocell. So long as a torch shines on its photocell, it remains quiet. If the light is interrupted, a bleep sounds. This can be used for the endpoint in PT – ensuring that press-ups go all the way down, or to control rifle drill exercises: if the weapon drops the light beam is interrupted and the alarm sounds. Yet to be tested in anger – another product of RMR-Togie's fetid imagination . . .

respectfully in training
and
ready to sweat
potential brig-rat 24207516 salutes you, SIR

Canal-Towpath Running

December 1992

When I arrived at Leighton Buzzard railway station the outing became a disaster – the gym had apparently been destroyed by fire the previous day; however, he did take me in his car to a canal towpath, had me strip to army boots, socks and a pair of no-jock Adidas football shorts that really were the minimum necessary for decency in a public place. It was misty but not actually raining, and I was ordered to run along the canal towpath and he would be waiting for me two bridges further along. Fine, nice and muddy and I was careful not to slip into the dirty canal water. Two bridges along – maybe 4 kilometres – he was nowhere to be seen. I had been suspicious all along but he'd always appeared trustworthy, but I was very quickly thinking about how long it would take him to drive to London and break into my house or to use my credit cards to the limit. And more immediately, what do you do in rural England dressed in boots and nearly indecent shorts, eighty kilometres from home with no wallet or keys . . .

It turned out OK – he was 'merely' incompetent and was waiting at the *third* bridge along, but this made the whole situation impossible and I had to get back to the station as soon as possible. I was amazed actually how helpful the two people I approached were – one offered to lend me a sweat-top and the other knew the canal route well enough to advise me that the third bridge was more likely for a rendezvous because it is a road bridge: the second bridge was for farm animals only.

Hard-steel Gift from Otto

Christmas 1992

Internet e-mail to an auto-erotic bondage contact, 4.30 a.m.

Hi mate,
I'm writing this frustrated.

I locked on myself the stainless steel chastity globe yesterday and posted the key first class to my own address, so at this moment I am wearing a tight cockring, enclosed by the stainless steel globe, I can't jack off and I dearly want to. It's not really even been possible to have a good piss to let the hard-on down a bit and it's getting painful where the cockring is tight round my cock and bollocks. But I'm stuck … hopefully Royal Mail and the postman won't let me down but there does exist a 1 in 20 chance that the packet won't make it today. I'm not working today so lack of sleep and potentially going around with this thing on won't matter but it could be a problem tomorrow. I don't want to go on too much about my own pains but it's a sort of relief. I woke up trying to pull the globe off, which just makes it ache more – and I get no sensation at all from my cock inside, except the pain of confinement in unrelenting steel … I can't move my cock to thrust it around to get some 'relief', even pushing (you know the muscle you clench deep inside) just makes it hurt.

All the other erotic areas are more sensitised – buttocks, tits, guiche area, hair around the cock but not inside the globe. Pissing gave me some relief but I didn't piss much and the cockring I have inside just makes it difficult for the hard-on to disappear again. Lying on the bed it's difficult to decide whether to lie face down, which is good because the weight of the metal package is supported but bad because it's a reminder of shagging, which I can't do just now, or lying on my side – most comfortable for the body but most painful for the cock because of the way that the steel package pulls on the cock, or on my back, which is almost impossible because of the weight of the steel package. So I've been tossing and turning . . .

9.30 a.m.

The key arrived. My hard-on never went down since I awoke with it and the pain of long-term engorgement just got worse, driving me almost frantic like a crazed animal. The more I wanted to relax off arousal the less I was able to do it. After I went back to bed after writing the above I caught myself manipulating the outside of the globe, trying to masturbate unsuccessfully, simply reminding my hands and the thinking part of my head that had disowned the rutting-animal side that, yes, my cock and balls were still encased in steel and no, I couldn't do anything about it.

I tore the key out of the package in a controlled but desperate way and released myself from the stainless steel globe. The cockring was still stuck hard and fast round my cock and balls. The whole area was dowsed in clear pre-come and although I felt considerable relief from the pressure of enclosure, I was still suffering from the constriction of the cockring and approximately six hours of constant engorgement. Serious masturbation followed with the longed-for relief as expected . . . The hard-on persisted and I wrung another charge out before my sore cock finally allowed the constricting cockring off.

Military Training

January 1993

Suggestions for Playpen's next Gay Soldiers' Camp offered in appreciation of the event of October 1992 by #921031067

Recruits receive *Joining Instructions* to report to a remote railway station wearing minimum civilian street clothes: jeans, sweatshirt, trainers. No underwear, no socks, no cap, no gloves. Transport is provided to the Training camp.

Induction processing consists of checking street clothes to safekeeping for the duration of the Training Camp, keeping only PT and combat uniform kit and boots. Recruits strip naked in front of uniformed staff, a previous-service questionnaire is administered humiliatingly by the Staff asking questions aggressively and writing down the Recruit's replies.

Next to *Medical Examination* where naked Recruits are medically investigated (including testicle check and rectal dilation test) and then inspected for cleanliness, measured (height/weight/clothing sizes) head hair cropped to #1, body hair including cock balls arse hair shaved completely away. And a big one-litre enema, then a cold shower. Recruit's number written in large letters across the chest by marker pen.

Still naked, Recruits next ordered to arrange bed-space and locker for their first *Strip Kit Inspection*. This means the Recruits stand naked 'At Attention' with all kit neatly laid out or squared off in a pile whilst the Inspecting Officer checks every Recruit. Any errors, untidiness or lack of cleanliness result in immediate punishment and the Officer throwing the whole of the Recruit's kit on the floor. Further Strip Kit Inspections are held during the Training Camp. The discomfort of the Recruits is enhanced in the winter as the sleeping barracks are not heated and the floor is cold to the feet but

MORE AND HARDER

Recruits must stand rigid, soles flat on the ground 'At Attention'.

Recruits are permitted to dress in singlet, no-jock shorts and running shoes for *Physical Training* (PT). After an exhausting 'warm up' for the Recruits there is a Physical Readiness Test as used by the US Army – how many press-ups in two minutes, how many sit-ups in two minutes, how long for a two-mile run. There are punishments of extra PT for those that are below the standards laid down in the training manuals. And extra exercises for the super-fit to encourage them and to make sure that they are also tired out for the following Training. The standard punishment is to run-on-the-spot eating a packet of dry Army hard-tack biscuits without water. The running-on-the-spot continues until the biscuits are consumed and the Recruit's mouth will be as dry as a monk's sandal.

Marching Drill: by the end of the Camp each Recruit will be part of a squad that can march together in step as a Unit. Those who persistently march out of step or keep going when required to halt are relentlessly censured by the Staff and made to perform additional Remedial Drill after the other Recruits have been dismissed.

Punishment Drill includes being ordered to march on the spot facing and just in front of a brick wall; any movement forward and the shine is immediately destroyed on toecaps of the Recruit's parade boots.

Rifle Drill: this means holding a Rifle smartly in various positions which are not related to firing the Weapon but are designed to place physical stress on the Recruit and test discipline. Examples are both arms straight out to the front holding the Weapon horizontally at arms' length (this is called *le planton* in the Légion Étrangère) or holding the Weapon vertically in one hand again at arms' length to the front. Advanced Rifle Drill includes moving the Weapon smartly from one position to another, in time and to Command.

Eating, etc. as required. Officers separate from Recruits.

Punishments part administered at the time of the infraction, part accumulated for a Final Punishment Parade as the last thing before the end of the Camp. On *Punishment Parade*, the offender wearing Punishment Uniform is marched out front, bent over and held down by two Corporals or Sergeants for Corporal Punishment.

Poor uniform turnout increases the punishment – *Punishment Uniform* is made from particularly thin cotton material, shorts and shirt with lanyard and badges as usual. It must be ironed and the creases exactly right. The meticulous preparation of the Punishment Uniform is part of the Punishment because the Recruit is no longer wearing the same Uniform as the other Recruits so he is marked out as being in disgrace; the Punishment Uniform is thinner so he is more vulnerable and it is more difficult to keep it looking smart so he is more likely to be punished additionally for not being sufficiently smart.

Other Training Camp events are of a physical challenge nature:

Construct an *Assault Course* and run competitions over it either individually, paired off or in teams of four. Winners get to give the losers punishments of the winners' choice – examples would be press-ups, corporal punishments, cold showers or whatever the winners or the Sergeants decide.

Tug of War: Two teams pull in opposite directions on a rope. Conventionally they hold the rope with their hands, but it is also possible for each team to be yoked by their testicles or their tits. The Staff use cat-o'-nine-tails encouragement on the competitors' shoulders.

Military Crawls: Bunny Hopping and Leopard Crawl are well known but not easy ways to move across rough territory whilst maintaining a minimum profile. The traditional correction for a bum that is too high in the air is a good kick from the Staff's boot.

The Recruits can alternatively be blindfolded and formed into a circle on all fours, doggy fashion, nose in the arse crack of the Recruit in front. The Staff encourage the Recruits to crawl faster and faster, the Recruits must keep their noses pressed firmly in the arse of the Recruit in front or else the chain breaks with resultant Punishment for the defaulter.

MORE AND HARDER

Water Bottle Drinking: First to finish one litre. Some of the bottles are unexpectedly contaminated with piss or salt.

Pissing Competition: Winner produces the largest volume or pisses the furthest distance.

Running: With weighted webbing or rucksack or Bergan and/or respirator.

Respirator Drills: For one hour or more a gas attack is expected and NBC (Nuclear/Biological/Chemical protection) kit is worn. Training continues.

Press-up Race: First to 50 or 75 or 100. Also sit-ups or pull-ups. Failure to complete the set number is punished with the award of Corporal Punishment of the deficit number of repetitions.

Wheelbarrow Race: Requires soldiers in pairs, one stands upright and the other propels them both forward by 'walking' on his hands. Even more arduous on soft sand rather than grass.

Handcuffs Front-to-back Race: Recruits cuffed with hands behind back. First to get the hands round to the front wins. Last gets awarded a period of the American West Point Military Academy Plebe's Rest. The recruit has to stand on one foot, raises the other leg so that he can rest his elbow on the raised knee, and rest his chin on the hand supported by the raised knee.

Buddy Guiding: Like radio guidance. In pairs, one soldier is blindfolded and naked, the other has to guide him by calling 'left', 'right', 'straight ahead' round a mini obstacle course which of course will be wet and muddy with prickly bushes and stinging nettles.

Fire Building: First to boil a can of water using one match only. This race can be made more urgent as the Recruits will have not been fed or watered before the event.

Bulled Boots Inspections: The Recruit to have the best mirror-shined boots is the winner. The wearer of the worst shined boots gets the traditional British Initiation of being Black-Balled – the Recruit is pinned down whilst black boot polish is rubbed into his cock, balls and arse-hole.

Guard Duty: Not moving. This is organised as a team event. The Teams take turns to be the Guards and the Provokers. The Guards must not move and the Provoking Team must not touch the Guards. A valid provocation would be to make as if to punch the Guard but to stop the fist just before making contact. The Guards win if they remain motionless for the set time period – two minutes.

Sentry Duty: A variation of Grandmother's Footsteps. The object is to attack the Sentry from behind who must look straight ahead all the time. If he thinks he is being attacked he blows a whistle – if the attacker is judged by the Staff to be moving at that point, the attacker is dead and out; if the Sentry has blown falsely, he is dead. And if the attackers touch the Sentry, he's also dead.

Stun Gun Resistance: How many stun-gun zaps on the buttocks, standing At Attention, can the Recruit take before the hands move? The current Champion gets to administer the jolts to the next contestants.

Ball (testicles) Weight-Lifting Competition: Filled water bottles can be used as weights.

Non-Physical Competitions: Carrot and Stick motivation and the same principles as strip poker apply: for each mistake, clothes are removed and when there are no more clothes, the Recruit gets CP as well.

Number Recall: Either in own language or a foreign one, a multi-digit number is read out and the Recruit has to repeat it.

Naming Ranks: In seniority order in another country's army.

Phonetic Alphabet: Learning and recall in various languages and forward, backwards and every other letter: Zulu Yankee X-Ray Whisky Victor Uniform Tango . . .

Turn in to bed except for: 2 a.m. or 3 a.m. – *Night Exercise*. Running, or direction finding, or 'attacking' the Officers' quarters.

Early morning *Reveille* and *Strip Kit Inspection*. At this or any Inspection, Recruits standing 'At Attention' must stand completely rigid except that showing a stiff cock is a severe disciplinary offence and results in immediate punishment of standing 'At Attention' for two minutes under a cold shower outside.

More Physical Training (PT) and running. More Marching and Rifle Drill and then an hour or more in NBC kit

Final Parade and *Punishment Parade*. All the accumulated offences are punished in front of the entire Training Camp. Recruits accept their Punishment without showing any signs of pain and then thank the Punishment Officer for his effort in helping them to reform themselves and achieve proper motivation.

Final Parade also includes *Jack-Off Duty* in which recruits are ordered to strip to boots (no socks), and cap only and stand 'At Attention' for inspection. They submit to a tight cock-ring and grab their ankles to receive lubrication and a buttplug. The order 'Attention' is given again and it is explained that the recruits are to masturbate into a condom with one hand whilst the rest of their body (including the other hand) remains in the correct position of 'Attention'. The Staff enforce this with a cane or sticks giving sufficiently stinging cuts to remind the recruit of his lowly status but not so hard as to preclude a successful conclusion. The recruits must of course ask permission to ejaculate and then successfully ejaculate immediately or risk punishment or simply have their jack-off duty terminated without relief.

March-off parade, end of exercise, clean up and get out.

Obedience Training and a Living Sculpture

March 93

I met Sticks, the editor of *Nozzer, the magazine for real men*, Friday night ten days ago in a park for some discipline, obedience training and PT workout.

He got me stripped down to boots and rugger shorts, the rest of my kit in my pack – you'll remember the previous escapade where I ended up separated from my pack, running along a canal towpath, boots and shorts only, and the guy wasn't at the rendezvous. I *do* learn!

Anyhow, he had what he said was a Borstal Cane and Strap and we did quite a good session – running, mud press-ups, sit-ups, obeying orders at the double, arse-hole inspection for drugs, etc. Until I noticed a torch light coming straight towards us through the branches of the bushes.

We scarpered and left the place by an alternative route.

Next day, now striped across the arse by his original, thick, genuine and warranted authentic Borstal Cane I was on the train once more to The Fox in Liverpool. I got a cab to his place and was immediately sequestered from the other guests to his party and tightly enveloped in my double-skinned leather hood (no eyes or mouth holes and only two pinholes for breathing) and considerately handcuffed to a warm radiator.

Various abuses were perpetrated on 'the thing on the floor in the bedroom' whilst the guests were arriving or the other 'staff' took rest periods from preparing the rest of the household.

Finally, genitalia encased in the stainless steel sphere chastity device, boots-no-socks on the feet (I'm getting into that – much rougher than wearing socks and fine indoors) and still in the hood, I was led downstairs to be a display in the dining room: hands cuffed at my back, chest out, chin up, etc., legs in stocks keeping my legs spread.

The guests then arrived – I can't tell you much about their

reactions except that some came over to touch the goods; the hood precludes hearing much except for one's own breathing. During the meal I had been prepared to expect to be standing wearing webbing and a tin helmet but in fact I was attacked with shaving foam and razor, scrubbing brush, tit-clips and roped on the balls and tugged . . .

There was another 'display', who I never saw or had any contact with so that, along with the identities of more than half the guests, will remain a mystery . . .

After dinner, when I had now been hooded over four hours and similarly without food or drink, I was led into the drawing room – leather furniture and decor reminiscent of a rather tasteful Pall Mall Gentleman's Club – and placed on the floor. Various attacks were perpetrated on me: cock and balls now released from the stainless steel prison.

There was a certain amount of feeling like a 'stay in the ring' wrestling challenge – attacked from several quarters at once. I indicated that punching was far preferable to me than slapping and took some good heavy ones. In that hood it's difficult to judge the severity of a blow because you don't hear it and the feeling is actually a bit delayed. Once you get accustomed to the restricted sensation it's quite interesting . . .

Display time was over and I was taken off and dealt with relatively privately by someone. Who? And then appropriated or rescued by The Fox. I was then let loose around the house sampling the muffled sounds and smells of the various rooms over three floors. Tiring, I located The Fox again (or he located me) and the hood was removed.

After six hours it was a considerable mental jump to return to reality. Really one of the most severe mental dislocations I have experienced: firstly over a dozen strangers were around and I had been totally exposed and overtly humiliated in front of them all. That would have been more easy to cope with if I hadn't have also known that one or two of my friends (RMR-Togie and Mr N, the guy who had me running naked through the forest at night a year ago wearing white gloves and white socks/boots) were also there so I couldn't inconspicuously wimp out . . . The mental state was rather close to clinical paranoia; the impression that everyone was out to get me.

I lay down in a darkened room, shattered, then out of the house to a fish and chips shop for a bag of chips to eat walking along the street. I had the impression that other pedestrians were crossing the road to avoid me; high and tight short-cropped hair, Woodland Cammo trousers and a MA1 'bomber' jacket might have had something to do with it, and this is an area of Liverpool that was, until recently, relatively rough.

Back indoors, I found it hard to cope either with party kitchen-talk or with hard sex: I'd completed a six-hour scene that probably The Fox was the only person there who could understand. The origin of his idea of the human bondage displays was from when he was doing his National Service in London at the start of his career as a soldier at the time of the Coronation. He made cash on the side by nude-waiting at select parties and also by being a bondage sculpture entwined with another muscular man at receptions and parties.

However, next morning I got it together with a same-age guy similarly muscled and we had a good *sex* session with no equipment but a lot of pain from pressure points, ball squeezing, scissors and head-locks. He was well marked from a session over RMR-Togie's caning horse and another on Togie's ski boots equipment that is a fantasy of a punishment for the Soviets' Ski patrols.

Back on the train – kit in the washing machine!

Berlin, May 1993

Thursday

Met Berlin-Tegel airport by Haupt-Feldwebel Rüdelowski. He seems safe.

Travelled bus, S-bahn, U-bahn to the former East city dragging 20kg suitcase plus cameras in 27 degrees C sunshine. Lots of linden-tree pollen also.

From U-bahn to his house – must walk one pace behind to the right of Herr Haupt-Feldwebel. Much sweat.

Herr Haupt-Feldwebel has a flat on the sixth floor: no lift.

Inside, strip to shorts, glasses off, face the front door standing 'At attention' (*Achtung*).

Measured with tape.

Brought into next room which has wallpaper which is a realistic woodland photograph. Training rifle in hands to hold out front. Also heavy sea-bag for back. No movement allowed. Coffee machine noises from kitchen.

Tested OK, allowed down for coffee sitting on floor. Still '*Ja woll Herr Haupt-Feldwebel Rüdelowski*'. It's a tongue-twister; try to say it out loud yourself. He knew that and tortured me with that and other German language phrases.

Bathroom:

Strip, squat in bath. Cold-ish water applied which got progressively colder.

Stand in bath, face the wall, hands behind neck. Bum cheeks' hair shaved. The rest of body shaved (other positions).

Head cropped to USMC 'high and tight' crop with my permission.

Woodland Grotto (!):

Bundeswehr uniform was in the sea-bag: all of it, cold weather complete including boots, webbing, rucksack and tin hat. Put it on correctly. *Achtung*, stand for ages with another heavy rucksack whilst the training programme is explained. This house seems to have no shortage of heavy packs . . .

PT – check I could do what I said I could, which I could even after the journey and the rest.

Food – the *rekrut* serves Herr Haupt-Feldwebel at table. The dining room is a two-man table, two benches facing, built into a cupboard with military props all over the place. Including Légion stuff.

Herr Haupt-Feldwebel had ordered photos of previous training – showed those *mit Bier*.

Bed provided in the Woodland Grotto. Too soft (my choice) so other nights slept on the floor directly.

Given name-tags to tack over his own name-tags on Bundeswehr uniform. Intention is to wear 100 per cent correct BW (Bundeswehr, the West German army) uniform on the streets and in ordinary public places – restaurant, bar, etc.

Friday

0600 PT. Five laps of the square outside, 17 minutes.

Breakfast. White toast + cheese + ham + *wurst*.

Repack sea-bag. (Difficult). Put on full, correct combat uniform as a signals *rekrut*. (Yellow band on epaulette.)

Tote the sea-bag to the apartment of Feldwebel Stefan Vogel, said to be ten minutes' distant. Marching always behind and to the right. At five minutes, Herr Haupt-Feldwebel announces the halfway point. We pass a man who looked gay who says in German, 'Ah, the poor *rekrut*.' Other citizens just stare or get out of the way, lorry drivers allow us to cross the street, we pass town policeman no problem.

Mail postcard to Steve en route. It got wet with sweat in trouser pocket – sorry, Steve!

Twenty minutes later, the flat of Feldwebel Vogel turns out to be (even) smaller; the photos I had been sent did not do him justice: lot of pidgin German later I had established he was five years in an East German army (NVA) Jaeger regiment as a parachutist of 1009 jumps. Own-done high and tight crop, tattooed arms. Denies being an animal, which doesn't convince me; speaks no English: German and the obligatory minimum of Russian only. I suddenly find an urgent reason to improve my German, *schnell* (quick).

Also there is my *Kamerad-rekrut* Rheinhart. Herr Haupt-Feldwebel strips the Feldwebel insignia off Rheinhart's shoulders for the duration.

Kit is sorted out.

Leave for a meal in a local bar/restaurant. In full Bundeswehr uniform. I am assured that it is 100 per cent correct – I am not allowed a *rekrut* cap (*Mütze*) but must wear a Signals beret because I would not still be a *rekrut* at my age. I must not speak English if they are not secure about the situation.

Food + *Bier* OK. Feldwebel Vogel orders a second serving of the same dish. Do I provide him a gallery to play to?

Loaded kitbags into Rheinhart's car, which has karate stickers in the windows. Ordered to minimise boot noise on stairs – difficult.

Leave Berlin two in car, me + Feldwebel Vogel on his 250cc MZ. Traffic jams + imminent thunderstorm.

Forest near Prötzel – turn off on to track. Military training and discipline starts seriously. Kit up – webbing + rucksacks. Mine had been weighed previously at 33kg including camera and Bundeswehr ration pack.

Team photo, then set off into the forest. Rain starts in earnest.

Several stops, then camping place found. Taking off unfamiliar webbing is almost as confusing as rigging it. And making a Bundeswehr tent from canvas sheets was also a challenge.

No poles in the set I had been issued so used rope tight between trees: + five points.

Rain now serious. Dug drainage ditch round outer line of 'tent', then a few other holes for practice or possible fire pits. Feldwebels obviously in conference.

Marched off lightly loaded into the forest, eventually back at car – different route. Rheinhart's step is impossible to follow.

Back to walking-out kit – berets not tin hats. Practical sense prevails, we are off to the local restauration facilities.

After a good meal + *Bier* I want to march the 5km back but told there is a Bundeswehr barracks nearby and don't want to attract attention to ourselves. Filled water carriers from restaurant taps.

Tied to a tree surprisingly efficiently. Respirator put in place, some kicking, throttling and punching goes on then I'm left. Rain still coming down, tin hat keeps it off head but into neck – can't move anyhow.

Dunno how long – untied after not replying to the question 'Do you want to stay here all night?'

Saturday

Slept well and the 'tent' was actually waterproof – still raining when a whistle blows loudly outside and a boot connects with my feet in sleeping bag.

PT – three trips to the car and back along the track. Stripped my combat jacket, shirt and T-shirt off while running – completed it in BW-combat trousers, boots and tin hat. Great! Other *rekrut* did one circuit only.

Turning around and stamping type drill.

'Rat-pack' breakfast. Bundeswehr ration pack doesn't have many brews – four and only two whitener packets.

Tents secured, all my kit back in my rucksack, webbing and water bottle full up again also.

Marching around the forest: halting, running, anything sweat provoking. Running over piles of logs, climbing ladders up into game-shooting hides. But the weather was as unremittingly wet as the Feldwebel and Haupt-Feldwebel were relentless with the training.

We came to a halt near another huntsmen's hide and did some ABC drill (German for NBC, nuclear/biological/chemical); putting the respirator on in one go, no wrinkles, less than thirty seconds for the whole drill.

Then I was tied up against a tree, this time with my feet

not touching the ground . . . Left to escape – i.e. they ran to shelter from the rain in the hide.

Conference ensued – nobody had any rain gear and all were wet. The Feldwebels were using ABC suits as rain protection – I turned one down because carrying a fully loaded rucksack would just have produced the same wet-kit effect from extra sweat.

Result was – return to camp for lunch, unless the weather radically improved, strike camp late afternoon and return to Berlin.

Rheinhart and I ended up handcuffed together in a forest wooden hut – but we had my whole pack with us so tried to use the sewing kit needles to pick the locks – unsuccessful in the time.

Lunch was a cooperative affair, shackled shoulder to shoulder. Cute!

Knife combat training – I wasn't happy about this but it brought a gleam to Rheinhart's eyes.

Weather still inclement – packed up and returned to Berlin, and it rained harder.

Unpacked, kit in drying room.

Waiting to go out – Rheinhart and me each in old pattern iron fetters – Feldwebel Vogel gets a call on a radio walkie-talkie and does something with a revolver . . . Looked as if he was threatening us but it was about trespassers on the railway near his flat.

Out in civvies for food, *Bier* and German language practice.

Sunday

0700 PT. Six laps of the square outside, 22 minutes.

Breakfast, then back to Headquarters Two – the apartment of Feldwebel Vogel – *rekrut* waiting at table, etc.

Rheinhart leaves. In UK DPM kit + lightweights I am tied up, blindfolded with an NVA respirator with the eyes blacked out and enticed into a cage which is then secured shut. The Feldwebels left at 1130 and did not return until 1505. The cage is 2 feet square and 4 feet high: 10cm squares made by 16 gauge or so plated rods.

Parting words: 'Here's your lunch' – packet of rat pack 'Harteck' biscuits + water bottle. *Rekrut* reply: '*Bon appetit, Herr Feldwebel*' – nice thought but in French not German!

They return, make some photos and coffee but not for me.

In non-military mode, Feldwebel Stefan is then locked into the unused part of the cage above me and played with as an SM slave. Unfortunately I have to shout 'halt' as this results in my space being even more confined to impossibility for the time. Embarrassing for everyone.

To try and restore things I ask for twelve of the belt from Feldwebel Vogel's belt on the arse as demonstration. First of all he gets out his green webbing belt and I refuse to count 'one' and demand the leather Bundeswehr belt instead. Taken OK.

Relocate to 'Headquarters One'.

Feldwebel Vogel must work 0500 so early food + *Bier*.

Monday

0600 PT. Five laps of the square outside, 17 minutes.

Breakfast, etc.

On S-bahn to Grunewald in the former-West. Mountain troops' leather rucksack at 20kg.

Forest march. Herr Haupt-Feldwebel marches with me on the way there (10km) and takes the S-bahn, back, uphill.

Time outgoing 1 hr 45. Time back 1 hr 30. Result – time for chocolate cake in Eis-bar at the S-bahnhof.

Route passed a US rifle range – some firing heard and some US personnel seen. Germans reacted as though a Feldwebel was beasting a *rekrut* – no acknowledgement to the Haupt-Feldwebel, furtive nod to me.

Return to Headquarters One, freshen up, local army shop (Légion pattern camouflage PT shorts) then Headquarters Two for rifle drill on my own with Feldwebel Vogel. Rifle was a deactivated G-3 (*G-drei* in German).

Drill fuck-ups earn belt strokes – twenty. Counted in German and wrong counts send the count back to *eins*.

NVA songs and BW video during rifle holding out to the front positions.

Demonstration: *rekrut* + Feldwebel for Haupt-Feldwebel. Same rules for fuck-ups – belt + count in German. Sixteen.

Demonstration – belt on bare. Sixty on shoulders and bum, various.

Demonstration – bastinado – twenty, belt.

Explanation – of difference between training CP and punishment CP. Punishment CP is a due penalty but training CP is voluntary CP to make you tougher.

1800 hours – end of Bundeswehr day, Free time.

Food and then much *Bier* in Feldwebel Vogel's *Lokal* where he has told them he is in the Bundeswehr. I work for the British Forces Broadcasting Services making television training videos for soldiers . . . Sounded convincing and my pidgin German is sufficient for a boozy night out in German. Considerable progress.

Feldwebel Vogel draws an arrow through heart tattoo on my left forearm in blue ballpoint pen. I believe we understand each other.

Reluctant *auf Wiedersehen* and back to Headquarters One. More *Bier*.

Tuesday

0630 start – No PT.
Packing.
Final *auf Wiedersehen* at Berlin-Tegel airport.

Gay-Soldaten Köln Uniform-Wochenede

May 1993

Hair newly cropped Number One, we left Steve's place in Brighton Friday 0655 en route for Dover.

Delayed by the Channel Tunnel roadworks, we abandoned thoughts of catching the ferry we were booked on and ended up on the next crossing. Ursus (Steve's military teddy bear) seemed to enjoy his first sea crossing and was eagerly anticipating the prospect of buying VAT-free, high quality chocolate in Belgium. Ursus is a noted chocoholic – when he's around the chocolate seems to disappear – of course it could be Steve but so far there is no evidence.

Finally arriving in Cologne, I located the gay bar and Walter was already there. We changed – me to British lightweights, DPM jacket, sleeves rolled up, no shirt and tight webbing belt. Steve was *de la Légion* in lizard pattern DPM shirt and trousers, complete with a couple of badges and brass-tipped red *fourragère* (lanyard) correctly arranged for walking-out. Neither of us were wearing any socks, for toughness.

The bar wasn't that full and I think there were only just over a dozen listening when Walter made his speech about arrangements for the next night. We helped Walter fetch some camouflage nets from the disco to the bar – this meant four of us walking on the streets in Cologne in uniform but there was no problem. But apparently until about ten years ago it was illegal to appear in public in Légion uniform because it was associated with Nazis when so many SS joined it after World War II.

Michael from Hamburg (but he's working in Bavaria just now) arrived, his face familiar from the mauling he gave me at the 'Playpen' weekend in February.

Steve was in his second gay bar ever and his first foreign

gay bar as well as having driven his car on their side of the road for the first time and a long list of other 'firsts'.

Steve was soon circulating in his own orbit – leaving me free to set him up for the next night's drill training as a tough-nut soldier.

We left the bar, crashed out on a friendly floor and tried to stay asleep until a decent hour next morning.

The afternoon we relaxed sunbathing until a thunderstorm brewed and finally broke about the time we left for a restaurant meal. Gloom and doom in case the whole thing was called off.

We left in convoy for the training ground, the sky flashing with lightning although the torrential rain had passed. We found ourselves parked and changing between an industrial estate and the woods bordering an autobahn. Steve was in Légion combats with water bottle and spade, I was in UK DPMs with webbing including sand-filled pouches. We don't remember seeing any of the Germans wearing webbing or water bottles . . .

We followed a line of night-light candles through the dripping woods – Steve was disgusted from the military reality viewpoint but it was practical and, actually, they had been placed so as not to be too obvious except on the assigned route. There were many cases of food and beer to hump from the cars to the barbecue site.

Finally everyone mustered – I counted 18 total which included 8 *rekruten*, and Michael said they had expected 28 total, 18 *rekruten*. But it was enough.

We *rekruten* were formed up in a line and a Haupt-Feldwebel introduced himself and two Feldwebels. Enough English was available either from the Feldwebels or up and down the line for us to stay with it.

The first order was to lower our trousers and to produce our condoms, lubricant and ID for checking. Two *rekruten* were detached and the rest of us kept waiting. They returned and another two detached, etc. This proved to be for medical examination which included cleaning off cock, balls and arse with beer, having one's arse-hole poked, balls held while you coughed, and questions asked about night vision and any other problems.

Torrential rain intervened as we were marching around and we huddled under trees which actually wasn't too bad for morale and team-spirit, although it must have been nerve-wracking for the Feldwebels.

The weather abated, again leaving the trees dripping and puddles and mud underfoot, and we were marched up and down, drilled on the spot and finally herded across the road into the dark unknown and much denser forest opposite.

A period of training ensued which I can't remember exactly but the result was that I was obeying the German commands as fast as (if not faster than) the others; we had been running through the trees, up and down slippery muddy inclines, across long grass, dropping to ground and running back, through muddy puddles and avoiding running through ponds. In order along the line, shortest to tallest. Left and right turns on the spot, etc. My obeying of the orders had become instinctive, ear to body directly without the brain interpreting. I can't recall the words at this moment, but have the impression I would know what to do if (when) a Feldwebel shouts at me again. Comparing experiences with Steve afterwards, we concluded this was pretty close to the position we would find ourselves in had we walked into the Gendarmerie at Calais and signed the papers to join the Légion Étrangère.

We *rekruten* were lined up front to back drawn up across a track for one particular exercise; cocks were ordered out and standing on legs wide apart. The front *rekrut* had to crawl on his back from front to back and take his place at the back, then the next one, and so on. When we did it, the view was very special but also we suddenly all found ourselves with itchy necks because the line had progressed backwards into a stand of stinging nettles. That was about the moment when we *rekruten* formed some real team spirit about the thing.

Some time later a relay race was organised along the same piece of track: two teams. What didn't come over very well in German was that the *winning* team got to take a punishment administered by the losers. I was running against Steve and he was in front of me. If you can't win fair, use your head, so I tried to trip him, fucked up and fell myself. That settled it – his team elected for him to take the victors' punishment, which was twenty from a German belt which I laid on him across the shoulders. He took it without moving *at all*. I think they were impressed.

In another part of the forest later on, we *rekruten* were again ordered to take our trousers right off, boots back on. The German *rekruten* were impressed by my modified UK DPM trousers that come off over boots. We were arranged for wrestling pairs – I drew Michael first who pinned me conclusively and secondly the skinhead, Jörg, who was always at the front of the line because he was the shortest. He beat me also, mainly by pinning me in a clump of nettles, which panicked me good and proper into submission . . . the stings are still noticeable now, thirty-six hours later.

Meanwhile, Steve had been selected for special treatment – in between wrestling I had seen him following the boots of Feldwebel Frank which seemed to be taking him round in figure of eight tours of puddles, nettles and rocky paths. Apparently he also had to use the shovel to dig a shell scrape hole to lie in, and also at some point ended up rolling about in a pond doing press-ups and other exercises to ensure his kit was thoroughly soaked all over both sides and with his head under water kept there by a Feldwebel's boot pressing down on his head.

By now we all had dry mouths (except Steve who had tasted the local water!) and I distributed some English water from my webbing water-bottle amongst the other *rekruten*. We marched back to the main site – I had by now 'lost it' through exhaustion and could not get my feet to march in time. We crossed the road slightly more to command than on the way out and I managed (closely followed by Steve, but no one else) a *Danke* to the Feldwebels after they dismissed us.

We rejoined those back at the barbecue and drank lots of water – I immediately demolished almost a complete bottle of mineral water and Steve and I between us finished a bar of plain chocolate before the *Würste* were ready. Ursus was in the car so had none on this occasion.

The weather had held off and really the thunderstorm had added to the atmospherics of the event, lightning in the skies and plenty of mud. The Feldwebels had known to keep us moving and it had worked out great, tremendous, fantastic. I hope we communicated our gratitude to our hosts who had obviously worked hard and planned effectively to ensure the event's success. One of the Feldwebels had translated the fantasy I had written around the time of the Playpen-organised Brabant Soldiers Camp; he must had understood that piece more intimately than anyone – it was great to meet him.

Steve and I humped the remaining vittles back to the cars (several trips), cleared up the rubbish and were escorted to a well-organised floor for the night, indoors and dry again, bedding down as the birds were singing and the sky well lightened by the dawn. Even meathead Steve noticed the birds so he must have been feeling good!

Sunday morning came on fast – breakfast and repacking for the long haul back to our Island. Steve's kit was intact, my DPM trousers had taken a tear from my fall and we each itched from the excursions into the nettles.

Berlin Military Training

August 1993

Herr Haupt-Feldwebel Rüdelowski met me at Tegel airport and we travelled to his flat near Friedrichschain – Headquarters One. He has been buying much Légion Étrangère equipment – and also been kindly passing the addresses of these suppliers to me. So he was in Légion combat uniform – the green, heavyweight F2 – and took me to the bathroom for a full shave. Head to a 2mm crop (#0) at the sides and 4mm (#1) on top. Chest and cock hair all shaved off. Ball-weight in place.

Feldwebel Stefan arrived having escaped from work early. German olive woven name-tags had arrived with my real name on them; sewed one on to the Bundeswehr combat jacket I was being lent. Also Signals (yellow) shoulder ring. The other two are as Fallschirmjäger (=Paras); Stefan was with the NVA Fallschirmjäger for five years and left as Feldwebel.

Slept on the floor in HQ1 as previously. Up 0600 Friday for PT: pull- and push-ups in HQ1. Did 10 10 8 pull-ups and 50 40 30 sit-ups.

Breakfast and cramming kit into sea-bags for travel in uniform on the S-bahn. On our return I weighed 75kg in uniform + boots, 99kg with pack no water or food and 68kg naked. The air temperature was getting to 34 degrees C midday.

We met Feldwebel Vogel on the S-bahn platform and enjoyed riding in uniform also waiting in uniform to change trains. We arrived at Falkenhagen and rerigged the kit for marching – Bundeswehr webbing, rucksack, etc. I ended up with a rucksack back and front; the front one had a metallic rattle and weighed a lot.

The footpath through the forest was way-marked in old German script, *Jugenherberge* (youth hostel) with signs that looked from the Hitlerjungend era; Herr Haupt-Feldwebel said that this terrain was used by the Russians for training until re-unification. About 5km onwards, over a road and through mixed forest, we turned off the tracks and a camping place was found. I put up my English poncho bivvi, they made their canvas Bundeswehr tents. I finished first so was hand and foot cuffed to a tree.

We broke into ration packs and had lunch. I began to be worried about water – I had only one small Bundeswehr water bottle, smaller than a British one. We were in circumstances where one needs the water more, at least until acclimatised.

Afterwards we went to explore the forest in patrol formation and halted at 'danger points'. The tracks are on a rectilinear grid so it's not too hard to navigate. Some crossings have dug-in control places, others have high lookout points like game-shooting hides. There was also a central command point with many dug-in cabins. It was a bit like exploring Iron Age tumuli and hill fort remains on Dartmoor: defensive mounds and underground chambers but all in the forest and flat. I was carrying the kit so sweating the most and the water situation wasn't too good . . .

We stopped by some stacked logs and did an hour or so of PT. Running over the logs, carrying them, wheelbarrow and piggyback racing. And straight running, me with pack, Feldwebel Vogel with no pack; when I got exhausted, he was pulling me along by the arms. It was good to get exhausted . . .

In a clearing we dug a shell scrape and buried Herr Haupt-Feldwebel in it up to his neck. Last year, somewhere else, Herr Feldwebel buried him in ABC kit, only the respirator above ground. This surprised me further as the mother of Herr Haupt-Feldwebel died between my previous visit in May and now.

My water situation was getting bad and almost out of *rekrut* character I had to insist on more water. They weren't using all their water and anyhow they were using larger water bottles so there was enough. We did some crawling and running and dropping to ground racing. I'm sure Herr Haupt-

Feldwebel was aiming to get me to drop into the thistles in the terrain!

We split and Herr Feldwebel took me back to the S-bahn station and we obtained water from the tap in the booking office – the *Fräulein* seemed to like the para-Feldwebel at least as much as I do!

Back at the camp, I made up a large isotonic drink – half a litre of ration pack grapefruit drink with a couple of sugars and all the salt in it and felt a lot better.

Evening meal, then tied to a tree and hit in various ways and left.

Night-time: it was surprising how much sound travelled through the forest. I could hear the S-bahn public address loudspeaker as well as the trains and cars, and the aircraft taking off from Tegel airport. When these quietened down the dogs and wolves could be heard barking and howling and once a deer walked through our camp.

Next morning I wasn't cold – they were: it can't have been colder than twelve degrees Centigrade! Breakfast, then packed up all the NVA ABC kit, marched off into the forest, put it all on – it's rubberised cloth – and went patrol-marching along the tracks again. I couldn't see well from inside the respirator and as ABC is more their thing than mine, they decided to put me in front doing the lookouts and calling them on when clear. I still managed to get my uniform underneath soaked through and to empty a mug full of sweat out of the ABC suit boots after over an hour of patrolling in this kit.

We dried out, did some punching training – not reacting to being hit, which got my self-respect back a bit after having being told not to do the whole patrol with the respirator on.

Then back to camp, clearing up and marching back to the S-bahn. On the return journey Herr Feldwebel Vogel and I were both dog-tired. I broke into the ration pack chocolate and dozed off, again getting hallucinations from it . . . We tried later to buy some but that make is specific for the ration packs.

We split and took the kit back to the respective HQs and met again at HQ2 – Herr Feldwebel Vogel's flat. In his kitchen (*Küche*) he has constructed a *Kerker* or maybe the word was

Klinker. Would I like to see it? Silly me said 'yes' and spent at least half an hour restrained in a dark cell.

Then we went out for dinner in a *Lokal*. I mentioned that walking from HQ1 I had seen two men drinking with tarts outside a bar, each wearing muscle singlets (one maroon, one green) revealing fleur-de-lys tattoos far into the centre of the back on their right shoulders. Légion Étrangère presumably – we went back for a second look but it seemed a bad idea to interrupt the chat-up in progress.

Sunday Herr Feldwebel Vogel worked an 'early' so he could have Monday off. This was convenient because Herr Haupt-Feldwebel took me to the *Flohmarkt* (flea-market). I caught a pair of NVA rigid-alloy handcuffs and a rubber riot truncheon.

Back at HQ2 we went out for Sunday afternoon chocolate cake and coffee.

Between chocolate cake and dinner Herr Feldwebel Vogel tried out the NVA handcuffs and truncheon that I had bought in the *Flohmarkt*. And his 30-inch leather thong cat. That was 394 + 173 + 40 + 17 strokes, 624 total, front, back, bum, backs of knees. Also much standing at attention and being poked with the rubber truncheon. He was more gentle with that, perhaps because it is a work tool for him and he must be careful with it. No marks but that doesn't mean that the training wasn't hard.

Monday was the best and most special day of all but it will take the fewest words to describe: Herr Haupt-Feldwebel dispatched me to HQ2 early; I shopped for cans of isotonic drink and fruit en route. HQ2 was informal – we changed into Bundeswehr uniform, packed cameras and other kit for a bike ride.

Thirty kilometres out of Berlin we passed a large army barracks with a prominent red star – Russian army. The other side of this town we headed off the road: this was Ruski panzer training ground. There was a railway siding full of vehicle (tank) carrying trucks and also the sort of cattle trucks that the NVA still used for troop movements. Over a railway track and set back by some pine woods there was a building looking like a UK polytechnic: a disused NVA barracks. And parallel to the railway line was the complete assault course, overgrown with grass but virtually intact except for the climbing ropes.

I can't really describe the day in detail – Herr Feldwebel took me over each jump, first showing me the correct movements; then I went over the obstacle once without timing to try it out, then a timed attempt. He knew times for Class 1 and Class 2. Worse than Class 2 was 'fail'. He then had me over each obstacle individually until I achieved a Class 1 time. Then we had a short rest and then he ran me over the whole course end to end. You run directly south, into the noon high sun. End to end took seven minutes and had me very much out of breath and my heart rate good and high – not many things have that effect on me except the rowing machine at home.

Lunch under a small oak tree was great. No sex – in the bar later he thanked me and said that this had not been necessary. I think we both had a curious feeling about the place, almost reverence. He, because this had been a standard NVA assault course and although he could still demonstrate the jumps, there must be many memories associated with this sort of place – he said he also trained here in ABC kit, in both winter and summer. For me there were echoes of past conscript *rekruten*: the mud under the 40cm high metal poles you crawled under and jumped over was corrugated by previous use like the steps up the inside of a church tower or monastery ambulatorium; those ripples got there the hard way.

The barbed-wire perimeter fence was in places constructed not to keep intruders out, as at a NATO camp, but to make it difficult for the conscripts inside to escape home. Later, exploring together the derelict barracks building, we realised that the single central staircase had locking cages at each landing, quite against Western notions of fire safety. We had a thought-provoking discussion about the difference between compulsory army service and gay fantasies.

The apple tree orchard was clearly visible on the far side of the railway line, tantalisingly out of reach of the sweating *rekruten* with their small NVA water bottles.

Demolition was clearly in progress elsewhere on the site.

We also explored the parade ground, the barracks building with ransacked library, gym with motivational cartoon characters on the wall, culture room with large windows looking down on to the parade ground and outdoor gym. It must have been bleak, locked into one floor at night, kept within one building and small training area. There was also a sauna and cold plunge pool, but the size of the facility must have meant it was for officers only.

Outside there was a pine copse, the ground between the trees disrupted by continual shell-scrape digging. Some barbed wire X defences and a complete set of shell scrapes and command dug-out were still intact – like elsewhere, when the place was abandoned, no one thought to put things straight before leaving. Finally, down at a far corner of the pine wood there were two ABC buildings, still smelling – we didn't go too close. And an electrified fence for training on.

The place had ghosts – Stefan said he would not go there at night. It was good to see, to photograph and to train on before it is demolished.

Back to Berlin, some coffee and cake, making a cassette of NVA Fallschirmjäger songs, and another meal and then further German language conversation practice, otherwise known as a drinking session in Herr Feldwebel Stefan's own *Lokal*.

Recruit Training at the Bunker

July 1993

RMR-Togie and I had long dreamed of a location where we could play sadomasochistic games in atmospheric surroundings without the constraints of domesticity. Many Americans we have visited have elaborate 'playrooms' set up for their leather SM interests and in Birkenhead there had once been an ancient coastal tower which was regularly cut-off by the tide, providing a secure venue for leather parties.

With the ending of the Cold War, the Home Office was starting to release further properties which had been commandeered around the time of World War II. Following an announcement in a farming newspaper, we successfully bid for one of these and became the owners of a genuine ex-military bunker.

Ordered to arrive Walthamstow Underground station 1030 hours wearing DPM combat kit and Crusader rucksack. Met as arranged by the Major, who was wearing Rank and Insignia as a Captain of the Parachute Regiment. He was annoyed that 'Goldfinger' surplus stores had not been able to supply him with Parachute Wings and Dispatchers Wings. Drive to the Bunker – he drives fast – we stopped at the usual roadside halt for a bacon roll and tea. Both of us were in uniform.

Walked from the usual lay-by to the bunker carrying Crusader weighing 27kg, also the Major's black leather kit bag. Very humid, my T-shirt satisfactorily marked with sweat as the Major didn't go any slower because I was carrying the load. Opened up, stripped to T-shirt order, kettle boiling whilst shown the property and installations.

After a brew, the Major had me learn the commands and positions associated with 'At Ease', 'Stand Easy' and 'Attention'. And moving from one to the other correctly. The difficult one was to move from 'Stand Easy' to 'At Ease' halfway through the command 'Squad A-shun'.

'Left-turn', 'right-turn', 'about-turn'. These proved difficult until I got it that you turn on the heel of the direction in which you're going to turn – right turn, right heel, etc. There was also some confusion between my head and my arms and legs because they had previously been most used to obeying German drill commands . . .

At various times the Major gave me a short time to change from combat kit (working dress) into PT kit. The quickest time achieved was just over five minutes and no amount of shouting managed to improve it. And I ripped a large hole in my combat trousers which left me feeling even more vulnerable around the cock and balls area.

He punished me in various places – arms outstretched on the canvas shelter tubular metal frame, at first on the top bar; subsequently he had me lie on the ground and grab the two uprights whilst he cuffed my hands to them, roped my boots together and yanked and tied them upwards, so I was spread-eagled on the floor, boots tied high above me.

The Major was using a black leather-covered Officer's Cane, lead-weighted, usually for use on horses. It was equally effective through PT shorts or combat trousers, its weight cutting through the material. His aim was always to the same point and by the end of the day the target area was well swollen and today is bruising colourfully.

His other punishments were physical – hit the ground and then do push-ups. Run around the circuit, and when that wasn't enough he ordered me to carry my Crusader, still heavy with kit. And halfway round he'd order an about-turn, and another and so on, so that the number of circuits prescribed actually turned out to be much further in total distance.

The next bit of Drill was then performed wearing the Crusader, etc.

The Major located two bricks and had me hold these out to the side, in front and above my head. Both standing still and then running the circuit holding the bricks in position. Obviously he used his cane as a go-faster encouragement when I passed him and these circuits were subject to the about-turn commands as well. The maximum he had me achieve was to run the circuit in combat kit, Crusader and holding the bricks above my head. The T-shirt was getting to show sweat on this.

When the local farming activity had subsided he had me marching up and down along the track outside the Bunker. This led to starting, halting, saluting, about turning. Finally we had got to a degree of proficiency on my part where it began to get to be fun when I got it almost right. Of course there was still quite enough to find fault with so the officer's cane did not stay under the Major's arm all the time.

The Major also explained three different sorts of British Rifle Drill but I'm sorry to report that these largely went in one of my ears and out of the other – or not in at all.

There were one or two respites for tea and cake. And my size of cake slices was commented upon. Steve will make a Para of me yet!

There were also one or two unsuccessful stunts – tying the bricks to a rope around my waist and having me run the circuit, the bricks jangling in my cock and balls. And also running the circuit dragging a weight tied to a rope around my balls – analogous, I guess, to the Guards' renowned trick of tying a rope from a soldier's balls to the leather loops at the top back of his boots underneath his trousers before going on Parade or Duty. Every 'Attention' stamp yanks the rope. The Major spent quite some time in the Guards as well as the Paras and also MCTC Colchester ... It is good to be in authoritative and authentic hands ...

The punishment record shows:

SLOWING AT BASIC DRILL AND PT: three hours including kicked round Parade Ground. Requires Additional toughening up: 50 + 50 Officer's Cane.

DRILL STILL NOT SATISFACTORY: Extra Drill, PT, toughening up. Required to use cane to remind him of his place. Required kicking. 20 + 20 + 20 + 20.

PT: SLOW AND TARDY; requires practice: required hands chaining to instil into him discipline 20 + 20 Cane.

REPORT: Requires more drill for longer period. PT should be doubled with extra weights.

Cotswolds Adventure Training

November 1993

I got on the train from Paddington and changed into full DPM combats and newly bulled boots in the toilet on the Sprinter after Swindon.

At the destination station in the Cotswolds, I looked out into the station car park but couldn't see any obvious army transport – heart sank. But there is a footbridge over the lines and Sergeant Blue was on the bridge in full kit, beret, cap badge and all. In the alternative car park was a very obvious army one-ton transport vehicle. This turned out to have carpet in the back and a filter coffee machine – the Officers' gin palace!

He drove me around the countryside a little, looking for a quiet spot. The four-wheel drive capabilities were great – and we eventually ended up at the side of a quiet road and I handed over the East German rigid handcuffs and key. He soon had me flat out on the floor in the back of the vehicle in search position. Crossing my legs and hands to maintain control he checked out the meat on the body and punched and kicked a bit. Then he introduced me to his Danner Matterhorn boots and I had a good lick. He commented on the good state of my DMS boots – I'd played a CD or two the previous day bulling them to a reasonable state.

Some more checking out involving various not particularly restful search and control positions and then he tied me spread-eagled to the floor of the transport, covered me with a ground sheet and some kit bags. The plan was to take me into the depot, park the vehicle and then a bit later 'some of the lads' would unload me on a stretcher and into the gym where they would check me out for PT. And I was to keep strictly quiet as we went through the MoD Police on the gate and also to keep quiet when the vehicle was on the park.

All seemed to go OK – I had a few minutes bricking it as

we went through the gate checks but no problems. Then all went quiet as he abandoned the vehicle and all I could hear were occasional drill commands 'Squad halt' etc. Some time elapsed – I was in a stable position so there was no great worry except working out a possible cover story in case I was discovered!

Someone got into the vehicle and drove it off rather more roughly than previously. I also heard 'bloody hell', exclaimed in a voice I didn't recognise. The vehicle evidently wasn't just reversing a little bit around the depot from the park stand to the gym as planned . . .

There was a period of travelling at some speed and also some tight corners, then the ride got rougher – you notice because you have to hold your head from being knocked to pieces on the bumps. At some point the kit bags fell on to me but with no particular result. And I had to 'pop' my ears, presumably due to gaining altitude.

The vehicle drew to a halt and a voice said, 'Well, Mike, it's your birthday – and your present's in the back under all the kit.' Some moving around and then a bit of an exclamation. 'You always said you wanted a Glo'ster to play with . . . He responds to "Mark" but you'll have to work out where he comes from . . .'

Mike was now evidently well surprised but pulled the ground sheet further back and revealed the whole of his 'present'. Sgt. Blue then said he'd better do the introductions – 'This is Mike, Cpl. Mike to you.' There were also some encouraging 'Try that bum – lots of muscle there' comments.

They then had a mug of coffee each and didn't offer me any. The weather was still chucking rain and wind at the canvas sides and roof of the vehicle and they asked me how much PT I was able to do. I replied with stories about taking my bricks and webbing for a run for The Fox on Southport beach on December 31st last year in a freezing gale, boots and shorts only, etc. Cpl. Mike apparently likes that sort of thing but hadn't brought the right kit!

They decided on a short excursion, me in PT kit with the webbing and bricks, them in full foul weather protection! I got a mug of coffee and a slice of cake.

We made it outside, me still with no glasses; not that that would have made much difference in the driving rain. We ran a few hundred yards and then gained the comparative shelter of the forest – with the disadvantage of the slippery leaves and the larger raindrops blown off the branches. Running downhill then uphill again, I was in the front, webbing rattling slightly and apparently steaming somewhat also.

At the top of an incline, Sgt. Blue asked me what was ahead – I replied that if we went straight on we would be back to the transport, the left was the route downwards that we had taken. Another brownie point for not getting disorientated.

We took the straight-on option and then lost the shelter of the trees, going off the road on to an exposed headland. The rain was turning to sleet and hail and they pointed a vague blur in the distance – one of those topographical markers that, on a clearer day, would point to the various landmarks. Out in the full blast of the weather we shared a Twix chocolate bar – and turned back.

Inside the shelter of the transport they stripped me off and gave me a thorough rubbing down and cracked open another thermos flask of coffee.

We got talking and somehow Cpl. Mike got to try on the East German handcuffs which was the cue for a bit of torture to happen on him – I wrestled him to the ground and, despite his failure to get where I had come from out of me, got the name and organisation details of the Scout Company he had belonged to previously. The secret was tickling. He finally agreed to do anything I demanded so he ended up doing twenty press-ups outside, wearing only my shorts. He was more worried about not doing the twenty than the weather . . . Sgt. Blue and I put helping boots on his shoulders and bum to ensure that he went fully down into the puddles each time.

Then it was my turn again – except that Cpl. Mike couldn't get the cuffs on me – and very nearly ended up cuffed himself. Sgt. Blue helped with a few well-placed bits of assistance. Then they tried to get my legs which also took a while. It was finally disappointing because even with my hands cuffed and held down and my legs attached to the roof of the vehicle they didn't manage to crack me with tickling although it was quite close and they had a jolly good attempt, several times!

Finally they saw me off at the railway station.

Recruit Training

May 1994

I travelled up to the bunker with Corporal Psycho on our bikes. Mr J was expected from Denmark arriving Gatwick 2020 and at the bunker around midnight 30. I had supplied him with detailed directions and maps by fax that morning and Cpl. Psycho had received Orders from him on the phone at my place in London before we set off.

Thus at 2300 I found myself in complete darkness, stripped off to boots and a searched overall, locked into the cell with the outer door shut. In the main room of the bunker my kit was laid out neatly for his Inspection – combat uniform and plenty of toys. The stainless steel globe was secured over my cock and balls precluding masturbation.

The phone went twice and I eventually heard the Cpl. Psycho escorting our guest down the access ladder. Cpl. Psycho had me 'Brace' against the back wall of the cell, informed me that the cell was in a disgusting mess and ran me out to the back wall of the main room of the bunker.

Mr J performed his inspection with me stripped naked. I don't remember the details but the procedure left me feeling mauled – and not a bit cold, as I had been standing barefoot on the floor. At one point he sent Cpl. Psycho out of the room and informed me of a code word which it would be his and Cpl. Psycho's intention to get out of me during the course of the weekend – there was a £10 bet between them as to who would get it out of me first.

I was returned to the cell and permitted my sleeping bag for the night and slept as well as can be expected in the circumstances.

Despite his journey Mr J was awake in good time next morning and accepted a mug of tea from Cpl. Psycho. Two cups of Cpl. Psycho's strong tea were administered to myself, hastening use of the piss bottle, a potentially messy procedure considering the cock and ball globe was still attached.

I was let out and told to change to PT kit – V-neck red T-shirt, army navy-blue rugger shorts and boots and socks. The chastity globe came off.

Cpl. Psycho supervised an exacting hour of PT on the surface using most of the facilities of the obstacle course with plenty of sit-ups and pull-ups as well as much running round the course, dropping for 'Cover' and crawling through the long, wet grass, scented herbs and pretty meadow flowers. Mr J supervised and used a whacking stick when he considered I needed it or his boot if my bum showed too high when crawling.

Cpl. Psycho introduced some new exercises and when I wasn't learning the moves he sent me round the course a couple of times until I did.

There was also some CP on the triangle to punish fuck-ups.

Breakfast was informal – Mr J's first friendly words were something like 'You're running quite an operation here', to which I agreed.

More training downstairs – Mr J exercised a preference for drill and PT performed naked as well as some timed kit changes and boots on/off practice, again timed and with handcuffs.

I got to a point of exhaustion and was returned to the cell – I believe they had a light lunch upstairs.

Mr J returned and demanded that I clean his boots in the doorway of the cell whilst he stood in front of me, next Cpl. Psycho's. Then they took me into the main room and checked the boots – there were many faults, to be punished with CP.

I needed a break – Psycho helped with getting me back on track – and Mr J used his hire car to get petrol and re-supply water, I also showed him some of the local sights: the local TA Camp and a possible route for a night march.

Cpl. Psycho prepared dinner, his first main meal cooking at the bunker, and loaded his bike to return home.

Togie phoned and I think told Mr J to hit me harder.

After dinner, Cpl. Psycho gone, Mr J did some more on

me downstairs – including a session naked and hooded but with mouth open so that he could get replies from me.

We reached a conclusion and, after a hot chocolate, he turned in downstairs, me in the Radio Cabin.

First thing next morning Mr J collected his car and then supervised an exhausting hour of PT round the course. With all the experience of the previous day he had become very precise in pushing my performance close to the limits of endurance whilst effectively maintaining motivation – in other words he got me well shagged, confused with rapid changes of direction. Tornadoes overhead provided authentic calls to drop for 'Cover' – I counted a dozen aircraft in all.

He asked me if I was 'fresh' and I said 'yes', so he checked that my press-up, sit-up and pull-up performance was as I had indicated in my letters. I passed.

The PT session finished off with a circuit consisting of laps of the course including the parallel bars, jumping the hurdles, pull-ups on the triangle then motivation CP from the NVA rubber stick, sit-ups, press-ups and star-jumps. Not restful and he kept me moving all through it.

After a quick breakfast he left me clearing up and waiting for a visit from Togie.

I never divulged the code word . . .

Training at the Bunker

July 1994

This weekend just past the Major arrived from Glasgow in Scotland and also new recruit Harry. To prepare for the Major's Inspection, Harry and I laid out our kit on the bench down below in the bunker. This comprised uniform combat kit as well as a buttplug, ball-weight and condom each. On his arrival the Major checked it all and told Harry to change into uniform.

Then we had an afternoon of running around the obstacle course, over and under the jumps, variously in combat kit, with and without respirator (gas mask), timed changing into PT for some more, and then back again into combats. The Major had not passed the cleanliness of the glass on our respirators so he said he'd get us to clean them with sweat ... Also we'd got our webbing there – mine loaded with bricks, Harry's with stuffed newspaper so we ran round the course with that on too.

Harry found that the correct reply to 'Are you tired, soldier?' is 'No, Sir' even when he felt the opposite: saying that he was tired evoked a response of 'Two more circuits, now'.

I got to a degree of tiredness where I lost count of hurdles to crawl under and was miscounting circuits of the course. Harry couldn't hold anything above his head for tiredness but he stuck at it. We both had T-shirts soaking wet with sweat to the delight of our Instructor. Harry turned out to be quicker than me at getting his boots on and off and more coordinated at drill.

As an athletic respite, the Major alternated PT with Drill. As we were already a bit tired this was quite amusing and the regrettably frequent cock-ups resulted in more PT on the obstacle course and a change of uniform so that the Major could see exactly what the bodies were doing, unencumbered by respirator, webbing and combat kit.

When we finished, Harry was a zombie, sitting down and staring straight ahead. I don't think I was much better, but somehow we got it together to prepare the stew that Harry had brought, which we ate with a bottle of good champagne to celebrate the Major's and my birthday. Nature obliged with a decent sunset!

Slightly tired and lubricated with some Kronenbourg, we set to cleaning boots for the morning. Somehow I spent the night locked up in the cell while the other two slept on the bunk beds down in the bunker.

Next morning we went for an informal walk in the woods then had breakfast. Harry left and the Major and I went for a walk to survey a field as a possibility for training.

The next day I got a severe half-hour of PT, then breakfast, and an hour and a half of simulated route march on the obstacle course, loaded with webbing, full combat kit including combat helmet and respirator. My large breakfast was walked off fairly swiftly. Punishment parade and then cleaning up. I took the Major to the railway station on the back of my bike, the weather still fine and sunny.

There were a couple of disappointments – Harry didn't like the Major's continual mention of severe Corporal Punishment and I was disappointed that we didn't have a jack-off parade and that the boot cleaning wasn't carried out in Harry's '4B' uniform: beret, boots, ball-weight, buttplug.

The week before had been my birthday and I spent it at the bunker – RMR-Togie was invited, of course, but was too ill. As an indication of his state he didn't find a card or even phone. Previous years he's sent two cards, both typically of gallows humour, rather than choose which!

The weather's hot and dry – Saturday Steve and I travelled up there leisurely and enjoyed the afternoon sunbathing. Jack K arrived on his motorbike late afternoon.

Champagne at the bunker! Maybe we're going soft. Steve's made up my Légion combat uniform with 2REI badges and insignia so it looks smart and he's got a Walking Out uniform, also seriously smart.

Sunday the other bikers arrived: Cpl. Psycho and his friend Michael (two bikes) and David of London Gay Sadomasochists. All, except Michael, gave me thirty-eight whacks in various ways as birthday reminders, entered in the punishment book, of course. I have a few nice bruises and welts on my arse now.

The weekend before that we entertained Cpl. Mike – a real one, delivered blindfolded and handcuffed in the back of David's estate car. We ran him up the track from the road to the bunker, searched him and advised him he was standing at the top of a 5-metre shaft with a ladder down it, and ordered him to go down. Cpl. Psycho ('We call him "Psycho" but I wouldn't advise you calling him that') was at the foot of the ladder and Cpl. Mike found himself caged up in the cell and handing out his bootlaces and belt. Then we trained him to improve his decision-making – various positions 1 2 3 2 1 3 1 2 1 etc. for his hands and feet and any hesitation or dithering was punished.

At a later time we played 'Boot the Squaddie', a game I had adapted from a newspaper report of some actual army bullying. Mike was tied up on the surface and had to identify who was kicking him or hitting him with a nightstick. If identified correctly, he got a kick or blow from someone else; if he got it wrong, he got another from the same person. Interestingly he couldn't tell between Psycho and me kicking him but he could reliably identify our nightstick blows – which we'd been entertaining him with all the afternoon. Funny the skills you acquire, isn't it!

CP Frame*

October 1994

Thank you for phoning last night. I'm sorry that maybe it wasn't the best time for an extended chat: stripe-yer-bum Peter and I were still reeling from trying out RMR-Togie's flogging frame.

The arrangement between us is that we each take the same. I usually go first. We both like boots and PT shorts – he has a nice arse that is well displayed by Bundeswehr cotton shorts and on this occasion I was wearing East German NVA red shorts and yellow vest.

Peter has always previously insisted on no bondage during a caning, partly as a safety mechanism – if you really can't take it you can lose the position. But we've each administered to each other some of the severest floggings we've tasted. He knows me and doesn't let me wimp out, firmly insisting that I continue to the agreed dose. I know how he likes it – heavy and hard. I also see when he's trying to anticipate and know to take corrective action. As you know, I am anti-smoking and there's always been a tariff for smoking in my house: press-ups or stripes depending on the person.

The flogging horse has been in my Training Room since I inherited it from Togie's place in Southfields; before Peter arrived I tightened the bolts firmly with spanners and checked the straps.

Peter had previously seen with appreciation my vaulting horse: his reaction to Togie's horse was amazement at how big it is. Neither of us have ever been tied over anything like it for a real caning.

I went over it first. I wondered when it was last used – whether it was the infamous time in the village hall when the

---

* RMR-Togie died from an AIDS-related illness in August 1994 and I inherited the frame which he had made himself to his own design.

girls' tap dancing team were double-booked and Togie, strapped on the frame, apparently had to switch from grovelling bottom to Total Top to organise everything and everyone to safety. The frame has also made appearances at The Fox's party and also at demonstrations at an SM disco. But I don't believe any serious caning happened on those occasions.

'Lamb to the slaughter'. I wasn't trembling or anything. I had to help Peter fix the wrist restraints and the leg straps sufficiently firmly and then accepted the blindfold, traditionally so that the prisoner can't see which guard administers the punishment but it also has the desirable effect of reducing the possibility of anticipation.

The position over the horse is unusual. You are particularly exposed, pulled on to tiptoe, naked buttocks and thighs can't move and the main bar pushes well into your stomach. I felt slightly nauseous. In his turn, Peter was irrationally concerned that his bollocks would get hit – anatomically impossible with a stick, but indicative of his fear level.

A dozen each was the agreed dose. Peter used Togie's red-taped cane on me for sentimental reasons – we'd checked that it was clean.

I can't really describe how much worse this was than a regular caning. We're both experienced – scarred even – but nothing prepared me for the total feeling of having the stuffing whacked out of me. Three cuts only – yes, they did cut – and I was extremely unhappy. Somewhere around number five I noticed that I needed to consciously avoid pissing on my carpet. He paused after six and number seven was worse. By the last three resignation had set in and I'd stopped tensing my stomach so the bar was biting into me. I was light-headed with fantasies of HMS Ganges floggings, bullies being taken down a peg, etc.

Helped off the frame and hugged warmly by Peter, who was revelling in the amazing accuracy he'd been able to achieve on the firmly presented target area, I was totally washed out. Unlike some other CP we've done together, it was horrible. No erotic content. Just totally whacked. We checked the stripes in the mirror, nice and even with the centres on each buttock gone black. More bear-hugging.

I felt Peter didn't really comprehend the situation and it was his turn to take his stripes. A little cautiously he took the position and I took aim with one of his canes, similar in length and weight to the one I'd inherited with the horse.

Peter doesn't usually show much reaction to a small number of cuts but he too was moving about a little and his boots were trembling. I took my time but completed the dozen, as was our agreement, and hauled him back standing afterwards.

'In half an hour, or maybe tomorrow, we'll be saying that that was the best caning we've had but right now that felt horrible!'

The pain didn't wear off quickly – for the rest of the evening we were catching each other rubbing our own sore bums – a cause for further punishment under some regimes. Sitting down was unexpectedly painful; and the redness, certainly bruising, are still noticeable now, twelve hours later: most unusual for recreational CP.

Usually Peter accepts the tariff for smoking with equanimity even after a session involving many strokes and with varying weapons, cane, tawse, garden bamboo made into a birch. However, as an indication of the thoroughness of the caning, he was asking for a free cigarette. Seizing the opportunity, I said I'd take his stripes for him again bare-arsed but across my vaulting horse. He administered four and couldn't keep me down for any more (in my defence, it's even more difficult to keep yourself down if you've been tied down previously) and was also overcome with guilt at his mate taking his tariff for his addiction for him. So I persuaded him that the only honourable thing was to get over the horse and take four stripes himself. He said later that he didn't enjoy that cigarette!

Légionnaire Encounter

January 1995

Outside my employer's premises there has always been parked a long wheel-base Land Rover painted in army colours and camouflage. I have been keeping it under observation, intrigued as to its owner.

On this day there drew up behind it a grey 205 with French number plates, a French flag sticker inside the front windscreen and on the back door a Légion sticker and a triangular 2REP sticker. As you can imagine, I was immediately interested!

I talked to the guy inside – he had just arrived from Dover on a *quinze jours* leave pass. Cropped hair, nicely spoken French; the car's back seat was untidy including a hiking guide and a pair of Légion athletic shorts. He asked if I was military and I said 'No', pointing to my glasses. I suggested that my friend (Steve) would be very interested to meet him because he collected Légion uniforms. I offered him dinner or a small hike at the weekend.

We exchanged names and I left him my address and telephone number and asked him to phone at 9 p.m. and I went in to work.

Presumably he was an officer as he seemed French, therefore I guess he's intelligent and not a rogue. Impossible to gauge if he is gay because my sense of sexuality is confused by foreign culture. I didn't mention being gay at all, just offered daytime or evening hospitality.

The car was still parked in the same place at lunchtime but when I left work at 7.15 p.m. it had moved. I continued towards Victoria, late for my appointment for training by Mr H, running with my backpack and wearing singlet and shorts in the frosty conditions.

About a mile along my route, at the junction of Chelsea Bridge and the Victoria Embankment, my friend emerged from the shadows. My thoughts were 'great, he'll see that I really do train'. He started by saying '*Je suis perdu*' which I took literally as 'I have lost my way' although I suppose it could mean 'All my plans have gone wrong.'

I asked if he had a map and what was the address he was seeking. At his car, parked nearby, he had a street map and a flier for a hotel the other side of London to which I directed him. Already late and not wanting to get a chill in the freezing condition, I departed but I asked him to be sure to telephone me and he sent me on my way with a convincing 'Go!'

My workout was as thorough as usual but my mind was preoccupied with this second encounter. Had he staked out my route to seem to happen to bump into me? Had I been stupid to take his words at face value – would a Légion officer admit to getting lost? Should I have offered overnight hospitality when I saw he was aiming for a hotel? Should I have asked him to join my run?

I suppose that I should be thankful to fate for the meeting that I did have, and remember that he has my contact details; if he was interested enough to lie in wait for me then he may try again. If it was the case that the second encounter was genuine coincidence or that he was waiting there for someone else, then I am no worse off than had I met him only the once. But it's still annoying that I didn't have the quickness of thought to offer him a floor for the night . . .

The Masochism of Urban Running

November 1995

Today is Thursday morning and yesterday was training night when I go running to my Trainer in Victoria – it takes about half an hour. It's now fully autumn with pavements slippery with leaves and what seems like incessant drizzle that has clothing soaked in an instant. I'd escaped from work early so it was possible to come home and eat some fruit for fuel, but I was also only too aware of the climatic conditions.

There are two possible approaches to soaking rain: defence by wearing lots, or go on the offensive and wear as little as possible. Skin doesn't absorb water much whereas clothing does and, with a wind, it increases the chill factor. Thus it's actually likely to be more comfortable going out in the thinnest singlet and shorts available, consistent with not causing traffic accidents or getting arrested. Last night I took out the white Aussie Rules shorts and a vestigial nylon singlet I have.

The other advantage is the street warrior effect on slow-moving and defensive pedestrians of lightly clothed muscle running along the pavements. This can be an advantage because they get out of the way better, or else are too gobsmacked that someone is not adopting their cover-up and defend position towards the climate!

Situation is more complex away from the local rabbit warren street pattern around here and on the relative running motorway of the Victoria Embankment. Here one encounters the serious lot, taking a circuit outside from the various gyms within the area. This includes wispy females in non-aggressive pastel colours and – of course – total body coverage. There are also the executive joggers, neither jogging far or often enough to do any good. Then there is the hard core, whether they are pairs out from Chelsea Barracks or loners running solo from Battersea Boxing Club. One popular run is 'running the bridges' i.e. running along the Thames and crossing from North Bank to South Bank at every opportunity. Another is running circuits of Battersea Park, but including the North Bank and thus the Embankment.

Hard core don't have a uniform – some wear the kit of their sport, e.g. English rugger kit, others are in fashionable Lycra suits. In between the two extremes are the neighbourhood sports guys, the types running to and from tennis or rowing – these rarely on this stretch of the Embankment, more often encountered near Hammersmith en route for Chiswick Reach or Putney. Somehow soccer players don't seem to run or, if they do, they disguise their sports identity and don't wear the team strip.

Anyway, last night, quietly running along the Embankment, I was joined by a solo serious type as I emerged from the pedestrian way under Albert Bridge. Nothing unusual about that except that he wanted a race – he joined the Embankment at one speed, saw me and speeded up. I know a challenge and responded and we both sped along overtaking the others on that part of the route, spaced enough to maintain contact, not close enough to crowd each other. Next bridge along – Chelsea Bridge – has a slight incline up it which he sprinted and I did likewise, continuing across the traffic whilst he peeled off to the right, across the bridge, parting with a friendly wave. Encounters like that help everyone's motivation.

I arrived at Mr H's place as usual dripping sweat but also rain-drenched. He supervised a good session of exercises which seem tailored to exploit the holes in my fitness that I don't cover elsewhere: particularly stretching and coordination drills. He's also building the number of press-ups and sit-ups I can do – the performance isn't the same as when I'm fresh.

Coordination and muscle control has usually been intensified part way through the routine by stripping off completely and holding in my small size buttplug. On almost any exercise it's possible to hold it in but it's another muscle group to concentrate on and make automatic. The pressure inside is also erotic of course.

He's usually been kind enough to finish off the workout with a muscle rub-down massage – which is great but it's like a two-edged sword because of the knowledge that I'm shortly going to face the bracing Thames wind and rain again, debilitated further by his workout and relaxation. I assure you that the homebound run is by far the more difficult to keep going all the way without stopping. I have to consciously monitor myself to keep the running action fluid and not to run wooden and stiff, which (apart from anything else) is slower.

Last night on the return journey I picked up two runners going the same way and at similar speed and ran with them the same fast track between Chelsea Bridge and Albert Bridge. Matching white England rugby shirts and navy track trousers, they were alternately sprinting and running the sections marked by the numbered river lampposts. This suited me fine and we made a three of it matching paces and strides: stretching in the sprints, relaxing the pace in the 'off' sections.

They went back to Battersea, I continued home and, still dripping, wiped the gym horse leather top with sweat, rain and the remaining massage oil, feeding it so to speak. If I look after it, maybe it will look after me the next time I'm over it for CP.

Gay-Soldaten Köln: Eifel

January 1996

The instructions were to take a train at quarter past seven in the evening from Köln Hauptbahnhof, the busy main railway station in Cologne. The station seemed to have even more than usual Bundeswehr soldiers passing through in uniform; this made the game of trying to guess who were the other Gay-Soldaten Köln people at the station more difficult!

On arrival we were met by a few people in Bundeswehr uniform. We put our baggage in an open pickup truck and were assigned car rides. At the *Haus* which was the training base we collected our baggage and went downstairs to a tile-floored room. We were assigned dormitories and left to change into green kit. There were five in our room – one Bosnian, the rest German, speaking varying amounts of English: initially no one was speaking English at all but, as the weekend progressed, alliances were formed which helped a lot. There was a meal – bread and cheese, German cooked meats and salads.

Back in the tiled basement we *rekruten* formed up in a line and were asked to state if we were for *Kaffee und Kuchen* (coffee and cake, i.e. easy) or light training or for hard-core training. Then we were assigned into *Trainings Züge*. As I had arrived by train it took me some time to realise that this use of 'Zug' meant 'squad' not 'locomotive'. Organisation took quite a long time so there was a lot of standing around in the Bundeswehr version of 'Stand Easy'. As it turned out there were three *Züge*, *Zug drei* seemed to get a lot of CP, *Zug zwei* got the most drill and *Zug eins* was less hard all round.

There was a parade and the officers were introduced and one or two people who had been promoted since the last meeting were introduced at their new ranks. The layout of the place was explained: the barracks *Haus* with the three dormitories, the main *Haus* with the eating room, the off-duty assembly room and the other assembly room with the tiled floor in the basement, also the group showers; the bar and sauna were in another *Haus* 200m up the road. The total attendance was forty-nine, from all over Germany, the Netherlands, one Frenchman and myself from England.

That was the end of the formalities and we went to *Haus drei* for some beer and friendship. I ended up in the same bed as an ex-boxer GG who spoke excellent English and used to work for the British army in Munster, so we didn't sleep too well – lots of punching and muscle pinching.

Next morning at 0815 we were awakened and thirty minutes later paraded outside the front of the main *Haus*. The weather was a slight mist in the valleys below, old and frost snow on the ground, especially in the fields, and a slight wind. It could have been warmer but the Germans found it very cold. I'd not understood completely and ended up out there in T-shirt and lightweights but certainly wasn't going to admit to being cold . . .

After an Inspection by the Kommandant and his staff (there seemed an awful lot of them) we were allowed inside for breakfast, which seemed very similar to the evening meal, although measly, and the drink was the strong German *kaffee*.

Formed up outside, the three *Züge* were taken out to survey the area. We six skittled down a hillside track and marched a bit along a forest road. Then there was some running across a frozen valley with a stream in the middle, which provided some opportunities to practise *stellung* and another similar command to 'cover' which was inevitably given when we were in the muddiest bits. More running, marching and so on up and around the area. This was preparatory to the afternoon's exercise which proved to be *Zug drei* attacking the main *Haus* with the *Zug zwei* (us) defending the forest and roads and *Zug eins* defending the *Haus*. We practised asking for passwords ('*Parole*?') and what to do if we got the wrong one – excuse to interrogate the bastard. Two *rekruten* were picked on in this fashion and ended up searched against a tree, cuffed and tossed in the back of a pickup jeep; due to poor control technique, Fred (from Holland) kept escaping . . .

MORE AND HARDER

After lunch – fried fish and potatoes done school-kids style – there was a long meeting about Tactics for the exercise. The officers proposed the situation. Not understanding much of it, it seemed that there were a lot of different opinions . . . We were all sent away for a rest, regrouping at 1600. More opportunity for *Kamaradshaft* in bed with GG.

The next meeting was the two defending *Züge* only, and things were more definite. When the enemy passed specific places there were signals of red or green rockets or whistle blasts. We togged up against the cold: for most of the Germans this involved *Unterhose* (thermal underwear), T-shirt, shirt, pullover, jacket and parka or tank suit!

We marched away from the main *Haus* and took up our positions – I was with one of the *Gruppenführer* guarding a jeep at a path crossing a track and we laid hidden in the forest for ages, seeing no one.

It all ended when we heard the whistles indicating that the *Haus* had been taken – the enemy had used a route round and through the forest rather than the direct route we had defended, although this could be seen as a cock-up because the majority of players saw no action. Remember that to organise an event of this magnitude is not at all easy and that no other groups are even attempting this sort of thing.

Dinner, then group showers. I expected this to be lots of soap and lathering but the numerous handcuffs were fully used as *rekruten* were picked on, cuffed and then cold-showered and cold-hosed with the large bore cleaning hose. In the barracks *Haus* there was quite a lot of unruly activity also – I ensured GG got his arse well punched and kicked, held down by the other *Gruppenführer*. Fred was also picked on and ended up being transported to *Haus drei* tied up and rolled in a camouflage net to be toasted in front of the log fire there . . .

The evening exercise was to be no longer than forty-five minutes' duration outside, on account of the cold, and we were transported to our positions in the back of the Land Rover and the jeep. Some of us were of the opinion that we should do a flying disembarkation, like in the magazine pictures of soldiers, but in the end we got out slowly, stood around for a meeting and then dispersed. We patrolled our bit of road and challenged an innocent rock which failed to give the password but which was allowed to survive: Germans are very ecology conscious and anyhow we were only armed with white stickers to designate 'kills'.

We set up an ambush around the track in the darkest part of the pine forest and put up a torch to attract attention: 'Please come here and let's have some fun!' Just as the enemy patrol was cautiously creeping along, the jeeps returned and we were cheated of them. Oh well.

Back in *Haus drei* there was more beer and mulled red wine. Me cuffed and gagged, my bum got well and truly punched by various people in succession. It didn't go much further than that as I was a bit cautious about the situation; GG, for example, got the full works, but not from the NCO he wanted. The sexual dynamics of the situation were complicated: there was partly the NCOs manipulating activities so that they got what they wanted, the *Offiziers* coordinating things to give a good show, and the *Kaffee und Kuchen* lot watching when they were permitted to. Then the *rekrut* on *rekrut* alliances, friendly fights and horseplay. There was also the sauna but I didn't try that.

I'd had my bit and wanted some sleep. GG was away elsewhere and when he returned there was a long chat including our *Gruppenführer* and some more after that also. 0815 Sunday morning we were up again; the *Stabsfeldwebel*'s whistle saw to that. Another parade outside but it didn't seem so cold. Another breakfast that seemed the same fare as dinner, except some *Apfeltorte* (apple tart) had appeared. A meeting about the next one, to be held at Easter, then a group photo in front of the vehicles for publicity purposes.

Finally we got out for an exercise – two groups each armed to the teeth with . . . nothing: hand to hand fighting to save the shell of your very own egg! If your egg broke you were dead. Various ingenious measures were employed as mess containment, including a new use for condoms . . . The winning team was the one with a survivor. Instead of heading directly for the enemy I circled at a slow run and no one got me, so our *Zug* won.

Then some marching on the forest tracks, more training around the frozen stream and some marching – we were getting to be quite together about it. Back at the main site I demonstrated the US Grass Drill to a couple of our lot and got a dose in return which ensured I was nicely washed out as well as a bit tender from the previous night's punchings.

Lunch, presentation of new rank slides to our *Gruppenführer* and then the sad business of splitting. Our two *Gruppenführen* took me and GG and Hans-Peter to the station . . .

Adventure Training – Dartmoor

March 1996

Busy time of the year – I got away on Friday evening down to Sgt. Blue's gay soldiers' group who were on adventure training exercise in Devon. They'd hired a whole bunkhouse for the weekend at a beauty spot just off Dartmoor.

David and Harry met me at Exeter station in David's olive green Land Rover, much to the chagrin of another character who'd been intermittently eyeing me since we'd left Paddington. The decision was taken to leave him waiting at the station rather than to offer him a lift.

The bunkhouse turned out to be a charming 1930s wooden construction with modern bunk beds and a wood-burning stove. Rasher-Splasher ('the Catering Corps') greeted me with a lasagne and shortly the others returned from the pub. '350 Alan (who has been visiting me at home for training and also went to the bunker as '350) seemed to require some tying up so he was tied to a bunk and quizzed about the phonetic alphabet. This included Jeremy, Llama and almost everything for G except Golf.

Next morning '350 Alan and I went out for a run before breakfast: the daffodils were coming out and the sap had made a twig that I took from an elder bush quite whippy. '350 took a dozen as morning toughening-up without trouble.

After a cooked breakfast and a group photo the company set off for a hike across the moor. Billy, an ex-Royal Marine, did the map reading and we yomped leisurely across the heather. Lunchtime saw us at a pub in the middle of the moorland. We drank outside, still in full kit with berets.

The famed Dartmoor mists were rolling in so we headed back to the vehicles via some ancient Stone Rows. Alan and I did a further hike across the moor despite the worsening weather but did manage to follow the compass bearings into a bog. Billy and David picked us up as arranged – Billy with a very convincing 'Get in the back there faster, you maggots.'

Splendid evening meal – '350 Alan was perhaps a bit rushed for it as he seemed to cop boot cleaning duty for almost all of the eleven pairs of boots available.

One detachment went off to a gay bar in Torquay: someone had phoned ahead midweek and asked if a bunch of squaddies would be welcome. Silly question of course – the gay club was agog with anticipation. The group got in for nothing and were the star turn of the night.

Meanwhile back at the hostel, David, Rasher Splasher and I had a quiet evening and went to bed. The beer monsters returned with predictable noise and '350 Alan was definitely gagging to be tied up. Things had quietened down a bit but I was wide awake and in an early shift schedule, so we moved the dining room tables round so that he could stand on one with his arms lashed to one of the roof cross-members. Blindfolded, and with a few dripping candles around, I got him counting clothes pins as I put them on and off: the audience were amazed how he was convinced that two dozen actual clothes pins got counted as three dozen!

After some more sleep, David and I went for a walk in the meadows by the side of the river with Sergeant Blue who set the whole thing up and had taken his one-ton Land Rover there as the main transport. Breakfast was fresh bagels, scrambled egg with smoked salmon . . .

Then an excursion to Haytor, which was windy, and some recruiting among some other ex-army blokes there who David said (after an impenetrable conversation in Gaelic) were also gay. More riding around on the moor in the vehicles and back to the hostel for high tea. There were three birthdays to celebrate and the Catering Corps had produced an iced cake with the group crest on it as well as lots of fruitcake and marzipan.

I had to leave to catch my train home. This was more painful than expected as someone had convinced the group that this weekend was the occasion for the clocks to change to Summer Time. I wasn't sure and hadn't changed my watch but everyone else had: the railway clock still showed GMT . . . A real reality check!

Gay-Soldaten Köln – 'Fälscher Hase' (Funny Bunnies)

Easter 1996

Easter Sunday morning at 0545, the Military Policemen (MP) woke us in the dormitories with their whistles. The previous night we *schütze* had each prepared an 'alarm chair' with our rucksack battle-ready with handcuffs and rope, water bottle, whistle and spare clothing. Folded and stacked in order of donning was combat kit and boots, except that a couple of us chose to sleep in boots and kit for a speedier response to the expected alarm.

As the stars disappeared from the Easter sky leaving a nearly full moon, we mustered outside and Oberleutnant Hermann ('Lucky') assigned the two *Züge* their battle areas. Ours (*Zug zwei*) had the furthest distance from the neutral points but had the advantage of high ground. A short time later we marched off to establish our bases.

The previous day we had thoroughly reconnoitred the area: a deep valley in the Eifel mountains; we were using about 3km length and 200m height of one side of the valley. In the base is a small stream and a few springs feed this from the valley sides which are pine forest with two forest roads zigzagging up the sides.

A hidden base was established to dump our kit – hidden in thick (not impenetrable) pine and another (the 'sun spot') for grouping. Also an interrogation point. Much planning had established the rules: at 0700 a number/letter cipher in the range 1–9 and A–M assignment for each *schützen* arrived from HQ; the list was destroyed after issue.

The object of the game was to obtain three of the opposition's ciphers. The expected method for this was capture and interrogation. The captive would not be released until the cipher he had yielded had been checked against the list held by the triumvirate running the game. If the cipher checked true, the captive should be released at one of the Neutral points; in the case that he had given a false cipher, further interrogation would be necessary.

These rules had evolved through a planning meeting held a fortnight previously at the same location and much discussion on the Easter weekend. It was important that the captive had the possibility of controlling the amount of discomfort necessary.

At the mustering on Good Friday afternoon, all *schützen* had been stripped of their travel clothes, searched and medically checked (blood pressure, anal search, testicle check, etc.), asked their sexual and physical preferences, available punishments and exclusions/limits, and issued with an ID card recording these responses. These were also recorded in coded form on a master list which was available to the *Gruppenführer*. Those of us who travelled without underwear showed all – including my eighteen stripes which were the 'price' of the snappy haircut I'd received from one of stripe-yer-bum Peter's 'Singapore-weight Dragon canes' a couple of days previously. Expensive haircut, pay in advance!

At all times since then all *schützen* must have been carrying these green ID cards: the three MPs had authority to challenge a *schütze* at any time and report infractions of this and any other of a dozen *Verhaltensregeln* for immediate punishment or assignment to the *Strafkompanie*.

For the whole event there was also a stop word *Weihnachtsmann* ('Father Christmas') with the meaning 'stop this activity immediately'. A less severe stop word was also available meaning 'stop this part of the training but don't stop the training'. I had occasion to use this during my voluntary (!) participation in the *Strafkompanie*: twelve *schützen* had been handcuffed to a chain and were pig-sticking – gathering wood for the bonfire to celebrate Easter Saturday with special bread and schnapps. We'd exhausted wood in one location and were sent up a steep path we'd previously experienced as being slippery; I didn't fancy a broken wrist due to the mechanics of being in the middle of a chain gang. My call of the English stop word was heeded and the *Strafkompanie* returned to the forest track, were ordered to remove socks and boots and sling them around necks and to return to base barefoot, silent and carrying the firewood.

In the forest on Easter Sunday I shared a Mars bar around our four-man patrol as we moved away from the baggage dump. I'd explained the concept of an attack patrol and sweeping through the forest clearing area of suspicion as being tactics likely to yield prisoners. There was much keenness among the Germans for concealment and cover but there were no guns or knives allowed for the whole weekend so attack had to be by hand-to-hand contact and some risks should be taken otherwise no contact would be made.

Our first attack patrol was tight – four of us speaking German and English but mainly hand signs and remaining in formation. We checked a larger area including the two neutral points and turned to base where breakfast was predicted to arrive 0900. On regaining high ground I spotted another patrol – two, possibly three. We attacked – war cries and all – and after a short grapple realised we'd attacked our own side. No one had thought to issue a *zug* password.

The sun was becoming stronger and was melting the last of the lying snow under the trees. Inspiration provided a pass- and answer-word of 'Get Lucky': 'Lucky' being the nickname of Oberleutnant Hermann. Some practice interrogation and eventually breakfast and supplies arrived in one of the jeeps.

Next patrol had the concept of two men in front as 'bait' and four behind. In a disciplined situation it might have worked with the two out front being noisy and the four behind sneaky-beaky quiet, but in practice it became an unwieldy six-man patrol that split into three plus three when the going became tough. Nonetheless we cleared a large area.

Lunch was assigned to be at one to the neutral points and we arrived marching smartly in formation and whistling the tune of 'John Brown's body'.

'Lucky' and his HQ staff dished out three different menu Bundeswehr ration pack boxes. Some of us got worried that we might be out for twenty-four hours from that point onwards until the game was actually decided rather than stalemated, as had been the case so far.

Soft interrogation of a member of *Zug eins* revealed that a spy patrol had located one of our bases so after *Zug eins* had melded into the forest we made measures to move our interrogation *Lager*. I was ordered to choose a location; my preference was for a rather comfy headland between two big zigzags of one of the forest tracks with good overlook to the valley floor and somewhere to stash kit. Topping it all, there was a stream to cover some noise – it also had other uses later.

We left Haupt-Feldwebel Schmidt and a lookout and went off to find some prisoners: lunch was good but prisoners would be better!

The MPs and various other distractions were around to provide false alarms but eventually we located a patrol of four enemy. There was some tittering whilst we observed them crawl through an area of forest in which one of us had taken a shit earlier in the morning. Oberfeldwebel Fritz led the charge as we attacked them on the forest track as they emerged. A tough fight ensued – one of the opposition's favourite tactics included throwing handcuffs out of immediate reach. We concentrated on subduing them and immediately asking for ciphers whilst we had the screws on them, so to speak.

I'd also been equipped with two of the common handcuff keys so was at one point able to release Oberfeldwebel Hermann who hadn't yielded his cipher. After cuffing one of them I moved on to his mate, who called to the already cuffed one for help. 'Not likely,' was his reply, 'that's a wild animal attacking you!' The last of their four ran off but we had three ciphers and three prisoners.

After some *Feldwebelarbeit* – which meant sucking the cock of the Feldwebel – we were returning cautiously to our new base but heard the noise of further battle. Our Haupt-Feldwebel Schmidt had been captured and GG (*schütze* Georg) and Unteroffizier Klaus were roping up our lookout Erich. I attacked GG – he was the only opponent who succeeded in knocking off my cap; eventually I cuffed him and turned to the bigger prize – Unteroffizier Klaus, 6'4" and the military brains of *Zug eins*. Not an easy fight, we were eventually three on one, but it was possible to untie Erich and our reinforcements arrived soon after we yelled for them.

Picture the scene – two of them tied up in a small valley next to a stream underneath our interrogation point. Close by, the neutral point, convenient for checking ciphers. We have two of them immediately subdued, three ciphers but unchecked. Others of their *zug* arrive and are captured. As gentleman fighters we have been giving the vanquished water and squashed Mars bar chocolate from my stash. Visitations to the scene of battle by the HQ staff and MPs.

Then it transpires that the captured have been giving out false ciphers.

Gloves off. Methods employed included portable TENS unit; battery hair clippers and ordinary discomfort. 'TENS' means Trans-subcutaneous Electrical Nerve Stimulation by a small portable electrical unit and skin electrodes used to induce mild electrical shocks and muscle twitching.

The next set of ciphers also false.

The stream comes into use. Captives dumped in watercourse, mud in hair, trousers and boots. Nose held – mouth opens: mud can go in!

Next set of ciphers: one false, one true. Methods proved effective! Their remaining *schütze* interrogated further and this time kept in water until his cipher is verified.

Finally, one of the HQ staff comes over and starts boasting how he has been carrying the complete list of ciphers around all day. We ask him to show it, snatch it and then suggest that he can only have it back in exchange for *his* socks and boots, as he was the bastard that ordered the *Strafkompanie schützen* to march barefoot on the forest track. A chance to show he can take a dose of his own punishment.

He won't march so now we have the complete list of ciphers!

Our march back to the neutral point was completed by arriving whistling and singing the words of the European Union anthem from Beethoven Ninth's 'Ode to Joy', with the adjustment to one line *'alle menschen werden brüder'* became *'alle menschen muste gefangen!'*

Back to the main house to clean off a lot of mud. After

evening meal there was some free time and a short show by the Entertainment Committee which mimicked some of the characters present. I finally located the sauna; it was fun cooling outside in the frosty air but the snow had melted by then.

The last thing I did before going to bed was a night walk around the area with Loibl, from the same *Zug*. We had to arrange with the Fire Watch to let us back inside.

Finally on Monday there was a debriefing meeting (I did some extra sport, supervised by one of the MPs) and a final parade at which Stadts-Feldwebel Wolfgang (ex-Navy) made sure that his superior in the group, Oberleutnant Hermann, didn't confuse left with right and called the commands *exactly* correctly. Everyone appreciated the friendly humiliation of the boss.

Weekend at the Bunker

August 1996

Alan and I left London in his car on Friday night; the traffic was surprisingly quiet. When we arrived in East Anglia, we stopped for a fish meal and reached the bunker well before nightfall. The first night was relatively friendly although I was woken several times by furtive shaking noises that can only have been Alan jacking off.

Saturday morning PT was an hour – before the sun became too hot. We concentrated on aerobic stuff: it turned out that this was an area that he'd recently neglected. Lots of running, crawling and running again. Then round the obstacle course, adding a new station on every circuit routine. Breakfast and the delights of cleaning up naked outdoors – the one not washing kept a lookout whilst the other used the cold water.

Alan had been to a 'Prison Camp' organised by a German group and had expressed some disappointment that their event wasn't sufficiently prison in character. Therefore I had him strip off and placed him completely naked in the cell, hands cuffed through the bars of the gate so he couldn't jack off. Additionally I padlocked a dog-chain around his balls; he switched into name and number responses naturally and I settled into some gardening whilst checking him at intervals. When I checked his hands he grabbed back warmly, indicating he was enjoying himself.

Eventually the amount of moving around noises coming up the bunker access shaft became greater and his fingers started to feel a little cold. It was time to release him. He surfaced a little slowly; the sun had moved round and the above ground temperature had risen significantly. His arms and shoulders were stiff from the cool and the enforced position after the PT.

We went for a short hike in the countryside and explored

an area of forest that has been recently logged. The padlock and chain remained around his balls – this was part of a complicated set-up with David: David had requested the use of the stainless steel chastity globe whilst I was on holiday to Wyoming and had mailed me the keys to the padlock on it. After a month of enforced abstinence he had requested the return of the keys, anxious to ensure reliability at a time of postal service strikes. I suggested that these should be returned by motorcycle courier, i.e. Alan. To ensure fair play and rapid delivery, I suggested that David should hold a key to something locked on Alan so that they both had a mutual interest in the key exchange. Thus the key to the chain on Alan's balls was with David.

In the evening we made dinner and then put Alan in the cell for the night with the padlock and chain still around his balls. To try to ensure a night not disturbed by unauthorised masturbation, I also put Alan in the transport belt that he and another recruit gave me for my birthday – it's a five-inch-wide thick leather belt with steel Hiatt old pattern cuff either side. Quite difficult to reach your cock and your shoulders cramp after a while.

As it turned out, he tossed and turned in his bedding in the cell quite a lot but didn't manage to jack off. More PT next morning after a wake-up mug of tea, lots of running up and down the track to the road. Breakfast and then clearing up.

Severe Pain on the National Health Service

I find myself with a verruca that my doctor is treating with cryotherapy; he fires liquid nitrogen at minus 200 degrees directly at the lesion. It hurts.

Strange how the pain from the cryotherapy changes my perception of other pain. I guess SM masochists know how to eroticise pain but it's not quite as simple as being turned on by the pain from the verruca.

Firstly, my appetite for 'voluntary' pain from Corporal Punishment is much reduced. When I've been close to receiving CP I have backed down – mostly from the fear of the pain. Yep, I know that I also get off on fear and that if the person administering the CP would force me then I would probably accept it – or get into a voluntary 'forced' situation. It's usually been 'stripe-yer-bum' Peter who has been doing this on me and although he knows me better than anyone, I haven't let him force me into taking the CP.

Secondly, in the same way as getting striped is painful at the time but arousing afterwards, there is a slight erotic overhang from the verruca pain. When I return from the surgery I am horny. Possibly endorphins still buzzing around the brain?

Thirdly, I have been finding that jacking off masks the verruca pain. Quite explicable because some other sensation and/or train of thought predominates. The sting in that tail is that after ejaculating the verruca pain returns full whack, no defences. It would be interesting to work out how to manipulate pain response to achieve that effect from SM pain.

I remember something similar when I was recovering from having my dick pierced for the Prince Albert; maybe that's a contributory reason why people get addicted to piercings.

On that line, I also tried the TENS unit on the pain blocking routine, which worked fine – minor discomfort from the TENS electrodes blocked the verruca pain, but with the same dastardly effect when removing the TEN stimulation.

Squaddie Train Trip

October 1996

Arrangements were made such that my Orders were to phone him when I returned from work on Friday, yesterday at 1315. I had prepared and laid out my kit (OG uniform and boots, PT shorts and shoes, no shirt, punishment uniform – RAF tropical shirt and shorts) and was to phone naked except for cock and ball strap and rubber buttplug. Orders received on the phone were to proceed to Victoria railway station to catch the 1418 to Ashford and details of where to advance on arrival: I was to stand at 'Attention' facing the railway embankment at the end of a footpath tunnel under the railway. For the journey I was to wear OG (olive green) T-shirt and lightweight trousers, boots cock-ring and buttplug. Actually this was his second choice of kit: he'd initially asked me to travel in the Punishment uniform but the shorts are cut back so much as to be indecent so I suggested this wouldn't be safe. I was also unhappy about travelling in OG uniform as it looks official, so I was allowed to travel in black tracksuit trousers and OG T-shirt. I didn't realise it but this was equally treacherous because tracksuit trousers allow no concealment for a hard or half-hard cock. But at least they don't show moist patches from buttplug lubricant or oozing pre-come.

It was an interesting journey – Ashford is ninety minutes from Victoria and I was unusually stimulated for quite a lot of the time. I don't typically travel with a hard cock, let alone wearing too few clothes to conceal this. Orders were not to sit, but to stand in the carriage vestibules and I obeyed this faithfully. I was allowed to drop the pack from my shoulders between stations, but standing like that means that you must retain the plug actively. I developed the technique of facing the wall to conceal my stalk when other passengers were passing.

On arrival at Ashford I was stunned and embarrassed

further to hear my name called out on the station public-address loudspeakers, requesting to report to the station information office on Platform Two. This was quite a problem of potential embarrassment as my cock was quite noticeable. I used the rucksack to maintain decency and received a message to phone a telephone number. The BR staff offered me the use of their phone but I turned it down and went to find a less exposed place.

The new meeting place was arranged and I proceeded following the instructions. At the edge of a rugby-club playing fields and near a stream there was a small hut and I waited facing its wall. Shortly afterwards I heard a voice ordering me to press-up position and then to perform thirty press-ups. He told me to walk forwards along a path, eyes front. In this formation we proceeded across a plank bridge over the stream, into a wood. The next orders were that from now onwards everything would be done at the double, so if walking I was to double-step and when in one place was to run on the spot. I was not to attempt to look at him and that any infractions would be punished with CP. Then he moved ten foot away, still behind me and maintained that sort of distance throughout.

Now in the woods, he ordered me to strip and stow my tracksuit trousers and spectacles. Remove the rubber buttplug for inspection and insert the stainless steel one: this requires continual muscular contraction effort to maintain retention. Dress in the RAF stone-grey tropical kit without removing my boots. He threw tit-clips at my back and told me to put them on under the shirt, then to stow the rest of the kit in the pack, and to carry it. Stepping through the shorts I had got some mud on the light grey material and this occasioned the first punishment: five minutes' punishment drill leading up to a dozen of the cane BB. He moved me to near some bushes, selected and ordered me to break off a hazel twig for his use. It wasn't easy – it was quite springy. I can't remember the exact sequence of drill he used: he maintained his voyeuristic distance and had a combination of turns, marching, halting, running double-step knees up on the spot that had me working like a robot. The five minutes seemed like an eternity, the tit-clips and the little chain between them pulling incessantly and emphasising the motions. Several times he had me touch my toes but it wasn't yet time for the caning at the end of the drill. I began to yearn for the caning because it would mean the end of the drill; then I stopped thinking and gave in to the suffering.

He halted me near some bushes and ordered me to drop the shorts to my knees and to touch my toes. Although the shorts have been cut down to be quite vestigial, I felt particularly exposed and vulnerable. He striped my buttocks, the twig wrapped round my flanks also, stinging as it striped red. The dozen came fast and hard, the twig was lightweight and caused pain without weight or noise of impact; just the whippy noise as it whistled through the air. There was also the base pain from the weight of the tit-clips and chain pulling downwards and away from my chest and shifting inside the shirt.

Shorts back up and at 'Attention', he then rested me 'At Ease'. Except that 'At Ease' is not a restful position and it's the most difficult one to control the metal buttplug. Then snap to 'Attention' followed by a series of deep knee-bends. He was definitely trying to get me to drop the plug and those shorts wouldn't hold it one bit; it was up to me. I tried hard not to give in but he surprised me with a snap to 'Attention' after I thought I had got used to the sequence. Out came the plug at a high rate of knots . . . It fell in the mud and he ordered me to replace it with the rubber plug, which was still clean.

Obviously, dropping the plug was a punishable offence and the sentence was the same: five minutes of drill and a dozen from the horrible little twig. After that he had me change into the PT shorts, no shirt and he allowed me to release my tits standing at 'Attention', one hand only and waiting for a minute or so between each release not showing the pain as the blood resurged . . . We returned to the rugger field and there followed a demanding PT workout which included much work on the ground (i.e. in the mud) and crawling. He had me run down the bank of the stream, through the water and up the other side, touch a tree and return the same route. Then some more crawling, keeping the butt down, running on the spot, star jumps, press-ups, sit-ups and so on. Inevitably I caught glimpses of him but without my glasses all I could make out was a navy-blue tracksuit, big Umbro logo across the back, white shoes. I think he was wearing glasses and had white receding hair. His appearance didn't matter: he was controlling me adeptly, playing me like a piano, and I was submitting in automatic obedience mode and sweating away as he drove me, flashing out the limits of my endurances.

This is England in October and the overcast skies began to give drizzle. Even I noticed in my sweaty fatigue as it pinged cool on my exposed chest and legs. He drove me back into the woods, ordered the metal plug and tit-clips and pack back on and told me to jack off into a condom I'd brought, standing at 'Attention'. This took a little while but he left me completely alone, no further orders, watching me from three-quarters behind. Afterwards he demanded that I remove the condom, tie a knot in it to seal it and hand it over to him. I was allowed to wash off in the stream, tit-clips thankfully off; no towel was available so I used the inside of the PT shorts, and then redressed to return home: rubber plug back in, cock and ball strap still in place.

I knew the route back to the station and ran off. There was time for a large railway catering tea, then another to take on the train with me; I dozed a bit as the stations went by on the homeward leg. Ashford's a long way out . . .

Well – actually what happened was that the message at the station information office was that his car had broken down and would I phone him. He was most apologetic and offered to pay for my train fares but suggested I should return home immediately. The next train arrived on time but departed late. I kept the plug and cockstrap on for a while as I fantasised and when the train started filling up with people as it neared London I found that both toilets were locked 'out of order' so I was stuck with wearing the toys . . . I completed the journey feeling well fucked but unable to jack off until I reached home.

Pony Day Out – Shropshire

July 1997

We had a brilliant day out in a secluded field with about half a dozen other ponies and their riders. At first it seemed that the weather would spoil things but the sunshine and showers and a light breeze turned out to be ideal.

My driver Mr N first showed off his control of me on a lunge rein, having me trot and circle at some distance. He'd fitted a tight brown leather head-harness and metal bit as usual and padlocked a buttplug inside the lower body chain harness I wear. Additionally a stainless steel ball-weight on my newly shaved cock and balls and a pair of light tit-clips across my chest with little bells which jingled and tugged as I trotted and performed on the reins. As usual my arms were crossed behind my back, hands in mitts chained together, hand to bicep, leaving my buttocks exposed for the rider's crop. Cock and balls bouncing up and down out and proud in front, inaccessible to me.

Firstly circling on the reins, then blindfolded so I was completely dependent on receiving control through the leather reins and the bit strapped across my mouth. I'd long since learnt to pull on the reins to feel and depend on the control from them through the metal bit irresistibly forced across my lips and tongue. Blindfolded, arms strapped behind, plugged and tit-clipped, the pony obeys the reins or else feels the crop.

After a break, I was harnessed into Mr N's newly constructed cart. This proved to be extremely light and manoeuvrable and conveyed him around the bumpy field at some speed. However, a mechanical fault developed and we were offered the use of one of Sir Rupert's carts. Mr N, wearing shorts, found that it was comfortable for him to spread his legs and rest his feet on the shafts. Unfortunately this posture resulted in his sensitive inner thighs being caressed by any thistles or nettles that his pony happened to pass through. Ponies are not stupid animals and the possibilities for 'revenge' were fully exploited to much laughter and merriment and use of the whip.

Another break for a packed lunch and intense discussion of pony-cart design and comparison of different tack. 'Roman Candle' was sporting a particularly well-crafted harness with many attachment points and his cart was much admired for its mechanical engineering and elegant design. Lady S, the rider of Roman Candle, was the sole beneficiary of spring suspension on the bumpy field.

Races were arranged. I'm afraid as a pony I didn't get a chance to note all the names but in the first heat we raced against the silver-bitted 'Two Ways' driven by the redoubtable Sir Rupert and also a very plucky third outfit. The course started slightly downhill to a muddy bridge over a stream and then up a long hill, round through some rough ground and back down through a wooded area with an alternative route through some nettles. Myself, 'Squaddie', came to win from behind after gloriously overtaking the opposition, firstly on the back straight and secondly on the stiff climb up the home run.

Cool rain intervened and the sweating ponies sheltered under some trees next to the stream. Afterwards the second card was Lady S driving Roman Candle, Mr N driving Squaddie, Sir Rupert driving another of his stable and one other whose name wasn't declared to the Starter Michael, also known as Shep the dog. The smart money was on the favourite Squaddie at 4 to 1. Under Starters Orders, one horse pissed on the ground entirely in role: no one minded.

Roman Candle and Lady S made a good start but started labouring on the hills, incurring heavy use of the whips; we finally overtook them through the thistles on the back straight to the delight of the crowd and the discomfort of Mr N's inner thighs.

Demonstrations followed of blindfolded cart driving – this is where the pony is deprived of vision and is entirely guided by the rider using rein and crop commands. It's very intense and very rewarding, particularly afterwards if the rider dismounts and sexually arouses the pony, still plugged, tit-clipped and harnessed tightly: submissive and restrained by the shafts and unable to resist the welcome stimulation.

The denouement of the afternoon was the harnessing of two ponies side by side to pull Roman Candle's excellent cart. Specific shafts and pony tack had been made for this and soon Roman Candle and Squaddie were harnessed side by side, arms laced across backs, shafts attached to the wide waist belts. In this position the pony is completely dependent, cannot move except forwards or backwards with the cart and with the cooperation of the other pony or under the command of the driver. Twice as much pulling power and stamina is available to overcome hills, etc. Additionally the reins are now arranged so that on one side the ponies' bits are joined by a strap and on the outer sides the bits are attached to the reins. Also the bicep straps on the pony harnesses are attached so that the ponies work together. The ponies feel the closeness of the other animal but can't actually touch: more submissive bondage.

Working as a team, Roman Candle and Squaddie gave rides to several of the riders including a couple of the ladies; I'm told it was a magnificent sight to see one of the girls in red and black and wielding a six-foot crop driving two ponies round the field.

After completing their work, the ponies were left alone awhile still harnessed in the shafts. This emphasises the submission of the pony role but unfortunately there was no way to relieve their sexual tension.

'Playpen' Slave Night

June 98

> ON THE NIGHT OF THE 'PLAYPEN' SM SLAVE MARKET AND SM PARTY I AM INSTRUCTED TO ARRIVE AT THE 'PLAYPEN' B&B AT 2000 TO ALLOW TIME TO CHANGE FROM MY MOTORBIKE LEATHERS INTO SLAVE KIT AND TO GO DOWN TO THE CLUB AT 2100. MR J WILL ARRIVE AFTER 2100 BUT BEFORE 2200 AND WILL OCCUPY THE REST OF THE ROOM WHICH I WILL HAVE LEFT TIDY.
>
> I AM TO BE LOCKED INTO A CELL NAKED AND BLINDFOLDED AND WITH A SIGN WE WILL SUPPLY. IF THERE IS SHORTAGE OF CELL-SPACE THEN IT IS OK FOR ME TO BE LOCKED IN A CELL WITH ANOTHER SLAVE WHO IS ALSO BLINDFOLDED.
>
> IT IS OK FOR ANOTHER MASTER TO REQUEST THE KEY TO THE CELL TO CHECK ME OUT FOR A SHORT SESSION BUT HE SHOULD CLEARLY UNDERSTAND THAT I AM MR J'S PROPERTY FOR THE NIGHT SO I SHOULD BE RETURNED TO THE CELL.
>
> MR J WILL CLAIM ME IN HIS OWN TIME.

Such were the instructions for my first SM slave night at the 'Playpen' club in Eindhoven, Holland. Note that Mr J does not meet me before the party begins as we arrive separately, from different countries.

As I rode off on my new CBR600F bike from Ralf's house in the pine forest south of Brussels there was another thunderstorm fast approaching. I travelled cross-country to rejoin the Antwerp–Eindhoven motorway near the Belgian border.

Hot and humid, the unlined one-piece bike riding suit I was wearing became like a personal sauna. The fresh olive oil it had received the night before during an arrival sex-scene in Ralf's kitchen was warm and sticky inside against my freshly shaved body, particularly around the cock, balls and slippery arse-hole and cheeks spread wide by the riding seat: nice!

The weather outran me and the rain started then the lightning. There was one fork which appeared to land less than a kilometre away and the rain soon became torrential. Fearful of aquaplaning, I stopped under a motorway bridge. The rain run-off was deeper than the toecaps of my steel-toed rubber site boots so at least 5cm deep.

I finally reached Eindhoven and knocked on the door at the Playpen and dripped rain on the cement that usually gets washed down with piss . . .

After coffee and a warm welcome from Rieks it was time to change into slave kit – on this occasion assault boots, cock-ring and lockable ball-weight. I'd shaved before leaving England. One of the Playpen staff – the slave-Master – was already preparing some of the other slaves. He was expecting me and locked me in a slave cage in the play area, asked me if I wanted to buy a drink and arranged an emergency word. The slave-Master was wearing dark glasses so I proposed 'Captain'. As I quickly drank Grolsch beer he fixed the sign I'd brought to the outside of the cage. It read:

> SLAVE OWNED BY MR J OF COPENHAGEN
> SEEK PERMISSION BEFORE USE

The slave-Master removed the beer bottle quickly and left me chained to the back wall of the slave cage standing 'At Ease' but chained.

Various chain and slave noises echoed around the play area. Shortly, another slave was installed in the adjacent cage. He was 'For Sale' and was supposed to submissively hold up to his chest a card with his details and price to be paid to the bar.

When the slave-Master wasn't looking we touched each other up. This was strange, having one's personal space invaded but not by a Master. We checked each other out – he tried to tickle me and then dug his fingers in my armpits. I hope I resisted thoroughly but my cock became erect and dripping from not having wanked for four days.

I got him hard by pinching him and also muscle-pinching but then the slave-Master discovered our games and gave my fellow slave a slapping and told me to stop.

Half a dozen or so other slaves were penned up but we couldn't see them. My cock erection subsided but I could feel my cock oozing pre-come juice even though it was now only half-hard.

Eventually 'Playpen' became open, the music started and the Masters were admitted. I could only make out leather-clad shapes as I wasn't wearing my glasses and the music covered any talking but the slave next door seemed to get plenty of attention and his cock went hard when he was attacked/provoked by a Master with a small horsehair flogger. The slave confided that this was the Master who had bought him at the previous SM night. He asked if I was for sale but I replied that it wasn't up to me. The slave-Master got wind that we were talking and gave us each a slapping.

I was beginning to get jealous of the slave next door – he was getting lots of action but I was solely there on display and wasn't even getting the benefit of being touched up or feeling noticed. It could be said that this is how life should be for a slave.

As it happens, I was later told that Mr J had arrived in good time and was around outside the cell displaying me. He was anonymous until he declared himself by claiming his slave property; he was enjoying watching his property on display in the cell and also observing the reactions of the other Masters who were out shopping for a slave for the night. One comment that was reported was 'Who the hell is this Mr J from Copenhagen?' in the sense of 'Why has he got a claim on this meat?'

When dreaming up this fantasy I hadn't considered the effect on the other Masters of a piece of desirable-looking meat which was labelled 'Unobtainable' – at least if you didn't know how to contact 'Mr J from Copenhagen'. Seems like the forbidden fruit always looks more juicy than the available.

As a slave in a cage I was exposed, naked and humiliated, my cock half-hard and dripping; but paradoxically I was quite safe, protected by the cage and the sign. A strange state, to be treasured.

And one effect on me as a slave was to start to wonder if indeed he would turn up to claim his property. Would I need to call 'Captain' to be let out? Had the thunderstorms delayed the aeroplane? The darkest time is just before the dawn; he did claim me and we left the cell for the comparative anonymity of elsewhere in the play area. Still without my glasses I wasn't distracted by cruising and was able to focus fully on serving him.

After some good play we were both interested to notice that a German guy had been watching quite closely. I got in contact with him and we played, including forcing me to ejaculate for the first time for four days using a TENS unit. And as a Master/slave couple we chatted to several people who had been watching our fantasy process unfold. We thanked the slave-Master as he left the bar – and also the others at Playpen who continue to make it a unique and safe canvas for so many interesting experiences.

More and Harder

October 2001

Mark's adventures continue. He's a moving target, he avoids becoming jaded by evolving as he comes. HIV is a continuing menace but no longer immediately deadly. Rest in peace ye who died through ignorance; we won't forget. Oh that we had more of your experience still with us now: you'd enjoy the toys and freedoms of this new millennium!

Internet messaging for instant obedience over the net. Webcams for cyber slavery without actual physical contact. JavaScript slave application forms which insist that all fields be completed before submission. Chastity cock cage made from plastic that's undetectable under clothes by airport security. This one works. Cock hard – Yes. Jack off – No. Oh shit!

And the enforcers raise the stakes too: the radio or internet controlled stun belt from South Africa. Once locked on, there's no escaping its incapacitating electric shocks delivered relentlessly. The pain's unmarking but the prisoner can't ignore its jolts. The webcam shows everything to the Master across the internet socket connection.

Mark's become emotionally mature and continues to balance his sadomasochistic fantasies with a successful real-life career. Typically he's on the internet in the early morning setting up his next stunt before walking off to work with his head full of fresh fantasies.

Maybe he's set up a day out shifting stones in boots ballweight and cammies labouring with landscape gardening contractors in Seattle.

Or sweating shirt-off in shorts filling skips in London; fill it 'too slowly' and he's ordered round the back of the site for a belting in private. Drop 'em, Bend over, take Six. Get up, Turn round, Kneel down, Suck this. Back outside he gets on with it smart like he should, shorts now dripping with piss from the Boss.

Next day, slight sore throat, his body hair's still cropped short and his arse hurts when he clenches. His balls hang just a bit lower still. The physical souvenirs remind Mark that yesterday he was a Master's real-life sub for a while.

Internet e-mail facilitates real boot-in-face fantasy sex, enchancing the moment when the real cat's tails first strike across shoulder muscles: the first timeless strike of reality, the discontinuity in perception and experience.

Mark endures punishment that is impossible to endure for long. Perspectives change. Immediate priorities are pain, pain and more pain. Fetters secure him. Leather straps bind. Inescapable real pain. And again the Master's cat strikes and again Mark's shoulders take the pain that men always take.

And then the last stroke; the taking down from the straps, the survival of pain and the manly endurance of primal experience become ever more precious to seek because a network connection and screen can't replace the warmth of a Master's arms when he's finished flogging you.

'More and Harder please Sir.'

'You'll have to come back for that.'

'Sir, yes Sir!'

Author's End Note

More and Harder may be taken as a historical representation of one individual's exploration of sadomachochism based in England. The AIDS epidemic and the continuing legal proscription of such activities have limited the factual accounts available to reseachers.

Morgan
London, 2001

Coming Up from Idol

idol

HARD TIME
Robert Black
ISBN 0 352 00000 0
9 May 2002

Three men are committed to Her Majesty's Prison Cairncrow on the same day. There's Paul – a young, tough inner-city robber. Simon, by contrast, is gentle, feminine, and obviously gay, and the third, John, an ex-vicar. The prison is a corrupt and cruel institution, run by sadistic officers and bullying hard men. It's also a sexual minefield – the old-timers prey on the newcomers and the guards prey on everybody. Will the three new inmates find their niche in this brutish new environment? A hot story of love, sex and redemption behind prison walls.

CHAINS OF DECEIT
Paul C. Alexander
ISBN 0 352 00000 0
6 June 2002

Journalist Nathan Dexter's life is turned around when he meets a young student called Scott – someone who offers him the relationship for which he's been searching. Then Nathan's best friend goes missing, and Nathan uncovers evidence that he has become the victim of a slavery ring which is rumoured to be operating out of London's leather scene. To rescue their friend, Nathan and Scott must go undercover, risking detection and betrayal at every turn. As their investigations take them from the leather bars of London and Amsterdam to the backrooms of New York, it becomes clear that they can trust no one, not even each other. Hard, horny and suspenseful erotic fiction!

TO SERVE TWO MASTERS
Gordon Neale
ISBN 0 352 00000 0
4 July 2002

Market day is a special time on the island of Ilyria. The goods to be sold are men, men who have learnt to accept their lives of slavery. Rock is one of these captive 'livestock', his only hope being that the beautiful young stranger, Dorian, will be the one who buys him. Even if he is lucky, Rock knows his life will not be easy. Dorian's adoptive brother, Carlos, is as cruel as he is handsome and Rock understands that, should he be bought by one, he will be owned by both. Fine homoerotic fiction with lashings of SM!

------ ✂ ----------------------------

Please send me the books I have ticked above.

Name ....

Address ....

....

....

....

.... Post code ....

Send to: **Cash Sales, Idol Books, Thames Wharf Studios, Rainville Road, London W6 9HA**

US customers: for prices and details of how to order books for delivery by mail, call 1-800-343-4499.

Please enclose a cheque or postal order, made payable to **Virgin Books Ltd**, to the value of the books you have ordered plus postage and packing costs as follows:

UK and BFPO – £1.00 for the first book, 50p for each subsequent book.

Overseas (including Republic of Ireland) – £2.00 for the first book, £1.00 for each subsequent book.

If you would prefer to pay by VISA, ACCESS/MASTERCARD, AMEX, DINERS CLUB or SWITCH, please write your card number and expiry date here:

....

Please allow up to 28 days for delivery.

Signature ....

Our private policy.

We will not disclose information you supply us to any other parties. We will not disclose any information which identifies you personally to any person without your express consent.

From time to time we may send out information about Idol books and special offers. Please tick here if you do *not* wish to receive Idol information. ☐

------ ✂ ----------------------------